Phoenix, Minnesota

A LOOZers Story

by

Rev. Chuck Waibel

authorHOUSE™

1663 LIBERTY DRIVE, SUITE 200
BLOOMINGTON, INDIANA 47403
(800) 839-8640
WWW.AUTHORHOUSE.COM

First published by AuthorHouse 07/08/04

ISBN: 1-4184-7055-4 (sc)

Printed in the United States of America
Bloomington, Indiana

This book is printed on acid-free paper.

Song, "Detour," ©1991 Carol Ford, used by permission-
Cover photo, "Desolation," © Armond Ferholz, used by permission

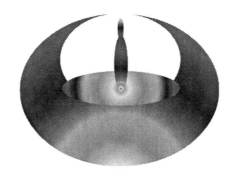

Phoenix, Minnesota:

A LOOZers Story

By
Rev. Chuck Waibel

Acknowledgements:

A book is like a quilt. The author is just the person who stitches together the blocks of ideas. Many people presented me with idea blocks, or showed me pleasing ways to arrange them. The blocks are theirs, the stitching mine. Any truth or beauty came from them. Any dropped stitches or frayed edges came from me. Here are some of the many to whom I owe thanks:

Carol Ford, for ruthless editing, relentless encouragement, and the use of her song, "Detour;"

Anne Kanten, for her political insights and knowledge of farming and the rural crisis;

Sisters Annette and Kay Fernholz, SSND, for their gentle yet tough spiritual vision, and the use of their father's photograph;

Professor Peter Whelan, for hours of schmoozing on science and philosophy- you will be missed, sir;

Richard Handeen and Audrey Arner, for showing how much can be done by dedicated people;

The Land Stewardship Project Crew, for their many and valuable insights and connections;

Adric Waibel, for understanding why Dad spent so much time alone at the computer;

and of course Robert Heinlein, Poul Anderson, Kurt Vonnegut, Margaret Atwood, Lois McMasters Bujold, Mark Twain, Spider Robinson, Ray Bradbury, Aldous Huxley and the others who taught me to dream on paper.

In Memory of

Prof. Peter Whelan-

Teacher, Philosopher, Friend

Peter was my first technical advisor on this book. This book may not have happened without his influence. In our last, too brief, conversation I told him that the book was finished, and I was looking for a publisher. He died a few days later of a stroke.

Table of Contents

Author's note7 xiii

Prelude-The Storyteller (2175 AD)............................. xv

Part One: Conflagration 1992-2020 AD 1

Chapter One (1992) The Beginning of the End 3

Chapter Two (1997) "You're either on the bus, or off the bus-"
Ken Keasey 11

Chapter Three (1998) Coming together 18

Chapter Four (1998) Pioneers, perils and revolution 22

Chapter Five (2001) "All you need is Love" John Lennon 31

Chapter Six (2001) Friend and foe in the Global Village 36

Chapter Seven (2002) Life will find a way 42

Chapter Eight (2002) "Life IS suffering" The Buddha............ 47

Chapter Nine (2003) Long-range planning by the short
sighted 63

Chapter Ten (2008) If it's not one thing it's another 74

Chapter Eleven (2009) Reaping the whirlwind 77

Chapter Twelve (2012) Boys will be boys.............................. 86

Chapter Thirteen (2019) Committing suicide as a national
sport 93

Part Two: Ashes 2020-2022 AD 101

Chapter Fourteen (2020) Mournings and Mornings 103

Chapter Fifteen (2020) Community is what you make it 119

Chapter Sixteen (2020) "Everyone has their story"................ 132

Chapter Seventeen (2020) The End of the Beginning 150

Chapter Eighteen (2020) Refugees from Paradise................. 156

Chapter Nineteen (2020) Back in "The Real World" 166

Chapter Twenty (2021) WHO goes around comes around..... 182

Chapter Twenty-One (2021) "A free Press is the backbone of Democracy." 185

Appendix: Excerpts from the writings of Karl Mueller.......... 197

Author's note:

I wrote this book for two reasons:

First, we are in a time of great change. Social rules and assumptions are changing. Technology is changing. The very climate we depend on is changing. That's the world we live in, like it or not. We need to squarely face what's happening. True and honest discussion of our situation and what we can and should do about it is vitally needed. I wrote this book to help get that discussion and action going.

Second, people from several places around Minnesota have told me that they see a new culture emerging in Western Minnesota. I wrote this book to try to express some aspects of that new culture, for it carries answers to our most vexing problems.

When I began to write this book, I thought of it as a fable, a cautionary tale something like Orwell's "1984." Little did I know how quickly reality would overtake fiction. There are policy proposals on the table right now at the Capitol in St. Paul that are a giant step toward the LOOZes.

This is a work of fiction. It is meant to entertain and provoke thought. You may think you see traces of people you know in various characters. They are not those characters- the resemblances are coincidental. You do not need to agree with everything I have written here. I don't even agree with all of it, but these are things which needed to be said. If we don't start talking and working, we'll be trapped when the fences go up, whether the fences are physical or metaphorical.

Read this book- you may need to be ready to live it.

Rev. Chuck Waibel

March, 2004

Prelude-

The Storyteller (2175 AD)

From above, Western Minnesota is almost as grey as the Moon. Great dunes, the remains of chemically-leached soil, march across the miles, driven by incessant winds. Here and there, an oasis appears around some deep pothole or gullied stream. Stunted cottonwoods and sawgrass cluster around these wet spots.

Occasionally, nomads can be seen, leading their often-blind horses from oasis to oasis. Sometimes they dig into the rubble-hill remains of old towns, looking for scavengable goods. But our story is not about them. We move on, westward.

A dark green line appears on the horizon. In places it sparkles with iridescence. As we come closer, we see that it is a massive hedge. Its tallest members are a kind of cottonwood, hundreds of feet tall. Their bark glints with crystalline highlights. At the feet of these behemoths grow great bushes, covered in pink flowers. Between them all hang vast cobweb strands of shining white thread, making a dense netting.

We pass over the hedge, and its purpose becomes clear: it keeps out the dust. We now see that the hedge encloses an oval land, perhaps thirty miles long and five wide. It is a rich land, with thick foliage of green and purple. Many small settlements of earth-sheltered houses can be seen. Towering windmills stand like sentinels over each.

Near the western hedge lies a shallow river. A large group of buildings huddles beside it. We approach, and see an amphitheater. On the stage stands an old man in white robes. His graying red hair swings about his waist as he strides back and forth, gesturing and proclaiming. His audience, mostly children, listen intently.

He is the Rememberer, as were his father and grandfather, all the way back to the beginnings of The Land. He speaks with the voice of his ancestors; for the sake of the great stories, he and his ancestors are one.

"My cousins, The Land is good. It has always been good. But it has not always been as it is today. I will tell you how it came to be this way. I will tell you of the people who made it as it is. That's what people do, we make things. Sometimes the things are good. Sometimes they are not so good. But we are always making.

"Here is what we made."

Part One: Conflagration

1992-2020 AD

Chapter One (1992)

The Beginning of the End

Jody Neihaus

Jody Neihaus wasn't what anyone would call pretty. With her straw-blond hair, strong jaw and broad forehead, some may have called her 'no-nonsense handsome.' Her shy demeanor did nothing to draw attention. There were thousands like her at the U of M; small-town girls of Northern European stock, still intimidated after years in the city.

She was feeling sorry for herself that day, her first day in Literary Research class. She was stuck in a dungeon room in an old stone pile of a building on the West Bank campus of the University of Minnesota. The windows looked out just at ground level. Seated, she could only see a patch of sky and the tops of some pine trees.

She was moping, waiting for class to start, when a tall, bony whirlwind with a ponytail dropped an REI backpack on the next desk.

"Hi, I'm Bill," he said, sticking out a hand. Startled, she let him vigorously shake her hand.

Then he glanced out the window and shouted "Mushrooms!" He snatched a plastic bag from his pack, and ran out the door.

Jody had noticed the toadstools on her way in, but thought nothing of them. She glanced up at the window. She could see his shadow as he was crawled around, stuffing them in his sack.

He stormed back in, then held the bag open for her to smell the fruits. When she shrank back, he said, "Oh, come on! I've been eating these for years. They grew in our back yard in Colorado."

She leaned forward, assaying a sniff.

"I suppose they're alright," she muttered.

"Alright? They're wonderful! Come on over to my place tonight and I'll cook 'em up for you. Waddaya say?"

"I don't know. I just met you…"

"Come on. I live in a big old house with a dozen other people. It's not like we'd be alone," he said. Then he spotted a familiar face in the room.

"Hey, Allen!" Bill called. "Ya wanna come over tonight to reassure this nice lady of my intentions?"

Eventually, she relented.

That's where it started. Where Jody had rarely even been outside of Minnesota, Bill had been everywhere, much of it on foot. Where she was a child of the prairie, he was a Colorado Rockies boy. Where Jody was retiring about anything but art, Bill was passionate about everything. To create in fiber was her one obsession; he wanted to see and know everything. She studied to be an Art Instructor, to share her passion. He wanted to be a Librarian, to swim on seas of information. They had one of those strange opposites kinships, perhaps a kharmic bond. He reminded her of her older brother Steve's far visions. She reminded him that a hearth to return to is needed by every adventurer.

In their early years Bill and Jody were the very image of the struggling artistic couple. They lived in the attic where they had shared that first meal. They knew all the great cheap, folksy nightspots. They found the best city parks for walking. They had a regular round of used bookstores. They paddled canoes around the lakes, biked to Hudson and Hastings, and camped out when they could.

Bill's attic apartment became their loft and studio. The sound in the loft from the sharply slanted walls during a rain was loud yet soothing. The slight mustiness was overcome by scents of baking, incense, candles, wool, flax and hemp. Low bookshelves sprawled all around the huge open space, even in the curtained-off bed alcove. Their camping gear lay piled in one corner. In a North-facing dormer was Jody's sanctum, with spinning wheels, two looms, a work table, and simple shelves holding the materials of her fabric arts.

Below the fan-paned front window hung the loose-ended Life Tapestry, which would grow as it depicted ongoing events in their life together. It was only a few feet wide, but she looked forward to one day seeing it stretching around a block.

The biggest change in Jody's life, besides Bill himself, was her introduction to activism. Like anyone, she'd heard of protests and petitions for things people believed in, but putting herself out in front just wasn't her way. She admired those who made a stand, but didn't see herself as having the courage to be noticed.

This changed on a visit to the State Capitol grounds. They'd come here before to see the statuary and the rotunda, and to walk about the mall which stretched westward to St. Paul's Cathedral. On this day there was a difference; a sort of clothesline was strung between trees. From it fluttered white tee-shirts bearing children's drawings. The drawings varied, but each had a name in large letters.

At the end of the lines was a table, behind which sat two women. A sign proclaimed RAMSEY COUNTY DOMESTIC VIOLENCE AWARENESS. The women explained to Jody and Bill that each shirt bore the name of, and a drawing by, a child who had been killed by a parent or other close adult. The display had been organized by the Women's Shelter to dramatize how many innocent children were the victims of adults' despair and rage.

Jody saw that there was a sign-up sheet for volunteering at the shelter. Her heart tugged at her, but she knew that she could never face such horrors first hand. She faded back into the crowd.

That night, Jody slept fitfully. She dreamt of her own safe, pleasant childhood, and had nightmares of it going wrong. She felt the guilt of the blessed when confronted with the reality of others' lives. She remembered her Sunday school lesson- "From him to whom much is given, much will be required." She had to find a way to contribute.

The next morning Bill told her, "Yeah, it's sad, and I love you for caring. Go for it, if you want. I'm just worried about you finding time. You've got to get onto that big project for your Master's, but if it's your kharma, you'll think of something."

She knew that he was right, but she'd begun to realize that she had always taken the easy way, the pleasant way, in life. She'd lived in The Cities long enough to realize that her hometown, Asyl, was a long way from most people's reality. But what could she do?

Then an answer dawned on her, a way that she could preserve her shyness around people, yet still participate. She'd call in the morning to check it out. Meanwhile, she slid out of bed and went to her desk; she had sketching to do.

She was still awake, knotting bits of cord together into shapes the next morning. Bill glanced over her sketches and trial efforts.

"Looks like a good concept," he said. "Will you take it down there today to show the ladies?"

"Oh, no," Jody answered. "I wouldn't want to be forward. I'm just playing with ideas"

Bill touched her face, and looked into her eyes.

"Art isn't Art if nobody sees it," he said. "This is good. You need to present it. I'll get the phone. You call them and ask what would be a good time to talk about it."

Four months later came the unveiling. The new Metropolitan Women's Center lobby was graced with Jody Ellis' masterwork. It was a knotwork banner, five feet high and eight wide. The massive-yet-delicate "super macramé" showed a community gathered around a mother and child. Jody declined personal interviews or photographs, but her "Heart of Community" became a symbol, repeated on brochures and stationary, known throughout the region. Jody shunned any credit or publicity, although the work was accepted by her Masters' committee.

Jody was working at her hand loom late one evening when Bill wearily flopped down on their couch. He'd gotten home late after helping at the Minneapolis downtown library with a recataloguing project. He held out a scrap of notebook paper to her.

"Honey," he said. "This is the best shot for us I've seen yet."

"What?" she asked as she took it from him.

"I found out the Morris Campus is looking for a Fiber Arts Instructor AND an Assistant Librarian."

"Reeaallly, then? Morris?"

"Yup. WE'RE the package deal they've been waiting for. I got phone, fax and e-mail contacts. We can polish up our online portfolios, and send things out to them tomorrow."

One month, and many calls and e-mails later, they nursed their ancient Honda Civic hatchback across the prairie to Morris. Soon enough they were walking down the echoing corridors of a grey and black concrete structure, typical of arts and theater building on campuses across North America. Jody found the wrought-iron spiral stair that led to the office level. Bill kept going across campus to the library; they'd meet later at the student center.

Division Chair Ray Sandte's office was one of several overlooking the main foyer from the shadows thirty feet above. Several doors bore posters announcing shows, or had been intricately painted by their occupants. One door was clearly newly bared.

Could this be MY office? Jody wondered.

Two doors down, she knocked.

"C'mon in!" a voice, familiar from phone calls, shouted.

Ray Sandte's office was cluttered with the usual floor-to-ceiling bookshelves, as well as odd gadgets and scale models. His specialty was the hardware of theater; prop making, set design, lighting, special effects- all those things which make the make-believe setting of a play look real. Since this meant working in almost all conceivable art forms, he had been deemed excellently qualified to coordinate the teaching of them all.

He rose from his chair. Jody saw a medium-tall, powerfully built man, with dark brown hair and beard. He wore a "Mister Rogers" gray sweater, and had kind, laughing eyes. He offered his hand.

"Jody! You're Jody?" he said.

"Yes, I suppose I am. Both times."

"Good! We're having a heck of a time filling positions lately. Nobody wants to teach any more. They all want MBAs and big bucks."

He grabbed a file folder from a shelf, then said, "Hey, let's go use Donny's old office. There's lots more room in there."

He stalked back the way Jody had come, then used his key to open the empty office.

"OK," he said. "Pull up a chair and we'll talk."

In half an hour Donny's old office had become Jody's new office. She met Bill at the Turtle Mountain Café in the Student Center. He had similar news: he was now Assistant Director of Tech and Media Services at the Library. Jody was happy, but not really surprised. She'd been raised to believe that if you worked hard, planned, and focused, breaks would come your way. Her life was sliding along the rails just as she had expected.

On the table in their booth were strewn maps of the area, a phone book, newspaper classifieds, and the U's pamphlet of local references. They had come prepared to scout out housing and amenities. First stop, as recommended by Ray: Alice Nevlund Realty.

Alice was a sweet older lady, who sounded like a character from the movie "Fargo." Jody didn't underestimate her; she'd known plenty of odd, capable women like her. Bill had some trouble stifling giggles, though.

"Hokay, so you two kids want something kinda big, but not too fancy?" she asked. "I think I got it- there's this place out by the research farm. The house is big as a barn, with a coupla acres. Da guy who lived there kept remodeling, right up till he died, so the inside is a mess. It was repossessed for taxes. Ya can get it cheap; ya said ya had some money put by, right? I betcha you kids qualify for the First Time Homebuyer program and the Fixer Upper fund, too. Ya wanna go take a peek at it?"

They did, and fell in love with the big block of a building. The "mess" inside wasn't much worse than the loft where they'd been living. They told Alice to start the process.

Jody had already made a mental sketch of the next panel of the Life Tapestry- the Morris skyline, featuring the U's water tower.

Asyl was a straight 40 mile run down US 59, so they went to give Jody's parents the news in person. Like many towns whose reason for existence had been agriculture, Asyl was slowly fading. The thriving 1940s town of 1400 souls had become a remnant haunted by only 350. Yet, it had spirit, and an above-average percentage of eccentrics, artists, writers and musicians, in a matrix of stolid rural folk.

The Neihauses were of salt-of-the-earth Norwegian farm stock. Their ancestors had settled just northwest of Asyl, four generations before. Those Norwegian pioneers had planted a solid shelterbelt of cottonwoods and poplar against the constant northwest winds. In its heyday the town had grown and shifted out towards the Neihaus Place. What had been a country house now stood at the head of Hill Avenue. The shelterbelt had merged with those of neighbors to form a small wood on the edge of town. The original homestead shack was only a ragged pit in that forest. A tiny cottage, "Grandma's House," stood just on the edge of the woods. The white clapboard house where Jody had grown up, built in the 1920s, stood just to the south.

As they drove up the short hill for which Hill Avenue was named, Jody's mother Inge came out to meet them. Bill always marveled at her; even in the late twentieth century of liberated women and working mothers, Inge was like someone from a Frank Capra movie. She came toward them, wiping flour from her hands onto her apron.

"Hey there!" she called. "What brings ya down here? Good news, I hope."

Jody hugged her mother.

"Mom, we both got the jobs! We start this Fall Quarter, but are going to get moved out to Morris as soon as we can."

They had found their El Dorado. Now the new professionals had to mount the expedition to claim it. The old Honda Civic went on many box-finding runs to CUB, Rainbow and the other big grocery stores. Bill sorted, boxed and labeled their library. Jody filled many black plastic bags with textiles, tying colored tags around their necks to keep them sorted. They ate lots of ramen and other quick foods while turning their loft from an artists' garret into a temporary warehouse.

Finally, "The Day" arrived. On a hot Friday evening their student friends, always drawn to happenings, swarmed up and down the attic stairs with bundles and boxes. Some bright folks set up a "bucket brigade." Jody's fabric bags, couch cushions, sacks of linens, anything soft, went out the front window, onto the third-floor roof, down to the porch roof, and onto the ground. From the piles and stacks on the front lawn, the big yellow rental truck was stuffed as evenly as Bill could manage.

It was a party for the whole house. In the side yard a motley assortment of grills, coolers, and a keg of beer were attended by volunteer cooks. Neighbors joined in, bringing more grills and musical instruments. Singing, Frisbee tossing, even a badminton game evolved, until packing the truck was just a part of the whole event. Jody and Bill slept soundly that night on a futon mattress in their bare loft.

The next morning, a bit blurred around the edges, they took down the Life Tapestry, rolled up the futon, and set out. Department Chair Sandte had arranged an unpacking crew, so all they had to do was navigate across 150 miles of prairie. No sweat.

Furnishing The House was much harder than filling a loft. Weekends were for scrounging. Bill and Jody kept track of auctions, and would rise early on Saturdays, map and want-ads in hand, to hit all the promising garage sales. High on their list was a decent bed. The futon was OK, but they were getting older. They had to turn at least sort of respectable eventually.

They found The Bed at the estate auction of an eccentric who had moved to Arizona. Among the gadgets and gewgaws left behind was a piece of furniture that had started out as a queen-sized, four-poster bed. It had acquired drawers under the frame, rope-lighting in the canopy, and a huge headboard, replete with sliding doors, cubbyholes, and a fuse-protected power strip.

Once they had it trucked home and set up, The Bed became a center of Bill and Jody's life. This wasn't just for the obvious reasons, but also because it could hold a microwave oven, telephone and PC. The bed curtains kept out mosquitoes in the summer, and made it cozy in the winter. Both spent many lazy, private hours with the curtains drawn, studying, reading or relaxing. It was their sanctuary.

9

The Life Tapestry acquired an ungainly-looking bed, with two smiling faces peeking from behind its curtains.

Chapter Two (1997)

"You're either on the bus, or off the bus-" Ken Keasey

Karl Mueller

"What the hell are you trying to prove?"

She really didn't know. Loni Mueller feared for her husband's sanity. Here he was in the kitchen of their beautiful new home, on a bright spring morning, moping again.

"You lock yourself away in your study! You sit around ohmming and meditating. You drag me off to coffeehouses and lectures full of fanatical students and geeks! Now this shit about some commune in the middle of nowhere!" she shouted. "If you want to have a midlife crisis, do something normal. Buy a sports car! Sail around the world! Even an affair would make more sense!"

Karl leaned over the breakfast nook table, holding his head.

"This isn't a midlife crisis. It's a LIFE crisis. It's like I've had amnesia for twenty years!" he moaned. "What's it all FOR?"

"You have two great kids, a huge house on the St. Croix, and the most successful small company in Minnesota! We go to a great church, and have wonderful friends at the Chart Club, your picture gets on the news every month- and you ask about FOR? This IS what it's for!"

Karl sighed, "I remember what it was like when we met. We cared about what happened in the world. We believed we could make a difference!"

Loni slapped the counter.

"We are not kids any more Karl. You HAVE made a difference: you've created hundreds of jobs; you've made a ton of money; you give buckets of cash to charity! Look around you! These are the goodies! This is sure all I ever wanted, and more!"

Karl wearily looked her in the eye.

"Just because we believed in something as kids doesn't make it worthless now. We wanted to save the world, change it for the better. What's so wrong with that?"

"You believed it Karl. You! Not me! I loved your fire. I knew I could create something practical with it. So I encouraged you, steered you. Look at all you've done- and you never would have without me! I DID IT!"

Dismayed comprehension overtook Karl's face.

"Then you never did get it, did you?"

"There's nothing to GET Karl! You've lost your senses!"

She slammed her hand down on the table and glared at him.

"This stops NOW, or I file for a divorce! I've already got my attorney working on the papers."

The drive out of Wilmar seemed endless, forty-three miles of arrow-straight road unrolling across the immense landscape. A person could feel lost, as if adrift on a raft on the South Pacific. *Still,* Karl thought, *that's what we'll need.* He could imagine how these roads would look in a decade or two, when Industrial Civilization's folly caught up with it.

He'd never heard of Asyl before some folks at a Minneapolis coffeehouse mentioned it to him. They knew he was searching for a place to build his research community. They said it was perfect- a funky little town, a low-key Mecca for artists and back-to-the-landers since the '70s.

Karl had looked over the map. Asyl looked promising; only forty-odd miles from the U of M Morris, and sixty-some from Southwest State U in Marshall. It had decent roads, but wasn't really on the way to anywhere. Services were good, and land was cheap. *Maybe, just maybe- it feels good.*

So, here he was, in his beat-up old Toyota Landcruiser, following Asyl's original white settlers of the 1870s on their path to a new life- he hoped.

He saw the water tower first, as its unusual orange peak thrust up from behind the approaching ridgeline. From the top of that ridge, he saw Asyl hugging the opposite wall of the shallow valley, a gathering of a few dozen neat houses in well-kept yards. The hamlet bustled that day, with pickups coming and going, farm wives shopping, and trucks and trains at the grain elevator.

Karl drove down the slope, across the tracks and US 59, and entered the two-block-long hub of the town. As with most prairie towns in the late Twentieth Century, there were several closed and boarded up shops, but the grocery and hardware stores were doing a brisk business. All parking spots near the café were filled, and the full-service gas station had a short line. He thought: *Hmmm, bank, blacksmith shop, parts store- good infrastructure. But something still tells me water and hills. Close.* Karl smiled at the rural kitsch of the Viking statue brandishing his sword next to the Public Library, and the carved granite "Velkommen til Asyl" sign in front of City Hall.

When checking out a town, start with the café.

The Viking Café lived up to its name. Over the basic Midwestern café ambiance was overlain a décor of Dala horses, rosemalling and tole painting, and Norwegian-flag banners. One wall was dominated by a round shield and crossed battle axes. OK, Asyl was proud of its heritage.

A tall, wiry blond woman called to him from behind the cash register. "Hey, you're new here, eh?" she said. "What can I get ya?"

"Just coffee and a roll, please." Karl said. "And where should I sit?"

"Anyplace is good. How about that booth over there?"

"Thanks."

Karl enjoyed the wait, watching and listening. He felt the usual buzz of people just going about their business, oblivious to the wider world. Still, the vibe held an undertone of greater potentials.

When a young waitress brought his coffee and roll, Karl told her he was looking into farming, and asked about available farms in the area. She suggested that he go check the bulletin board at the bank across the street; there were farm foreclosures all the time.

Karl thought, *Of course there are. We can get used to catastrophe looming. Do these people have any idea of what's coming?*

He sat nursing his coffee and sensing the vibes. He kept his eyes and ears open, bathing in the overlapping conversations. He could tell that his search for the place to build Phoenix was nearly over- but some piece was missing. He sensed that it might come to him here.

"Hey, you! Mister new guy!" the proprietress called. "You'll wanna know the fella who's coming in next."

The front door creaked open to admit a stout man in dark pants and a good cotton dress shirt. He carried a battered briefcase and wore a billed cap with a seed company logo.

"Hey Ed! Come and see this new guy over here!"

Karl rose and extended his hand.

"I'm Karl Mueller. And you are?"

"Ed Erhart. I'm with LaSalle Seed Company."

As their hands touched, Karl knew that the missing piece had arrived. *I know this man. In some other life, we were adversaries, or friends. We're only strangers because we've forgotten. The game's afoot.*

Ed sat, and the waitress brought him a cup of coffee and a menu.

"He wants to be a farmer, so I figure he should talk to you," she said.

"Is that so?" asked Erhart. "What kind of farming are you interested in? I can get you good hybrids, maybe some of those new GMOs, and all the chemicals you'll ever need."

"Actually, I'm planning to do some research." Karl told him. "I want to work with alternative technologies, unusual plants, that sort of thing."

"Ah, you sound like a Green or something. Not that I got anything against them folks, they got some good ideas, but they don't realize that the System works OK for people who are willing to work with it. All that doom and gloom stuff, uff dah! They can keep it!"

"I'm not as radical as those folks, I guess," Karl answered, "but I'm something like them. I'm looking for a hundred acres or so, some woods, open water, and several good outbuildings. I want to make it a study center, where people from other places can come to stay and work on projects."

Erhart rubbed his chin for a few seconds, looking into the distance.

"Hey! I know! It's a little strange, but you should check out the resort. They got open land, some trees, a few primitive cabins, and they're right on the lake. It just came up for sale this month- the Midgalls are retiring."

Oohh, that sings. Karl tried not to show his excitement.

"How do I find this place?" Karl asked.

"Easy. Get back on Highway 40. Head west four miles. You can't miss it."

The road west out of Asyl was not the straight run that the Wilmar leg had been. Ancient glaciers and their runoff had carved a network of valleys, creeks and ponds through this area, centering on the Minnesota River. Karl stopped at one large pond in a narrow valley. Perched on stumps and tussocks were at least a dozen graceful, long-necked, snow-white egrets.

"Thank you, cousins, for sharing your beauty." Karl murmured.

Around one last curve, the lake came into view: Lac qui Parle, "Lake that talks," named by French explorers. Their name was a translation of the Sioux name. During spring and fall, the valley was a cacophony of geese, swans, pelicans, ducks, herons and uncounted thousands of other migrating birds. Only about a mile wide, the lake was thirty miles long, and had grown deeper and broader after the dam was built at its southern end in 1936.

The Asyl Resort was strategically located on the east end of the one bridge to cross the lake. The resort had a campground, a few primitive cabins, a bait shop and 3.2 bar, an excellent boat landing, and a mid-sized ranch house. Judging from the many vehicles parked around "The Bait Shop," business was good.

Karl saw that it indeed had a big FOR SALE BY OWNER sign. *Would they take a check?*

Karl groaned as he left the C*O*S boardroom. *That could have gone more smoothly,* he thought. *Still, how easy is it to escape a thriving business you built without looking like a fool?*

He had scarcely closed the mahogany doors behind him when THEY swarmed around the corner- the Corporate-owned media locusts. He'd often wondered how Walter Cronkite or Dave Moore felt about these so-called "journalists" who didn't dare offend the huge conglomerates that owned them.

Then they were upon him.

"Mr. Mueller! Is it true that you've resigned as CEO of C*O*S?"

"What about the rumors of a mistress?"

"Are you leaving for health reasons?"

"What about the college kids you've been hanging around with?"

"Is there any truth to your wife's allegations? Are you crazy, or is she?"

That last one caught him. Loni wasn't content with her big divorce settlement; he'd defied her dreams and controls, so he had to pay.

"I have heard of Loni Weiman's stories," he said. "They show why she's my EX wife."

That brought forth chuckles, so he continued.

"I'll be fair with her. We've both changed since we were married. We no longer see eye-to-eye on where to go from here."

Mike Burns from Channel 8 asked, "What are your plans?"

"I'm going to find a place in the country and spend some time with my boys."

"Is there any truth to the rumor that you've bought a resort in outstate Minnesota?" asked Trudy Benbull of the Tribune.

"Yes, I have. It sounds like a nice, quiet place to fish."

Benbull persisted. "Some claim you're trying to cover up something. What about the rumors that you're starting a commune?"

Karl didn't really want to make the Phoenix project public yet. It rattled him that he'd been so poor at covering his tracks.

"I've invited a few friends to live there with us. We'll have a big house, and several cabins for privacy. We're going to research alternative technologies. That's hardly a crash pad. Check out the works of E. F. Schumacher, Buckminster Fuller, or that new fellow, William McDonough, for the general ideas."

"It sounds very noble, but aren't some of those 'friends' young women?"

"That's none of your business. They're grad students and assistants. Their sex doesn't matter."

"Are you so old that it doesn't matter?"

"No, I'm so old that I find paparazzi-style journalists to be insufferable. Good day."

"But Mr. Mueller…"

"If you'd read books instead of writing trash maybe you'd understand what I'm doing."

Karl and the boys had been living in a Dinkytown warehouse, in the middle of the U of M bohemian district, since the divorce. His student friends, Mary, Doug, Francie and Jules joined them to watch the late news, and to plan. Karl knew the media wouldn't show him favorably, but the younger ones had to see for themselves.

The talking head read a few lines about "the fall of the computer tycoon," then introduced the film clip (We apologize for the sound quality).

"Mr. Mueller! Is it true that you've resigned as CEO of C*O*S?"

"We no longer see eye-to-eye on where to go from here."

"What about the rumors that you're starting a commune?"

"Yes, I've invited a few friends to live there with us. We'll have a big house, and several cabins (rumble rumble) a crash pad.

Karl switched off the set.

"Those damn shit heads!" Doug shouted, the rest echoing him.

"OK, folks," he said. "I don't like it either, but we knew there'd be opposition. All we can do now is keep planning and working. I close the deal on the resort in three months; we have to be ready to jump by then.

"Mary, you're still in charge of organizing living quarters. Make sure your inventory lists are complete.

"Doug, get the lab and shop equipment on track. We'll need a clean set up ASAP once we're there.

"Francie, you're our librarian. I want every book, disk, and tape catalogued and labeled. Figure out your storage needs and pass them to me or Jules.

"Jules will handle overall logistics. Keep him updated on how much stuff you'll be bringing, and what special packing it needs. He'll be working on trucks, loaders, all that. Don't leave ANY surprises for him.

"I'll manage paperwork, permits, all of that legal stuff. Every one of you make sure that your grad study programs are approved. Any Profs needing assurances, any papers to sign, let me know. Keep up your meditations. Stay centered and focused. We'll pull this off, whatever 'they' say."

Chapter Three (1998)

Coming together

Andre DuPris

It's a long way from Hales Corners, Wisconsin to Morris, Minnesota, from Lake Michigan to the Great Plains. It's a long way from the son of a man who builds Harleys to an art instructor on a rural university campus.

Dad had been proud when I'd caught his love of bikes. He'd been proud again when I took to his instruction in welding and metalwork. He tried to be supportive when I took that teaching in the direction of art, not into becoming a machinist. He proudly introduced me as "the first DuPris to finish college," but away from his friends he was less than thrilled. Even so, he hugged me as I left, and warned me to "watch out for those redneck bigots."

So, here I was, rolling into town, with a moving van due the next day. I checked in with Ray Sandte, and then headed over to Security to pick up my office and studio keys.

When I got back up to the Arts Center office level, the office next to mine was open. In it a tall, very white woman was frowning as she rearranged her shelves.

I knocked lightly. She looked up.

I offered my hand as I said, "I'm Andre DuPris. I'm here to teach metalworking."

Her scowl disappeared, replaced by a shy smile. There was no trace of "that look."

"Oh, hey. I'm Jody Ellis, Fiber Arts," she said, taking my hand. "We'll be neighbors, then?"

"It looks like it. Can you tell me how to get to the bookstore and library?" I asked. "I want to check on what references they have on hand, and how easy it is to order more."

She strode out into the hall.

"Better than show you, I'll take you. I was just heading for the TMC anyway," she said. "Come on, then."

As we walked, she told me to look for her husband Bill at the Library. He'd know just who to talk to.

Jody had taught at UMM for a year, so she knew all the back stairs and shortcuts. In a few minutes we were in the Student Center. I found out that "TMC" stood for Turtle Mountain Café. As we stood in front of it she pointed to the stairs to the bookstore. The Library was right out the back door and across the patio. She went for lunch, and I went in search of Bill.

Bill was a sort of John Denver scarecrow; a smiling, open, outdoor type. He showed me through the stacks, explained the reserve process, and made note of books I thought the library should have.

"OK, that's business," he said after a fruitful hour. "Now, people stuff. Are you settled in yet?"

"No, I came on my bike with just a bag of personal gear. The movers are getting here tomorrow afternoon."

"Where are ya staying tonight?"

"I figured that I'd just bedroll it on the floor of my new place."

He slapped me on the shoulder. "A man of my own breed," he said. "But I won't have a friend sleeping hard when we've got a perfectly good couch. You'll come for supper, too, right?"

"I don't want to be trouble."

"Ha! If I didn't offer hospitality, then I'd be in trouble! So, I'll pick you up at, say six o'clock?"

I laughed at his insistence. "OK, ok, I give. But you'd better know where, hadn't you?"

"OK, where?"

"There's a converted old gas station on, I think it's Old 28?"

"Oh, sure. That place down from the Salvation Army, a kind of old concrete block Quonset?"

"That's the place."

Jody

An informal pleasure of UMM was a weekly gathering of jolly freethinkers called Fat Tuesday. The obvious reference to Mardi Gras was fulfilled in the potluck fare at the gatherings. After classes on Tuesday afternoons, a dozen or so faculty would descend on the home of Kate Mikkelson, an anthropology professor. They brought dishes ranging from miso to barbequed ribs, from tabouli to Buffalo wings, and all of it excellent. There were always a few bottles of good wine or home-brewed beer.

Jody remembered hearing of Kate when she was a girl. The older woman had grown up in Asyl, gone off to college, and never returned. She had traveled the world for years, sending postcards and exotic artifacts back to the Asyl elementary school. The collection still graced a display case outside of the library. Jody hadn't realized that Kate had returned to Minnesota, and was teaching a mere hour's drive from Asyl.

The conversation was as rich as the food. On Jody's first visit a debate erupted over the censure of a professor who had used the word "nigger" in class. Some contended that such a foul epithet was forever taboo. Others argued that, in contexts of discussing what a certain famous bigot was up to, it was allowable.

"You know my friend Andre," Jody said. "I can't imagine anyone calling him that, but I think it would be different if we were talking about someone calling him that. Ya know?"

The conversation drifted toward racism in general. One person said that they never listened to Wagner because he was a racist and anti-Semite. Kate silently put a CD on the stereo. As a rich tapestry of strings filled the air, she said, "That's from his *Siegfried.* Old Rikard may have been a racist son of a bitch, but from a man who can write that I'll forgive a lot."

Andre

By the next spring I'd gotten my shop and studio pretty well set up. The old office and front room made a nice, cozy apartment. The high-ceilinged garage made a dandy studio. It was everything I could want, but it was too empty. I'd never really lived alone, and I felt it. The friends I'd made in Morris didn't make up for that.

Things change.

It was one of those strange April days on the plains, when the clouds roll back and the temperature goes up. It was far too gorgeous a day to drive to work. As I was strolling home that afternoon, I spotted someone with a huge backpack sitting on my front step. As I got closer, he seemed familiar. Hmmm, with a beard and more meat on his bones, that would look like...

"Jason!" I shouted as I broke into a jog. "What in the world are you doing here?"

"I just got tired of Milwaukee, man," he said as I swept him into a hug. "It was time to get some air."

He knew that he wasn't fooling me. I could feel his tension. He was thinner than when I had met him two years before; way too thin. Something had happened to him.

"Come on in. I'll grab a couple of beers. You can tell me about it."

For a while we did catch-up small talk. Then I said, "OK. Spill it. What's really going on?"

Jason took a deep breath.

"I nearly died, dude," he muttered. "I got skin cancer. They called it a Stage Two Melanoma."

He pulled his Harley tee-shirt collar aside. His left shoulder showed an ugly, puckered scar.

"They dug it out and did some tests. I had to do Chemo. I was sick as a dog for a few months, but they figure I'm OK now."

"So, why'd you hit the road."

"Ha, you know my family. You could write the script."

Unfortunately, I did, and could. I'm hard to impress, but I'd disliked them as much as they did me.

"That's true," I said. "But tell me. I need to know."

Jason's parents, Imelda and Marco, were good Catholics. Pictures of the Pope and the Virgin of Guadeloupe hung in their dining room. And in the living room. And in the kitchen. They were decent, God-fearing, generous people. Unfortunately, they were also bigots. That their son should become "one of them" was shameful. That he was dating a non-Catholic black man was horrifying.

Like I said, they were basically good people. They never confronted me directly, but those looks were there. Jason had told me the hurtful things they said. They were praying for his soul and mine, bless them.

They knew, as a rock certainty, that Jason's cancer was a punishment. As soon as he was healed enough, he hit the road.

He wasn't sure where he was going. I told him that he'd arrived. He was welcome to stay.

21

Chapter Four (1998)

Pioneers, perils and revolution

Karl

I wonder what plants will come from the seeds these five vehicles are hauling? Karl mused. The three rental vans were stuffed. The box of the classic International Harvester pickup was heaped high and tarped. The rest of the crew followed in the old Toyota. *Am I leading this bunch of idealists to ruin, or to a productive, satisfying life?*

Especially for the lifelong city kids, the trip was surreal. From Wilmar to Asyl, nearly forty-five miles, there were no real curves, no towns, and only one stop sign. In places, the prairie was so flat that you could sense the Earth's curvature, and see buildings twenty or more miles away. It was like traveling to another world.

But we're all traveling to that "undiscovered country" all the time, Karl thought. *I just wish that the countryside and destination were always so easy to see. I wish that we always had the power to chart our own course.*

Young James Mueller wasn't so philosophical. He was bored with traveling; you couldn't get video games or TV on the road. And the geeks his Dad had them traveling with! Living in the warehouse was cool for a while, but he was starting to realize that he was doomed to live out his High School years in clod-hopper land, surround by these oddballs. This was going to RUIN his future!

The caravan pulled into the Asyl Resort at noon. Although the Bait Shop was closed, several pickups and trailers were parked at the boat landing. They wouldn't be in the way of the new arrivals.

After the crew had all climbed out and stretched, Karl gathered them together.

"OK." he said. "The guys Jules hired for unpacking will be here in a couple of hours. We need to know just what goes where before then.

"We'll set up HQ in the Bait Shop. Jules, you commandeer a couple of tables to lay out your maps and clipboards for everyone. Put out the picnic lunches. We can eat while we work.

"Mary, we'll handle food, laundry and such out of the Big House, so I want you to get a handle on supplies and equipment. Check the Bait Shop, too. Any household supplies the rest of you find, tell Mary so we know what we still need to get. Then somebody can run to the store in Asyl.

"Doug, you get your pick of the outbuildings for the shop and labs. There are a couple of garages and utility sheds besides the cabins. Figure out where we can put things for now, what remodeling we'll need, that sort of thing.

"Francie, we'll want the main library in the Big House, so you'll check that over first. We'll eventually put satellite libraries elsewhere, but for now let's get things organized in one place.

"I'll be circulating, answering questions and working things out. James and Alec, you'll be 'gophers,' so listen for your names. And everybody figure out who bunks with who and where. You have plenty of choices."

For the next hour everyone bustled about, looking and thinking and measuring. A few of the fishermen from the landing wandered over to help, too. Karl was just walking from the Bait Shop to the Big House when a pickup pulled up.

Ed Erhart climbed out.

"Howdy, Karl," he said. "I thought I'd bring a little something."

He reached back into the cab and pulled out a fruit basket.

"You didn't need to do that, Ed," said Karl.

"Karl, you're a businessman," Erhart said. "You know about keeping up client relations."

"But we aren't your clients."

"Yet." said Erhart.

Karl took Erhart into the Bait Shop, where they left the fruit with the other food, then on a stroll around the grounds. Karl knew that Erhart was fishing for business, and for juicy gossip. Karl felt uneasy, but knew there was a kharmic scenario playing out.

During the afternoon, they had a few other visitors, such as the Mayor of Asyl and a County Commissioner. Everyone in the area was curious about these peculiar newcomers, but the ancient rural protocols of who got to ask first were observed.

Atmosphere: aromas of strong coffee and rich soup; unpainted brick walls; plain wooden tables; wooden shelves with games, books, and musical instruments; huge, polished bar with pastry cases and bottles of flavored syrups; smiling cooks behind it; the jolly Irish proprietor chatting with customers; gentle Celtic music playing…

Karl was glad he'd found Joe Cool's Java Joint. The funky Montevideo coffeehouse was an added blessing of Phoenix's location. During the day, it was a great place to think, and to meet the area's most interesting people. On Friday and Saturday nights, it hosted live music, anything from Bluegrass to African drumming to cool Jazz.

This afternoon Karl was nursing an iced drink and waiting, waiting for something he felt coming.

"Hiya," said a friendly voice.

Karl looked up. A rawboned, lanky fellow offered his hand. He had a friendly manner, and was dressed in worn cowboy boots, blue jeans, a battered cowboy hat, and an almost illegally loud hawai'ian shirt.

"Hi yourself," Karl said, and stood.

"I'm Tommy Jensen," the newcomer said. "Danny Boy tells me that you're turning the old Asyl Resort into some kind of commune."

They shook hands, then sat down.

"Sort of," Karl answered. "We'll be doing appropriate technology research once we get going. And you? What do you do out here?"

"Far out. We can give each other ideas. I run an organic beef ranch out by Watson."

"Oh, really? How long have you been at it?"

"Since '73. I bought the old home place after my folks moved."

"I'd have liked to do that, back then, but I was a bit young. I got into computers instead."

"Hey! That's why you look familiar! Some TV station out of The Cities had a thing about you coming out here."

Karl winced.

"Jah, they did. I came off looking pretty stupid."

"Don't worry about it. The Media does that to everybody who thinks outside the box. So, what technology will you work on at your new place?"

This was just the opening Karl was waiting for.

"I'd like you to tell me, Tommy. I know that, since Reagan, pretty much all tech research has gone into making the big companies rich, not helping the people who need it. What sort of stuff do you need that you can't get?"

Tommy grinned, and grabbed a napkin.

"It's like this," he said. "Back when we started, we wanted to put in all solar and wind stuff, get off the grid, be self-sufficient. You know. But everything got so expensive and large-scale after Reagan cut research incentives that we couldn't afford it."

He began sketching on the napkin.

"Like this. How about a cheap, simple windpower unit that I don't have to lay out fifty grand for?"

"Hmmm," Karl murmured, then grabbed the napkin and added some marks of his own.

"We could make the blades like this, maybe of bent PVC, then…"

Danny Kelso had to chase them out at closing.

Phoenix puzzled Ed Erhart. He hadn't known such capable people who were willing to defy convention. Of course, his business was mostly with those famously conventional people, farmers. He generally didn't like "weirdoes," but was drawn to this bunch by their straightforward friendliness. He would often bring his wife and daughter out to play on the beach or chat with the young folks, while he and Karl went fishing.

Karl and Ed had an unusual relationship. To an outside observer it would seem that they had nothing in common, but Karl sensed otherwise. Ed was likable, once you made allowances for his salesman persona. Although shallow in many ways, he could be clever and compassionate. Karl began to think of him more as a friend than as an adversary, whatever their unremembered past had been.

That's how it was- for a while.

The Bait Shop was a natural place for gossip. Regulars brought the news that "the LaSalle Seed guy" had been in a car crash. He'd been on a long pleasure drive over in South Dakota with his family. Some old fart in a combine had pulled out on the highway ahead of him. Ed was just banged up, but his daughter had died and his wife was in critical condition.

Karl called Ed's number to see how he could help. A relative answered. She would pass on Karl's concern.

Ed never returned Karl's call. A few days later the grape vine reported that Ed's wife had come home. She was still weak, but improving.

25

Two days later Karl called again, to ask how Caroline was doing. The same relative answered.

"She's dead!" the woman shouted, and then slammed the phone down.

Caroline Erhart had suffered a massive cerebral hemorrhage on her first night home. She had asked Ed for a glass of water in the night, and then slid into convulsions. She hadn't even gotten out of bed before she died.

Karl arrived at the cemetery just before the service began. He only had time to take his place among the standing mourners before the Minister said, "Dearly beloved, we are gathered…"

When it was over, and Caroline's coffin had been lowered into the grave, Karl approached Ed.

"Ed, if there's anything I can do…"

Erhart turned his reddened eyes to Karl's, and glared.

"Anything you can do?" He snorted. "Can you people bring back the dead? I think not."

"I'm sorry."

"Sorry. Yeah, I'm sure you are, mister rich guy," Erhart sneered.

Karl was taken aback.

"I know you're hurting, but why are you angry with me?" Karl said. "I would do whatever I could to help, if you'd ask."

Erhart began shouting and shaking his fists.

"I couldn't figure you guys out. You were always so calm, so confident, so condescending to this working slob. Now I know what it was. It was all an act. I was welcome because I was cheap entertainment. Sure, you'd help me out. Gotta take care of the court jester."

Karl was stunned.

"How can you think that, Ed?" said Karl. "No one ever insulted you! No one ever made you feel less than an honored guest!"

"The doctors were friendly, too. They take classes in feeding BS to patients and families, you know. They did everything they could to help- on the budget plan. There were things they could have tried, but the HMO wouldn't approve payment at our coverage level. They sent her home too early- sent her home to die in my arms. What's one less working class cow to them?

"You know how I'm always saying 'The System works?' The System damn well works, all right. It works for people like you- rich, powerful and lucky. It works to keep you on top. I busted my ass selling, but my pitiful commissions and benefits couldn't save my family. Do you worry about losing your kids, Mister Millionaire?"

"I've learned not to worry," Karl said, "just to be prepared."

"You can afford to be prepared, you and your kind: The ones who sit in offices and draw up tables for who lives and dies; the ones with nice suits and manicured hands."

"The System isn't fair, Ed. I know that. I don't like it either."

Erhart spat on the ground.

"Now I know the rules." Erhart said. "The ruthless rich win. The poor watch their families die. No more. Now I play rough, too. Stay out of my way, Karl."

Erhart turned on his heel and strode away. Ed never came to visit at Phoenix again.

Karl took the southerly route, US 212 via Montevideo, back to The Cities. He'd dropped the boys off at Loni's two weeks before, for parental visitation. *She's still their mother, after all, even if she is a short-sighted hedonist. I'm sure that seeing the contrast will do them good,* he thought.

Karl mused on patterns of urban growth as he sat, the Land Cruiser virtually parked, on I-494. He remembered projections twenty years before, that growth would utterly outstrip the freeway system's capacity by century's end. That future was now, and the overload was here. He frowned and shook his head. *Too few people understand systems,* he thought. *They can't see the broad or long-term consequences of their actions.*

After two hours of stop-and-going, after breathing huge volumes of toxic fumes, after several near-misses from hurtling SUVs, Karl emerged from the east side of the Metro. He spent another hour driving through what had been rolling fields of corn and grazing cattle a decade before: Now they were crowded with cookie-cutter houses and strip malls. He eventually reached the gated community where his former home stood. Afton Acres Abodes had started out as a high-end development, overlooking the St. Croix River. The houses had been huge, the lots of several acres, and the access road unguarded: The nearest other neighbors had been ten miles away back then.

Not now. He showed his ID to the gate guard, telling him, "Karl Mueller to see Loni Weiman." The guard wrote down Karl's car plate numbers, and cautioned him to be out by sundown or the police would be alerted.

The house stood on the choicest lot in the area, right on the brink of the St. Croix River valley. Hundreds of feet below, the wide river was a playground for sailing sloops and fishermen. The steep bluffs were heavily wooded, although the trees had begun to die back.

Karl crunched up the curving white stone driveway, and pulled in next to Loni's new BMW convertible. Alec, who had seen him coming, ran around the corner to greet him. The boy grabbed Karl in a hug as he got out of the car.

"Dad! Am I glad you're here!" he said. "I was so bored!"

"Bored? Here? With all these things to do?"

As they walked toward the kitchen doors, Alec told him.

"You can't get down to the river from here. It's miles to the stores, and Mom says it isn't safe to bike there. Nobody visits anybody around here. You can't just walk around, or somebody will call the cops. All there is, is cable TV and video games. I wanna go home!"

"OK, that suits me, son. Let's pick up James and your gear, then blow this pop stand."

Alec turned sober.

"Umm, Dad," he said. "I don't think it's gonna be that easy."

It wasn't easy. In the kitchen where Karl and Loni had had their last big fight, lay the pile of Alec's bags and gear. Alec's, not James'. Loni and James came into the room as Karl and Alec were picking up bundles.

"C'mon, James, hoist your gear," said Karl.

Loni stepped forward.

She announced, "He's not a boy any more, Karl."

Karl set down his burden while saying, "No, he's not. He's a young man, with a man's responsibility and honor."

Loni sighed.

"That's your problem. You won't let your kids be normal kids. You try to fill their heads with philosophic nonsense."

He looked past her at his elder son.

"I'm in no mood for an argument. James, get your stuff. We're out of here."

"No, Dad," said the dark-haired boy. "I don't want to go back to that high school and that hick town. I don't want to hang around with geeks and hippies. I'm staying with Mom."

"Are you sure?" Karl asked.

James nodded.

"I respect your right to make decisions, even though this one is a mistake. You can always come home."

"Home?" Loni shouted. "That circus you're running is no home for my James! He has ambition, even if you don't! You've ruined Alec, but at least I can save James! He'll be twice the man you ever were!"

Loni grabbed James by the shoulders and marched him away.

"And get out of my house!" she shouted over her shoulder. "I'll call Security!"

By 2000 Karl's second book, "How Did We Get Here?" was selling modestly well. It was a critique of Industrial Civilization's philosophical and ethical bankruptcy. He contended that applying outdated worldviews and concepts of morality to a radically changed world did far more harm than good. He wrote of how Phoenix was working to establish the basis for a new way of thinking about humanity's place in the universe, where science and technology were as spiritually legitimate as art and music.

In July, Karl received a phone call from the University of Minnesota, Morris Campus. Would he be interested in teaching a course on the ethical implications of technology?

Karl jumped at the chance. He knew that any good teacher learned more from his students than the students did from him. This would give him a chance to banter ideas with fresh, young minds. It would also help in developing valuable contacts for Phoenix.

UMM had grown from an Indian boarding school in the late 1800s, through stages as an agricultural and teachers' college, to a highly respected public institution. It partook of the small-town, prairie culture of Morris, though its small student body and faculty were a community within a community.

Teaching there was indeed a learning experience, both for good and ill.

Karl had still thought of University in terms of his days at St. Cloud State. He expected students full of fire and indignation at the crazy state of the country. There were very few such radicals any more. Most were just seeking to "get their tickets punched," to get a degree and start their climb up the corporate ladder. That wealth was increasingly concentrated in the hands of the few, that global warming was an obvious fact, and that personal privacy was eroding, didn't bother them in the least.

The presidential election of 2000 provided material for many discussions. As various candidates put forth their ideas, Karl would relate them to the class topics. What did it mean that one candidate claimed partial responsibility for the existence of the internet? Or, that another favored drilling for oil in wilderness areas over developing renewable resources? Or, that one candidate's choice for Attorney General favored increased government surveillance of private individuals? Most students stuck with the positions they'd learned from their families or churches, not applying the philosophic tools Karl tried to give them to dig deeper. Their positions

29

boiled down to: "Who would be so immoral as to vote Democratic?" and "Who would be so stupid as to vote Republican?" It was disheartening, for how could such polarized groups even talk to each other?

There were a few students each semester who got it, though. They understood that humanity was neither a plague upon the earth, nor undisputed Lord and Master of all. They saw that, in Ralph Nader's words, they had grown up corporate, not civil. They broke out of their boxes, even having real discussions with those who disagreed with them. They discovered that "those people" weren't just contrary or crazy after all!

More productive was contact with the other professors. One, a sociologist, had regular gatherings at her home. These potluck affairs brought not only great cooking, but sharp minds and articulate conversation. Karl was able to hone the Phoenix philosophy in the fierce byplay.

Chapter Five (2001)

"All you need is Love" John Lennon

Jody

At least they had a couple of good years, Jody thought.

Jason had been a welcome addition to "the gang." Having him around was clearly good for Andre. The four of them, very much two couples, had had plenty of good times together. Andre and Jason's wanderlust was infectious- the four of them had traveled all around Minnesota, even as far as the Black Hills of South Dakota and Winnipeg, Manitoba.

The Life Tapestry acquired scenes featuring smiling people on motorcycles, posed before lakes, mountains, Paul Bunyan and teepees.

Then Andre had noticed that Jason was loosing weight. His color was off, too. Jason visited the clinic- the cancer was back. It had settled in his pancreas. Jason began a round of chemotherapy. He also adopted a special diet, and needed pills for the pain in his gut.

The four didn't give up traveling, though. They just switched from bikes to the old Honda. With blankets and pillows, Jason was comfortable enough to travel up until a month before the end.

Fortunately, Andre's health plan through UMM covered Jason as a domestic partner. The University community was very supportive, too.

A big problem was the unnecessary suffering that a few fools brought out. As Jason became thinner and sallower, the rumor began that he had AIDS. Morris' local crusading preacher decided to make an example of him, proclaiming that "the wages of sin is slow, agonizing death." What should have been a quiet tragedy among friends was blown up as a civic disgrace.

Jason had been known downtown, since he did most of the shopping for the two men. Storekeepers and acquaintances were still friendly and supportive as his condition deteriorated, but random strangers muttered foul names as he passed. He'd come out of the grocery store to find anti-gay tracts under the car's windshield wiper. There were days when he couldn't leave the house for fear of what he'd face.

Then he couldn't go out at all, except to make a last trip to the hospital.

Of course, once Jason was dead, the furor died out. Nothing had really been changed by the ninety day wonder of a dying fag- except that a young man's life had been saddened by hateful, ignorant scorn.

Andre

I suppose that they had to call Jason's parents. After all, a domestic partnership isn't like a marriage, is it? It isn't like being in love has any legal standing. It isn't like just any two people can commit themselves to lifelong partnership. Hell, no, that would be just too weird.

Jason had been fading fast. After three weeks in the St. Cloud hospital, any day could have been his last. I dreaded the trip from my motel room each day, not knowing what I'd find. I pictured a sudden, touching exchange of last words. Worse, I pictured finding that my love had passed on while I was coming to him.

I didn't expect to be stopped at the elevator by a uniformed guard and Father Jim.

"That's all right, Mr. DuPris," the grey-haired old priest said. "Jason's family is here now. You can go home."

"But I'M his family!"

"No," said the representative of a loving God. "You are Jason's friend. I like you. We've had some good talks. Everyone appreciates you helping him along, but his parents are here now. They'll take good care of him in his last hours. They specifically want you kept away."

"But how is he doing?"

"I'm not authorized to tell you. That's up to the Next of Kin. Now please excuse me. I must go administer Last Rites."

"But Jason isn't Catholic."

"His FAMILY says that he is. Good day."

The priest re-entered the elevator. The guard silently took my arm and walked me out the front entrance.

The good thing about haunting a hospital at all hours is that you learn all the back ways and shortcuts. I nodded politely to the guard, as I walked toward the parking ramp. He watched me smugly until I entered the elevator lobby of the concrete spiral.

He didn't see me run right out the other side. He didn't see me cross the parking floor and vault over the back retaining wall. I landed twenty feet from a laundry entrance. A few steamy minutes and back stairs later, I peeked out the door at the end of Jason's ward.

A small parade was exiting his room. Father Jim was trying to look consoling. Jason's mother was sobbing loudly. Jason's father was trying to look stoic. The guard looked embarrassed. The sheet-draped body on the gurney just looked very dead.

Dead. Dead and gone. Ripped away- by loving, caring people.

I don't remember leaving. I don't remember reclaiming my gear and hitting the road. I do remember coming to from the wind in my face. My bike was humming along between Avon and Melrose on I-94. I was riding, not driving. I remember coming into Morris, then hitting the liquor store for the biggest bottle of brandy they had. I remember going back a couple of more times- I think.

Jody

Andre had given Jody's number to the motel as a backup. The manager called her on Saturday morning. Mister DuPris had left some items there- three days before. Would he be returning to claim them? Would she?

Three days. Too long. She told the manager that they'd come right away, then hung up.

"Bill!" she shouted from the kitchen. "Andre's got himself in trouble! He left St, Cloud three days ago!"

Bill ran in, hair and robe wet from a shower.

"OK, ok. Did you try calling him?"

"No, not yet. I will. You please get the car ready- I think that this will be an all day job."

"Right."

Soon the sound of Bill's hiking boots stomped out the back door. Jody listened to Andre's phone ring for a minute, then slammed the receiver down, The Honda was waiting at the side door when she rushed out.

Andre's bike was parked in front of his shop, not in the garage as usual. The front door wasn't locked.

They found their friend passed out on the couch. The room reeked of brandy that had spilled when the bottle fell from his hand. Bill picked him up by the shoulders.

"Hey, man, hey!" he said, shaking his friend. "Wake up! Come on."

"Please Andre!" Jody urged. "You don't need to do this!"

Andre's eyes fluttered open. He smiled.

"Hey, sugar." He said. "You shouldn't be here. I'm dead. Only dead people in this morgue. Move along." He closed his eyes.

Jody touched his cheek.

"What happened!? Where's Jason? Why are you here?"

"You dead too? Hey, we deaders gotta stick together. Stick, quick, sick, prick."

Andre shrugged loose from Bill's grasp. He swayed to his feet. He clumsily straightened his clothes, trying to look dignified.

"Master Jason has returned to Milwaukee," he said. "His REAL family came to take him. No darkie fags allowed, loud, proud, shroud."

Bill and Jody exchanged dismayed looks. Bill took Andre by the elbow, and began edging him toward the door.

"Come on," he said. "Let's get you some fresh air."

"Air, fair, swear, pair- unfair" Andre murmured. He lurched toward the back rooms. "Just let me get Jason. Hey Jason."

"Jason's gone on ahead," Bill said. "Let's go see what we can find."

"OK, Bill. But who's gonna pay the Bill, still, swill, kill?"

They managed to get their drunken friend into the car. Bill sat in back with Andre, while Jody drove. Jody had never seen real grief before; she was glad that Bill was there.

Bill and Jody had talked about what to do on the way over. What Andre needed was fresh air, friends and beauty. They headed east, toward the glacial ridge country around Starbuck and Glenwood. They pulled into a rest area that overlooked Lake Minnewaska. The four had often picnicked there.

Andre began to sober up. He sat on the guard rail where the parking lot met the bluff's edge.

'"Jason," he said. "Where are you? You were here. Now you aren't."

He turned to Jody.

"They just fucking TOOK him!" he howled. "No goodbye. No by-your-leave. No forwarding address."

Jody tried to understand how her friend was hurting. She couldn't.

"Hey," she said. "I bet the Delgados were scared and confused, then, too."

"No, they weren't. They knew exactly what they were doing."

Bill saw that Jody didn't understand.

"Come on," he said. "Let's just drive. We'll grab some sandwiches and make a day of it. We can visit the places that Jason loved. He won't really be dead, then, not completely."

The day was a mobile wake for their missing comrade. The four of them drove a meandering loop through Central Minnesota. They visited Ole the Viking in Alexandria, and Paul Bunyan in Brainerd. They stood by Lake Mill Lacs and the Mississippi. They picked up Andre's gear in St. Cloud. They remembered Jason's humor, and his love for the road. Andre re-told the story of their meeting at a bike rally in Madison. That evening they ate at their favorite club near Alexandria.

Past midnight, they dropped Andre at his place. He assured Bill and Jody that he appreciated their offer to stay with them, but he needed his space. And no, there was no booze in the house.

As he got out of the car, Andre said, "It's over, then."

Jody answered, "No, it isn't. You still have to help me design Jason's panel on the Life Tapestry."

35

Chapter Six (2001)

Friend and foe in the Global Village

Phoenix

Kelly Jackson was minding the Bait Shop when a focused-looking woman strode through the door. She wore a calf-length, chocolate colored skirt and a cream-colored blouse. Her dark hair was up in a bun beneath her broad-brimmed straw hat. She carried a small, soft-sided brief case. She took off her sunglasses, glanced around, and strode purposefully up to the counter.

"I am Maria Carvalho. I come here for to see Karl Mueller," she said. To Kelly, a lifelong Chicago resident, she sounded South American.

"Yes, ma'am," he answered. "He'll be over at the Big House. Just out the door, turn left and cross the alley."

"Thank you."

Karl and Doug were discussing the state of the labs, particularly their shortage of biologists. Karl had assured Doug that the people they needed would show up somehow; then the doorbell rang.

Karl opened the door to find a short, no nonsense woman.

"You are Karl Mueller?" she asked.

"Yes, I am. What can I do for you?"

"I am Maria Carvalho. I am here for to work with you. May I come in?"

"Yes, please do," said Karl. He walked her to the dining room, where the lab schedules were spread out on the table.

"This is Doug, our Lab Manager," Karl said.

After greetings and handshakes he said, "Tell us about yourself, Maria."

"I am from Recife, Brazil. I am at the University of Minnesota on a post-graduate exchange program. I saw your postings for interns. I can help you, and learn from your activities."

"And what is your specialty?"

"I am a veterinarian and biologist."

Karl gave Doug an "I told you so" look.

"Why did you come to us?"

"In my country I have seen forests turned to deserts. I have seen the poor punished for their poverty by the rich and comfortable. We try to find new crops and new ways to raise livestock. You are developing things the poor need. I have seen. I can help you. I can learn from you."

One autumn morning Karl was taking a nap. Nothing in Phoenix needed his attention, and he'd been distracted by an odd feeling of foreboding. Karl was a lucid dreamer, one who is conscious that he is dreaming, and is able to act with knowledge in his dreams. He hoped that such a dream would give insight into his unsettled feelings this day.

He found himself in a glass-walled office, high in a tower over New York. Next to him, looking out over the cityscape was Juan Trippe, the aviation pioneer and founder of Pan Am airlines. Some of the world's greatest airplanes, such as the 747, were his brainchildren. In the shadows lurked robed and bearded men, grinning.

Trippe was pointing out over the New York skyline and crying.

"My beautiful airplanes!" he moaned. "Why did they have to do that with them?"

A few blocks away, smoke billowed from a pair of bluish glass skyscrapers. Karl could feel the terror of the people within, like a gale of ammonia and acrid smoke.

Why would someone do such a nasty thing to Juan? He wondered. *I'm glad I'm just dreaming.*

He heard shouts in the distance. As he turned toward them, the scene faded. Alec was shaking his shoulders and shouting.

"Dad! Dad! Wake up! Red Thursday came on a Tuesday!"

37

Karl sprang awake in a surge of adrenaline. That was a family high-disaster code, drawn from Robert Heinlein's book "Friday." *Oh, Gods, no!* he thought.

"Where? What," he asked as he jumped up, grabbed his pants, and headed out the door.

"New York! The World Trade Towers!"

"Again? How bad this time?"

"Terminal. Hit by an airliner. Maybe two."

Juan, I'm glad you didn't live to see this.

The TV lounge was crowded. The Phoenixites watched, mesmerized, as havoc engulfed Manhattan. When the towers fell, Karl told his people "The Reichstag has burned. It goes downhill from here."

Some were confused.

"It's an historical pattern. A Right-wing government comes to power on a technicality. It stresses nationalism, not international cooperation. Then a very public disaster provides the excuse for clamping down. Watch for increasing security demands, racial stereotyping, eroding of constitutional rights, foreign wars, the whole deal. Even if Mr. Bush means well, that's the path his philosophy, and history, will lead him down: to full-blown imperialistic fascism.

"Friends, we may have just gone from research center to Ark."

Jody

Jody thought Steve's funeral an odd affair. He'd pretty much lived on the road for NASA for years. He had never married. Asyl was his home as much as anywhere, even though his travels had ranged far beyond it. As in many churches across America that September, Asyl Lutheran Church brought together an odd assortment of mourners. They came to share History as much as Grief.

Just being in the old church was strange for Jody. The sanctuary, with its high beams and musky smells seemed an apparition from another life. All of her childhood Sundays had been spent there. When she was a girl, this place had been the center of all goodness and comfort; but at the U she'd drifted into an ill-defined faith. The old forms didn't mean so much any more- but on this important occasion, here she was.

All the formal trappings were out for Asyl's lone 9/11 victim. Candles burned on the altar. Banners draped every wall. There were friends of the Neihauses, dressed in their Sunday clothes, NASA acquaintances in suits from nerdly to elegant, Kate and Karl looking professorial, and the usual local "church crashers" in whatever presentable clothes they owned. Faiths ranged from Lutheran to Wiccan, from Buddhist to Atheist.

The ceremony opened with Jody and her parents lighting a large candle. Several classmates then spoke about Steve's High School days. A NASA astronaut described Steve's diligence and his dedication to expanding Humanity's frontiers. Then the minister preached about the heritage of Asyl's pioneer forebears. Jody was last, talking about his last phone call.

Jody barely got through her part; she was stopped several times by choking sobs. She spoke about the last time she'd talked to him. He had been in New York, consulting with subcontractors. He had one last meeting, early the next day. After that, he'd be coming to Minnesota for a visit. He'd bring her a souvenir of the World Trade towers, where the engineers' offices were.

"I'll be there day after tomorrow, Sis. Bye now!" were his last words to her.

In the lobby afterward Jody overheard an older woman saying to friends, "Such a nice boy, too."

Jody looked toward the woman, curious.

"It's a shame he had so many funny ideas. If he'd just settled down to a safe, normal life, he'd still be around."

Another added, "All this nonsense about running all over the country! And space ships! Uff dah! That boy should've just stayed put, like sensible folks."

Kate appeared at Jody's shoulder.

"'Sensible folks,'" she chuckled. "Don't let them get to you, kid. Their own great-grandfathers, who walked beside their wagons from St. Paul to get here, would disown them as yellow sheep."

Pastor Iversen tried, he really did.

"Jody, I never knew Steve well, but everyone spoke highly of him." he said after the service. "We can't understand why God chose to take him now, but we can know that it was part of His great plan. Hold onto that, and the grief will pass."

Jody heard him. She remembered why she'd lost her faith; it meant pretending that things were OK. It meant that being powerless pets of The Almighty gave enough meaning to life- but it didn't.

To Jody and Steve, only children of Mike and Inge, the wood behind the houses had been their private world. They climbed the trees, picked nuts and berries, and watched birds and squirrels.

Out of this all, what stood out in Jody's memory were nights of stargazing on its outside edge. The trees blocked the town's lights, and the flat fields all around gave an unobstructed view.

Steve was a giant to her. He seemed to have been born knowing the stars, their names, their constellations, and the myths they embodied. Model spacecraft hung from his bedroom ceiling. He played guitar, and sang songs of voyaging and discovery. He had shelves of books about an adventurous future, where war, poverty, disease and hatred were but a distant memory. In Steve's future, people took risks and endured hardship because they chose to, not because circumstances forced them to.

He always did a ritual on July 20th.

"Why is this night different from all other nights? On this night we crossed over. We went to the Moon. That's what people DO: We go and find out."

He sighed. "I'll go find out some day."

Steve proved that he had the drive for his vision in high school. He fixed up an outbuilding to be his model rocketry lab. He crammed in all the science and math classes he could. He lettered in track. He became an Eagle Scout. But while the vision of his soul was strong enough, the vision of his body wasn't. By the middle of his junior year he needed glasses; astronauts couldn't wear glasses.

Still, the fire burned. If he couldn't follow Neil Armstrong, he could follow Verner von Braun. If he couldn't go "where no man had gone before," he could help to send others. He graduated at the top of his class at the University of Minnesota. Then he claimed a double Masters in Engineering and Avionics from Cal Tech. That's where NASA found him.

Jody still had the shoebox of postcards. Beginning with Huntsville, Alabama, Steve had sent her picture cards from everywhere NASA sent him. He was a troubleshooter who made sure that vendors' goods met spec. He'd also been one of the team who finally tracked down the cause of the Challenger disaster in the '80s.

On the afternoon of the funeral, Jody received a postcard showing the World Trade Towers. In neat blueprint-style lettering it proclaimed, "Hey, kid! See you soon. Love, Steve." Jody had thought Steve would always be there. She had thought that she'd live in the future his visions pointed to. She was wrong, on both counts.

Fat Tuesday that next week was a somber affair. Some of the regular attendees were from the Middle East: That the 9/11 attacks had apparently been carried out by Arab terrorists made them fearful.

"Hey, we all know that you aren't that way," said Isaac, a mathematician.

Abdul, another math professor, said, "I thank you, friend. But we all know that Islam has always had its militant side."

"But so has Christianity," said Kate, "and most Christians are live and let live folks."

"True, said Fatima Iskedra, an Historian. "But don't forget that in ninety-nine percent of religious wars, one or the other of them was the aggressor."

"It's got nothing to do with religion!" declared Karl Mueller. "Any truly religious person knows better than killing and maiming. It's an excuse, or at best a shorthand cultural reference."

"So, what do you think it's really about?" asked Kate.

"Cultural imperialism, pure and simple," said Karl. "The rich western countries can dictate how markets work, what gets played on the radio, and what gets seen on TV and in theaters. People from other cultures are sick of it, and are fighting back."

"Precisely," said Isaac, while Abdul nodded vigorously.

Jody looked doubtful.

"But doesn't that apply to how the urban centers treat us out here?" she asked.

Karl smiled a sinister smile.

"It does, indeed," he said. "And what do you think is going to happen one of these days?"

There was silence for nearly a full minute.

"Jody," Kate said. "You're the only one of us who actually lost someone close. What do you think?"

"I think there are many people who kill dreams. They can't stand anyone who reaches higher than they do. Sometimes they kill with remarks and looks. Sometimes they cut your budget. Sometimes they blow you up. It's all the same."

☾Chapter Seven (2002)

Life will find a way

Phoenix

At first, the Phoenix labs worked primarily on developing small, inexpensive solar and wind energy units. The marketing for these concentrated on word of mouth, the Internet, and targeted magazines like Mother Earth News. The bigger markets weren't interested in devices to make people less dependant on centralized power. Phoenix sold plans and kits as well as pre-made units, so adventurous, capable souls could branch out, even get completely "off the grid." Business was brisk. Phoenix sometimes had to hire local labor to meet production deadlines. They eventually licensed other companies to produce some products.

The Phoenix people also wanted to address issues of toxic waste and cleanup. This was as much for themselves as for the market, since the Minnesota River was highly polluted by agricultural chemical runoff and upstream industries. The solution boiled down to biology; specifically, genetically modified organisms to soak up and encapsulate the waste. Karl thought it was a shame that GMOs were utterly taboo to their best clients: Even if they came up with a solution, it would be hard to market it. *One thing at a time,* he reasoned. The job needed doing, even if Phoenix never made a dime.

Quietly, Connie and her team developed a modified dwarf almond. They induced bacteria into symbiosis with the plants, like those in legumes. This enabled the bushes to concentrate heavy metals, PPCs and other toxins in their nuts. The team also made the nut shells literally rock hard. The nuts fell to the ground as golf ball sized stones. They were safe to leave where they fell, as breaking them open was very difficult. They smelled too bad for anything to try to eat them.

Many environmentally toxic chemicals had industrial uses. The nuts could be gathered and brought to a "cracking plant." These chemicals could be extracted and reused. Those that were useless poisons could be neutralized.

Soon the territory around Phoenix blossomed with pink-flowered scrubberbushes. Old factory and dump sites were favored plantation spots. The contaminant level in the soil around Phoenix, and in the upper Minnesota River Valley, began to drop.

Then the Pollution Control Agency heard about the scrubberbushes. Phoenix was slapped with a Cease-and-Desist injunction for releasing an unapproved organism into the wild. The bushes were a huge success- TOO much so.

One evening Karl got a phone call from Erhart.

"I have a solution to your little problem," he said. "You have a product without a market. I have markets who want that product. The Pollution Control people have you hog tied."

"Yes," said Karl. "What do you suggest?"

"Karl, don't be coy. We can help each other- I'm a dealmaker, remember? You sell the right to grow and distribute scrubberbushes to La Salle Seeds. We do the legwork; you get royalties, everybody's happy."

"What about the PCA?"

Erhart laughed.

"Karl, Karl, we've had them in our pocket for decades! Who do you think sicced them on you, anyway?"

"You bastard!"

"Ah, but I'm your bastard, Karl. I'm just looking out for you. Sometimes even your kind doesn't win; I really don't want to see you lose, Karl. You play with me, I play with you, we both benefit."

In the ensuing months, Phoenix scrubberbushes became standard tools in toxic cleanup, nationally. Phoenix made some money, LaSalle Seeds made a lot of money, and Ed Erhart gained in corporate stature.

A large man carrying a small bundle entered the Bait Shop. This wasn't unusual; he was a regular, and liked what the new owners had done with the Shop. It had been darker before, a musty "guy place." He appreciated the wider, open windows and brighter colors. His wife even visited here occasionally. She talked with the young folks; now that their youngest was off at school, the mother in her liked to be around them. She'd miss that. He walked toward the counter, past a few guys who were looking at the pegboard displays of tackle.

"Hey, Ben!" the blond woman behind the counter said. "What can I do for you?"

"Hey, Barb. I'm lookin' for your boss," he answered. "Is he around?"

"Yeah, I think he's out back. Go on through."

"Thanks. Say, won't you be leaving us soon?"

"Uh huh. I go back to the U in Moorhead next week."

"Aww. Us old guys will miss your face around here."

"Thanks. This summer has been good for me."

As he walked out past the burbling live bait tanks, Ben thought about the nice kids Karl always found to mind the Bait Shop. He'd sure miss them all.

He found Karl out back, talking with Jules about something or other, pointing out toward the campground and slowly sweeping his arm through an arc. As always, Jules had his clipboard.

"Hey Karl, Jules!" Ben called.

"Hey yourself," answered Karl, sticking his hand out.

"Hi, Ben," said Jules, also shaking hands. "I gotta run. I'll see you gentlemen later."

"OK"

"So, old timer, what's up?" said Karl. Ben was only five years older than Karl, but looked much more weathered.

"Well, kid. I brought back a couple of your books."

"Fine, thanks. Can we find you some new ones?"

"Nope, I don't think I'll be raiding your library any more."

"Why?" said Karl. He'd had a bad feeling about Ben and Marta all day. "What's wrong?"

"Ach, it's this weather. First we flood, and now no rain for weeks. We'll be lucky to get silage corn out of the fields. The banker and the seed company know it, too. I'm still in hock to them for this year's planting."

"So, how bad is it?" Karl asked. He looked grave; his friend was honest and diligent, but caught between the jaws of weather and economics. He wasn't the only one in the area on the raw edge of failure. And as the small independents failed, the corporate operators gobbled up the land.

"I got a call from the bank today," Ben said. "I need to come up with $20,000 or equivalent new collateral in two weeks. If I don't come up with something, we're for the road. But I've hocked everything I own already."

Karl hated to mention it, but said, "I can lend you the money, Ben."

Ben looked at Karl with a sick smile and moist eyes, and put a hand on Karl's shoulder.

"I know you could, friend, but that's just good for this time. There are still more payments to make this winter. With no crop to speak of, we'd be out then. I'm just too tired to keep fighting. I figure it's better to move in August than December. Our daughter Mandy says we can move in with her, down in Alabama."

"You're right, of course." Karl said. "I hate the squeeze you guys are in. In the long run we'll be developing more things to help folks like you, but right now there isn't much we can do."

The wealthy idealist and the stomped working man stood silently, sharing grief and frustration.

"Hey, I know," Karl said. "Now don't say no right off, but how about you join us?"

"Whaaat? I don't have half the education of the people here! I'm three times their age!"

"Don't sell yourself short. You have the kind of education we need right now- practical experience. These kids are bright, but they don't have the kind of hands-on knowledge you have.

"Besides, you're a native. You know folks around here better than I will for decades. You'd be a great liaison man. Here's my proposal- We bring in a nice trailer or something for you and Marta to live in. You two run the bait shop. You give our design committee a farmer's view of their ideas. Marta can teach the kids I bring in how to feed and take care of this bunch. You'd be Uncle and Aunt to a circus."

Ben stared into the distance, astonished.

"I didn't come here looking for a handout, much less a job, but…"

"No buts," said Karl. "It's no handout, and no job, either. We'll be partners."

The following two weeks were spent getting a house set up, and transferring the most important heirlooms and useful things from the Guthries' farm. On the day of the foreclosure auction, Karl watched with Ben and Marta as decades of memories were dismantled and sold to the highest bidder. Ed Erhart was there too.

"Hi, folks," Erhart said. "I'm real sorry it all came to this. I wished you'd taken me up on that contract when I'd offered it, Ben."

"Ed, I've known you for years," Ben said. "You know that all your contract offered me was a chance for your guys to tell me what to plant, what to spray on it, and who to sell it to. I'd have been nothing but a sharecropper."

"Ben, I'm sorry you feel that way," said Erhart. "That's just how things operate these days. People have to make a living by trusting the System. It works."

Ben eyed Erhart sharply.

"I wasn't trying to make a living, but to make a life. You don't get that, do you? So, why are you here?"

"I'm here to bid on the equipment, the house and the land. We have a young farmer who's willing to do things our way. We finance the place; he runs it, everybody's happy."

"Not everybody," Karl murmured.

At supper that evening, Karl said, "Folks, I believe that the time has come for Phase Two."

"What's that?" Ben asked

"Phoenix was planned as a research village," Karl explained. "Now that labs and production are established, it's time to move in more people. Not everyone here should be college-aged or a scientist. Our solutions must work in a real living environment, or they aren't really solutions."

He smiled at their newest residents.

"You and Marta are the first of the next wave."

In the ensuing months, entirely by word of mouth, dozens of new people joined Phoenix. Some found jobs in the area. Many were writers, web designers, artists or others who could live almost anywhere. Others formed work crews, which Phoenix hired out for projects in the area. Everyone had community duties, such as maintenance, cooking, security or childcare. The community paid its own way, and then some.

Phoenix experimented with construction techniques to house the newcomers and their needed infrastructure. Ecological change had come, and would continue; it must be accounted for. The engineers settled on sprayed concrete domes for most new construction. They were relatively cheap and easy to build, and could be buried for energy efficiency and storm protection.

Chapter Eight (2002)

"Life IS suffering" The Buddha

Jody

If I need anything, Jody thought. *I need everything.*

It was over. The Minister had pronounced the benediction. Folks had given the widow their IOUs of "if you need anything...," then hurried through the April drizzle to their cars. She knew that most would actually avoid her for weeks: people usually acted as though "Death of a Loved One" was catching. It was worse when someone so young had been taken.

Jody stood beneath the canopy, watching the workmen fill the wound in the earth. She stood alone, as she had been alone since her office phone had rung a week before.

The cemetery shared a fence with UMM. The Fine Arts Center was just across the yard. She could see her office window through the chill spring mist. She seemed to see a shadow there, as if the Self from her old life were watching her.

They had gone to hear the Dalai Lama's address at the Student Center Auditorium. Bill had volunteered to stay and help with takedown. She had some papers to grade, so she waited for him in her office. It was just a block or so, with one street to cross. He was overdue. Then the phone's pleasant cricket sound had announced the destruction of her world. After listening to a prophet of abiding peace, Bill had met sudden violence.

No more camping trips. No more debates over style and culture. No more "We'll have children when…" No more constant remodeling of The House. Although she could call up Bill's face and voice, and could still feel his love, it was the end of their life. A whole future had been swept away by a careless student in a hot car. She could feel the walls of restraint closing back in. The sodden canvas of the pavillion above her felt like her own shroud, waiting to wrap her in its finality.

It wasn't fair: first her big brother Steve, now her beloved Bill. She felt caught in one of those dank old Swedish films. *If they made a movie of my life, Liv Ullman would play me,* she thought.

Jody returned to The House; not Home, never again Home. She was tired, but she couldn't sleep in The Bed. The unfinished spare bedroom, with its gray sheetrock walls, suited her mood better anyway. She tossed a blanket onto the bare mattress, stripped off her severe black mourning dress, grabbed a quilt and drifted into fitful slumber.

Andre

I know how some artists are, Personal tragedy hits them, and they crumble. They live so much in their work that when their framework goes, they're lost. The weaving is ripped from the loom, unfinished.

Jody and Bill had known this. When Jason died I was ready to crawl into the bottle and never come out. They gave me a few days, then came out to our shop and bodily dragged me back into life. We drove all day. We went to Jason's favorite scenic spots, and then had supper at "our" steak house up by Alexandria.

It was my turn.

I dialed the number. She let it ring. When the machine picked up, I said, "It's me. You know why I'm calling. We need to give Bill a proper wake. It's five o'clock. I'll be there at seven with supper. Be ready."

Two hours was more than enough time. I called the Blue Panda to order take-out for two. I warmed up my bike and went to the liquor store for a bottle of Rhine wine. I stopped by my office for some Irish CDs. Then I picked up the food.

I'd been planning a surprise gift for weeks. I'd found the perfect one in the shopping news just four days ago. What better time? I called the number, told the people I was coming, swung by to pick it up, then went to Pamida for the supplies to go with it.

The House was a quirky old Victorian domicile with lots of scrollwork. The dormers even had fish scale siding. Various owners had added to, remodeled, and "improved" it to absurdity. It stood, out of place, on a farmstead a few miles east of Morris. It had been rather run down when Jody and Bill had bought it. They'd been whacking away at fixing it up for years, but in the end it didn't seem much nearer to completeness.

By the time I reached The House it was dusk. The rain had stopped, making for a bronze prairie sunset. It was just chilly enough for a fire. Perfect.

I used my key to go in the back door. I set the food and wine on the counter.

"Hey! I'm here!" I shouted.

"In here!" Jody called from the living room. She'd thrown on tan slacks and a sweater. She was on a stepstool, tying off the ends of the six-foot Life Tapestry that hung above the fireplace. Every event since her meeting Bill was recorded on it in symbolic form.

She had that eye-of-the-storm calm of a person who's cried as much as they can, for now. She tried to smile. I helped her down, and walked her back into the kitchen.

"Hi. You didn't have to do this."

"Yes, I did. Now, put the wine in to chill and keep the food warm. I'll be back."

I ran back out for the surprise and its sack of supplies. She crossed her arms and mock-glared at the box I had set on her kitchen counter. Scratching sounds came from within it.

"Now what have you done, silly?" she said.

"I know that you two were talking about getting a cat," I said as I opened the lid. I lifted out a diminutive ball of black fur, with blue eyes.

Jody's eyes got big. She uncrossed her arms and leaned forward, her lips parting.

"This is Isis," I said as I handed the kitten to her. "You two get acquainted and go start a fire while I set things up."

Soon we were propped up by cushions in front of the fire. Cartons of Sesame Chicken, Lo Mein and vegetables stood open between us. The fire pulsed and wavered, a good inducement to calm and reflection. Tommy Makem crooned in the background. Isis, after much begging and purring, had settled down to sleep on Jody's lap.

The tapestry glowered in the dimness. Jody pointed to its left side. She talked about meeting Bill, how he had charmed her loose from her timidity.

"He was like that," I said. "An agitator for us quieter types."

She nodded. "I'd never realized how sheltered my youth was," she said. "I had my little, warm world, and he made it a whole lot bigger. Steve liked him, too. They were both wanderers. Bill saw a horizon, and wanted to cross it. Steve saw the stars, and wanted to touch them. They both probably would have lived longer if they hadn't tried so hard."

"Probably," I said. "But they would have lived less."

"I suppose," she said

She sat looking at the fire for a minute.

"It's funny," she finally said. "An old buddy of ours showed up at the funeral."

"Oh, he's that stranger you were talking to." I said.

She smiled at me.

"I should have known you'd be watching," she said. "Yes, that was Allen. We were kind of a gang of three, back then. Sometimes it was four, when Allen would drag along his current girlfriend. When Bill and I started to get serious, he just faded away."

"And now he's back," I said. "How do you feel about that?"

"It's good to see an old friend. He's become quite a success."

"Really? How successful is he?" I raised an eyebrow. *No rebound fever for you girl, Huh-uh,* I thought.

"He's some kind of big shot at the Walker in Minneapolis, but he's not doing his own art. He used to do the most sublime stained-glass stuff."

She sighed and shifted uncomfortably.

"He offered to help me with connections back in The Cities."

"Are you going to take him up on it?"

She shrugged.

"I suppose I should consider it. I don't know. I thought I had my life figured out. Now…"

I raised a glass, and waved a salute to the tapestry.

"Let the future take care of itself," I said. "Professor, now we must celebrate the life of our dearly departed."

"Grandma's House" wasn't much, just a parlor, kitchen, bedroom, and a washroom lean-to on the back. A disused chicken coop stood across the weed-grown yard. Jody's great-grandfather Samuel had built the mini-Victorian house from a Sears and Roebuck kit in the 1890s, to replace the original claim shack. His daughter, Jody's grandma Agnetha, had still lived there when Jody was young. It was a place of transitions, pinched between town to the east, the woods to the north, and endless prairie to the west. Young Jody was reminded daily of what stock she'd come from; the handiwork of the past nurtured the future.

In three weeks, Jody had mostly settled into the cottage. Her busyness helped to mask the fact that she was rudderless. Her life had been all planned out. First Bill, then their "gang" had given her a framework and drive. Now, who was she? Where was she going? She was physically back in Asyl, but could never really return to her lost youth there.

It was past 10:00 on a Friday night. She'd been fussing with the old chicken coop studio for hours. She decided to take a walk. She popped Isis into her apron pocket, and then headed down the hill toward downtown.

It's funny, she thought. *I still think of it as Downtown, even though I've seen strip malls with more businesses.* She remembered Bill's light comments about "Gopher Prairie" and "Lake Woebegone" on their infrequent visits. It hurt to remember. She stopped to lean against a telephone poll until her heart steadied.

A teenaged woman walking two huge husky dogs came by, and paused. Isis gave a long hiss, then snuggled back into her pocket refuge.

"Are you all right, ma'am?" the youngster asked.

Jody fluttered a hand, belittling concern.

"I'm fine."

"Say," said the dog lady. "Aren't you the professor who just moved back into the old cottage? Mom says she knows you."

"Yes, that's me. Who's your mother, then?"

"Oh, Marge Sterne. She used to run the Brownie troop. I'm Kristy. She told me what happened. I'm really sorry."

"Thanks. Please tell your Mother that I said hi. I'll look her up once I get my feet under me."

"Cool. Well, nice meeting you, then."

Jody watched Kristy walk north down Fourth Street, then went south.

After walking past three blocks of houses, Jody came to the real center of town, where the spire of the Asyl Lutheran Church and the bell tower of the Asyl Public School faced each other across Fourth Street. The school still looked the same, although the High School grades now met in the big consolidated school eight miles west. She walked up and around the building toward the detached band room.

She stopped in surprise. It was gone. In its place was a fancy sort of jungle gym.

"What the heck," she muttered to Isis. "It was just an old one-room schoolhouse they dragged in from the country. It probably collapsed or something."

She remembered: creaky wooden floors and old high windows; coat rack in the hall; the scents of valve oil, rosin and dust in the air. School banners which she'd made had hung between the windows. She'd always been the first one there for rehearsals- it gave her "alone time." Her job in winter was to turn up the cranky stove and start the ceiling fans so people's lips wouldn't freeze to their instruments. Sometimes, she'd put a swing record on the old record player and dance around before anyone else came. She often felt that others were dancing with her, and wondered whether the building was haunted. She'd always meant to bring Bill back to see it.

All gone. Bill used to say that nothing in nature was ever really gone. It just gets recycled. Is he really gone? Am I? What does it feel like to be recycled?

She came around the building, back within sight of the church. Its high vaulted roof evoked more memories.

Even that's changed. I'm not in Luther League any more, and I'll never be a Circle Lady. I've gone too far, right off the edge of my world, without a parachute.

She kept walking, past the church, through two blocks of houses, down to Main Street. Of course it was deserted. Nothing was left that stayed open past six o'clock any more, not even a bar. She hadn't really been down here for years; the road from Morris connected close to her parent's place, way up on the North Side, six blocks away.

She turned the corner at the Fire Hall to go back up Hill Avenue, and stopped. *No. Can it be?* she wondered. There was a new building behind the Fire Hall, in the lot where the old horseshoe pitches had been. A metal junk sculpture of a farmer on his tractor stood among wildflowers before it. It was red, not white. It had Viking-style dragon heads on the ends of its roof beams- but it looked like the old band room! She walked over to it, stepping onto its broad porch. ASYL VILLAGE ARTS SCHOOL the sign read. The letters were in a kind of Gothic font, and were surrounded by richly detailed paintings of trees, vines, flowers, and figures in old-fashioned dress. A smaller, hand-written sign in the door's window proclaimed that business hours were more-or-less noon to five, depending on who was around and what classes were running.

I'll get down here to see tomorrow, she thought. *Hey, Andre'd like that sculpture, too. I'll call him.*

Andre

I was glad that Jody called me. I'd worried about her retreating from life, living in the old house around the old people in the old places. Even better, it sounded as though there'd been some interesting developments in Asyl. A decent junk sculpture? A dragon-headed art school? We'd just skirted the north end of town on our visits. I'd always wondered what else the town had going.

I saddled up my bike and headed out about 9:00. The highway south out of Morris was prairie-straight, but with enough long hills and gully-swerves to make it interesting. Several farmers were out spraying their fields. The huge, ungainly spray machines were like stretched-out go-carts with wings, bizarrely sculptural in their functionality. In other places, immense irrigation systems, like Paul Bunyan's lawn sprinklers, made rainbows over glistening fields of young corn.

I had to dodge several pheasants. I'd learned that these transplanted Asian birds liked to run AT trouble instead of away from it

At one point, about half way to Asyl, I came upon a vista worth stopping for. After a slow climb for about five miles, the ground dropped steeply away. From that ridge I could see perhaps thirty miles. Islands of farm sites dwindled into the distance. A mile-long train was creeping into Holloway, ten miles ahead. Hawks and eagles circled, hunting. A flock of pelicans danced their aerial ballet; I'd never known how beautiful those homely birds were in flight until I came to the prairie.

Past Appleton, around a bend and through an ancient, graffiti-covered concrete railroad trestle, was Asyl. I soon rolled up the hill to the Neihaus Place. Mike Neihaus was out mowing his lawn. He waved and smiled. As I pulled up before the berry-pink and blue gingerbread house, I saw Isis peeking from the parlor window. Her eyes didn't leave me as I parked and walked up to the screen door.

I walked in through the royal-blue door, pausing to admire its painted floral border. I shouted haloos, but the house seemed empty. I offered my hand to Isis, who finally recognized me and stretched out to be petted. I called out again, and caught a faint, "I'm out back." I passed boxes still standing in the kitchen and the laundry room lean-to. At the back door I called out again, then followed Jody's voice across a lawn of knee-high wildflowers.

She was in a long, low building with windows just under the eaves. I guessed that it had been a chicken coop. A door stood open near one end.

"In here. C'mon in!"

The scents of Pine Sol and bleach lingered in the air, but her studio was well set up. Her big loom stood in the middle of the floor. A huge work table sat at the far end. A wall of hen nesting boxes had been converted to fabric bins. Isis had followed me from the house, and leaped up into one with a worn blanket lining that was clearly "hers." In the middle of her sanctuary stood Jody in her apron, actually looking relaxed.

"Very nice," I said, looking over the bins. "But where's the Life Tapestry?"

Her face fell.

"Oh, I stuck it in this bin over here."

"Wouldn't it go nicely under the windows?" I asked.

"I suppose." said Jody. "But I don't know. It almost doesn't seem right, now that Bill's gone."

I put a hand on her shoulder.

"He's dead, but not really gone." I said. "Your story isn't over, so neither is his. Put up the tapestry. Keep the story alive."

I helped her to unroll the cloth, and tack it up along the north wall. As we stood back to admire it, I asked, "OK, now what? This town still has some surprises, it sounds like."

"OK, I'll show you." She said, then hung up her apron and led me out the door, stopping to give Isis a scritch behind the ears.

Sure enough, down the hill and over a couple of blocks, there was the school, just as she had described it. The rusty, metallic farmer rode his tractor through a field of prairie wildflowers. It was a competent piece of folk art. So was the building. Lovingly carved dragon's heads protruded from the roof beams. Rough-hewn timbers made front and side porches and a bell tower.

A sign in magic marker, taped to the door, said "HAVING LUNCH AT THE CAFÉ –MYRA-"

As we walked the block over to Main Street, Jody told me that there'd been two cafés in town when she was a girl. I counted half a dozen empty store fronts. Asyl was slowly drying up, like the other uncounted empty towns I'd seen from my bike over the years.

The café had an overblown Scandinavian motif. I must have looked like a tourist, gawking around. A tall blonde woman called from the cash register, "Hey Jody, what can I do for you?"

"Do I know you?" Jody asked.

"No," said the woman. "But everybody knows you. I'm Lois Greene. Who's your friend?"

Jody grumbled something about "small town gossip."

"This is Andre. He's another Art Instructor. We're looking for Myra."

"That'd be me," said a short, compact, red-haired woman. She rose from a group at the far end of the table and stuck out her hand.

We had introductions all around. It turned out that we'd walked in on the lunch for a master class. While Myra and the instructor were from Asyl, the seven students were from as far as Florida and British Columbia. I was impressed.

"What brings these people from so far?" I asked.

Myra answered, "Some of the best Traditional Scandinavian artists in the world live around here, and that's from international juried contests. Other instructors come here every summer to learn from them"

"I knew there were painters here," said Jody, "But, the best in the world?"

Myra sighed.

"Yah, that's been a problem," she said. "People tend to say, 'That's just so-and-so. I go ta church with her.' They don't recognize some things that are right in front of them. Besides, most artists are too busy doing Art to worry about getting famous."

"But somebody's got to know," said Jody.

"Sure. Lots of people in the Arts and Progressive communities do. We run classes on weekends all summer, and even most weekdays. We get literally busloads of students and tourists," said Myra. She called out to the café's owner, "Isn't that right, Lois?"

"What's right?" said Lois, coming over to join us. "Oh, the busses. Yah, sure, a big chunka my summer business comes from people coming for the art school, the museum and the other stuff."

"There's a museum in Asyl?" Jody said. "When did THAT happen?"

"Oh, it was already here back when you were in High School. It's over by the grocery store. I bet you walked right past it a thousand times without noticing."

"I guess I did. What else did I miss?"

Myra thought a minute.

"Let's see. The artists were here, but the school is new. You missed the museum."

Jody nodded.

"Did you know that some of the local bands have CDs out, and even tour a bit?"

"No."

"How about the organic farms and Community Supported Ag outfits?"

"No. I've no idea what that's about."

"Damn, girl! We've got to get you plugged in! I know, there's a fundraiser of the Watson Town Hall next Saturday. Everybody will be there. You should come, and bring your friend."

About then we were interrupted by a quartet of men coming in the door. They were loudly discussing the ills of the world.

"Ha, dese days ya never know whose comin' ta town," one was saying. "Ya used ta go greet da new neighbors, but now de might be Mexicans or worse. De kin hardly talk English. Ya gotta be careful."

"Hey, Lois!" another shouted. "Give us some coffees all around, and whatever's the special."

I noticed each of them give me that fish-eyed look while trying to pretend they hadn't noticed me. They headed for a booth in the far corner.

On their way past, one waggled a finger at Lois.

"Watcha' doin', then?" he said. "Ya run out of suckers? Trying to get more people to help you with your big hobby?"

"Something like that, Frank." Lois answered, bristling slightly.

He chuckled, shaking his head as he stalked off to join his buddies.

We talked with the art students for a bit. Every once in a while the voices of Frank and his friends were raised in complaint about some new thing- new to them.

Afterward, we walked the art school folks back, then headed for Jody's place.

She was puzzled.

"This isn't my town any more, Andre," she said. "The old security I remember is gone. Those guys in the cafe were angry and afraid. So were the people we saw on the street; they smiled and waved, but underneath was apprehension. The only people that seemed genuinely hopeful were the artists. What's all that about?"

The show was to start at 7:00, but Myra had warned Jody to be very early. Andre had come down to Asyl, then they drove the Honda the eight miles to Watson. All along the road they'd seen shrubby bushes with pink flowers. There was an especially thick growth around the abandoned doll factory near the Watson Sag. Jody had heard that they were some kind of cleanup plants that Phoenix had developed.

Watson was a busy place on weekends, even though it was mostly a bedroom community for Montevideo and other nearby towns. The Lucky Duck Bar attracted hunters and fishermen in throngs. There were street fairs and dances every summer. The old Town Hall was one of the last of the classic prairie meeting halls: It hosted gatherings and concerts almost every weekend.

Even though it was only 6:30, the streets around the hall were parked up. Jody felt a bit intimidated, parking between huge pickups and jeeps.

Inside, it was only welcoming. The building was shaped like a middle-sized church. Jody could see a high, curtained stage at the far end, where the choir loft and pulpit would have been. The warm yellow hardwood floor before the stage was bare, clearly intended for dancing. Folding tables with colorful cloths and floral centerpieces were loosely arranged in the back of the hall. Along both walls stood tables with various goods on them, next to coffee cans bearing labels.

"Hey, I bet you're Jody," the man at the door greeted them, sticking out his hand. "I'm Tommy. Do you wanna buy any raffle tickets? They're only a buck apiece!"

"What are you raffling off?"

"Oh, hey, lotsa stuff," Tommy said, waving his hand at the long display tables. "We donated forty bucks worth of organic beef from our ranch. The Asyl store has a couple of gift certificates. People donated books, artwork, all kinds of good things. Just pick what you want along the walls, and put a ticket in the can by it."

Jody and Andre each bought five tickets, then split up to explore the echoing room. Several tables already had people sitting at them. Folks in one back corner ran a concession stand; its banner read LOCAL FOODS. Children from toddlers to teens variously skittered or prowled around the room. It was already loud with conversation and laughter. Ever few minutes some group would burst into song, which once enveloped the entire crowd in an old Mills Brothers number.

On the cleared dance floor before the stage, Jody found Myra. She was directing traffic, telling the evening's bands where to stow their gear, when they were going on, and where the changing rooms were.

She gave Jody a quick hug.

Andre

I hadn't seen such a mixed crowd since Summerfest in Milwaukee. Ordinary "dressed up" clothes mixed with overalls and flannel shirts.

There were several cowboys. I could see that they weren't just dressed as cowboys, they WERE cowboys; No one else could look that good in Stetsons, snakeskin boots, and rhinestone-accented shirts. Another fellow was a throwback to his Viking ancestors. He had to be seven feet tall, with long blond hair and beard. His fringed buckskin jacket and high-laced moccasins looked as though he'd killed and skinned the deer himself. A grey-haired man in a natty Old-World suit was in animated conversation with a twenty-something woman in a halter top. She had many piercings and purple hair. Little kids of all colors were watched by parents, grandparents and any adult who was handy.

I heard Spanish, Norwegian, and languages I couldn't identify.

The smells were great. The light scent of varnish and dust was overlain by that of cooking meat and sweet flowers.

Everyone laughed, hugged, and clearly loved each others' company. It had the feel of a big, noisy family.

Jody went in search of Myra. I put my raffle tickets in cans for a huge Styrofoam cooler of meat, a crock-pot, a set of pen and ink drawings, and a couple of CDs from the night's bands.

I wandered a bit, soaking in the scene. To this old Milwaukee boy it was the breath of life. I eventually found Jody and Myra up near the stage.

Jody

"Hey! You made it!" said Myra.

"It wasn't hard to find," said Jody. "Right in town, next to the Watson C Store, a block from the Duck."

She looked around, then asked.

"How many bands are there? And they're all local?"

"Yup," said Myra, grinning. "Five bands, all local. We're lucky that they could all work this gig into their touring schedules. Most of them have CDs for sale over by the food table, too."

"I'll have to look those over," said Jody.

"I think that the guy who came with you already is," said Myra, pointing toward Andre with her chin. "He was with you the other day. Is he just a friend, or maybe...?"

Jody laughed. "No, it's nothing like that. Andre's gay. He's an old friend, an instructor at UMM."

"Oh, hey, he'll have to meet Greg and Tony, then. They're reclaiming an old, abandoned farmhouse out towards Big Bend."

At about this time, Andre walked up.

"My ears were burning," he said. "Were you ladies talking about me?"

Myra batted her eyelashes.

"Us? Heaven forefend!" she said. "Hey, I want to talk, but I've got to get the first couple of bands ready. Here, hold this front table. I'll catch you later, OK?"

Andre and Jody hung their coats on the backs of two folding chairs. After a bit, Tommy drifted up.

"Hey, you guys OK?" he asked.

"Yup, fine," said Jody. "But aren't you selling tickets?"

"Well, yeah, but I talked one of the Phoenix kids into covering," Tommy said. "I figured you'd want some pointers."

"Pointers?"

"Yeah. I point at 'im, I point at 'er. Like, I'd point at this guy coming, but you already know him, right?"

The "guy coming" was Karl Mueller. Tommy stood to hug the big man, then they sat down.

"Jody!" Karl said, "Good you could make it!"

Jody was a bit skeptical.

"Are you behind this shindig?" she asked.

"Nah. We're just another bunch of locals," he answered. "These folks don't need any organizing help from us."

Karl and Tommy pointed out various people in the crowd, or as they came in. Though they were mostly "ordinary" local residents, folks from a dozen specialized farms were there. The Sustainability movement was strong in Western Minnesota- these folks produced organic vegetables, free range beef and poultry, Omega3-high eggs, and many varieties of apples and other fruit. One farm had their own grain mill, where they produced custom-ground flour.

Although these were adventurous entrepreneurs, they looked like everyone else. Jody would never have guessed at the high levels of expertise they represented, without Tommy's commentary.

Then it was time for the show to begin. Myra excused herself to go emcee. Soon she stood on the curtained stage.

"I want to welcome you all here to our hall-improvement fundraiser. We've got five bands tonight, Minimum Maintenance, Western Minnesota & New Orleans Railroad, Mama Turtle, Mustang and Blue Suede."

At the name of each band a burst of applause and hooting went up. Myra visibly warmed to the crowd.

"I remind you that all of them volunteered for this gig. Most of them have CDs over by the food table, so show your thanks by buying some.

"The food is over in the other back corner. The Watson Lions are selling chicken and roast beef sandwiches like you've never had before. All the meat, all the spices, even the flour for the buns, was grown and processed within twenty miles of here! There's contact info for all the farms and ranches at the food stand, so you can get some of the good stuff for home. Danny from Joe Cool's is selling flavored coffees and chai to wash it all down.

"We gonna open with some folks who'd normally be the headliners, but they've got an early gig in Des Moines tomorrow, so we're letting them go first. Ladies and Gentlemen- 'Minimum Maintenance!'"

The curtain opened to show a trio of standing musicians- a woman on bass, a man on guitar, and a younger woman with a mandolin. They broke into their trademark, a folk/blues number that Jody felt had been written just for her:

Here I am on the return from another trip to escape the city burn
Sniffin' the country air
And I find myself on some crazy back-ass detour
That has my direction completely obscured

CHORUS
Not too surprising, this detour's got me thinking of you again
A detour; not on the map, waste of time, way off the main track

Have you ever been on one of those detours
Where you wonder if they switched the sign
Just to mess with your mind?
So you tell yourself, "Make the most of it,
Uncharted territory can be great."
But in the back of your mind
You know it's just making you late
For what you started out to find

CHORUS

So maybe sometimes I still look back in the rear view mirror
But I keep on going, keep on hoping, looking for a glimmer
Of a sign that'll tell me
Yes, oh yes, I'm

Straight on course, found my road, headed home
I'm headed home

Jody's evening continued under that spell. She danced and clapped with the rest. She ate the flavorful food. She was introduced to dozens of vibrant people. But she was still haunted by the first song.

Where had her life gone, but on a detour? She'd had everything mapped out, but all the signs had been wrong. Maybe THAT life had been the detour, and now she was back on track for home. Whichever it was, this new life was interesting.

Bill had taught Jody to do what she did full out. Her new life certainly gave her that opportunity.

She became a member of the Board of the Village Art School. She also taught an occasional class in Fabric Arts. On Jody's recommendation, some of her UMM students were able to make some money teaching.

However much fun it was, AVAS was work. For fun there were Friday night concerts at Joe Cool's Java Joint in Monte, and the many celebrations her new network held. The music varied from Folk to Ethnic to Jazz. Andre told her that some of the local Blues performers were the equal of any he'd heard in Milwaukee.

Happy Cow Ranch, Tommy Jensen's place, hosted an annual Summer Solstice bash. It was a potluck affair, with a flatbed truck stage for bands and jammers, campfires and a sauna. The food ranged from teriyaki chicken and roast pork, to vegetarian casseroles and the ubiquitous Minnesota bars. All of it was excellent, and all of it came from local sources.

Living Earth Farms, an organic poultry, egg and vegetable farm, held spiritual gatherings through the year. Some were simple group meditation sessions, while others were intricate outdoor ceremonies with prayer, song, interpretive dance and storytelling.

Although Western Minnesotans could party hard, they worked just as hard. The organic farms produced excellent foodstuffs, and individually marketed them as far away as the Twin Cities and Moorhead. They had also formed a joint marketing group called Prairie's Own Produce, or POP. POP gave the producers pricing leverage, and the ability to jointly fill large orders. They also had joint cold storage and food processing facilities. Caterers in Morris, Marshall and Wilmar regularly came to them for high-quality, chemical-free, ultra-fresh ingredients.

Jody bought nearly all of her food from POP distributors, such as the Asyl Grocery. In the summer, she had a "share" with Living Earth, for which she got a large box of whatever fruits and vegetables were in season, as well as a dozen eggs, every week from May into September.

They were also politically active. Many had actively campaigned for Nader and LaDuke in the 2000 presidential election. Paul Wellstone, the strong populist senator, held his only non-Metro rally of the 2002 campaign at a farm just east of Asyl. Jody attended, surrounded by many of her friends, and hundreds more. Minimum Maintenance and Mama Turtle played. Roast pork and potatoes were served. As the senator spoke, Jody began to feel that people like her just might have a chance to turn the US away from the nasty course it was taking.

Jody was having lunch with Karl at Joe Cool's that October. They were talking about the immanent election, when Danny came out of the back room, ashen-faced.

"Paul is dead," he shouted to the room.

"Hey Danny, you're having a '60s flashback!" someone yelled.

"No! Paul Wellstone!"

The only sound was that of the vent fans over the grill.

Danny bent to turn on the radio.

"The latest word is that the plane went down on approach," said the announcer. "There were snow and freezing rain in the area.

"There were no survivors."

Some people started to cry. Several left.

Karl sat with his face in his hands.

"Damn. I'm too late!" he cursed.

"Too late for what?" asked Jody.

He raised his face to look at her.

"Bucky Fuller wrote, in the '70s, that if we didn't get sane people in office, if we didn't start applying rational design science to our world by 1980, it would all come unraveled in the early 2000s."

"So, how does that make you too late?"

"Guys like Paul needed the backup guys like me could give them in the 80s and 90s. I should have started Phoenix twenty years ago," he said. "I was too busy making money."

"But without the money, you could never have started Phoenix."

"Maybe, maybe not. I could have bootstrapped it somehow if I'd tried."

He rose and headed for the door. Before leaving, he said, "I'd better get home. I'll have plenty of fallout to deal with from this one."

Chapter Nine (2003)

Long-range planning by the short sighted

Jody

UMM had a very proactive approach to controversial issues: bring in speakers, let them present their views, then discuss those views in class, on the commons, and in the school paper.

In the early Twenty-First Century, one of these issues was the future of family farming. Most Americans had never seen, let alone fed or cared for, a cow. They couldn't tell a bean field from a pasture. They knew nothing of commodities and futures, of co-ops and weather worries.

They didn't know the satisfaction of looking across a spread and thinking, "God and I built this." They'd never know how it was to awaken to the sound of migrating geese. The comforting warmth of a barn full of dairy cows in mid-winter was a mystery to them.

The facts of daily life in the country, the facts of life where food came from, were a mystery to most people. Unfortunately, this included government officials. The majority-decreed government policies and business practices were deadly to the vital rural way of life. Family farms and small towns were disappearing. Yet, the urban masses demanded cheap, plentiful food. This made for a nasty split in worldviews.

Seed and chemical companies effected farmers directly. Farmers could not avoid working with these companies, which were increasingly becoming arms of huge multinational concerns such as Cargill and ADM. To present the business side of this issue, UMM asked a seed company representative to speak.

Jody had heard about these things from folks at POP, so she was in the audience that Tuesday evening, as were Karl and Kate. A massive podium with the UMM logo stood before maroon velvet drapes. A few minutes before the scheduled start, a movie screen descended just to its left. After an introduction by the Board of Events spokesperson, a smarmy, fat man in an expensive but badly fitting suit took the podium.

"Good evening," he beamed. "I'm Ed Erhart, of the LaSalle seed company. I've come to share with you our vision of the future.

"I bring a message of liberation! Just as Moses brought forth the Israelites from slavery in Egypt, Science is bringing us forth from slavery to the land."

He spoke for nearly an hour, his remarks emphasized by PowerPoint slides. There were scenes of immense farms, with swarms of combines harvesting grain. Suitcase-sized robot tenders used GPS to wander about fields, eradicating both insects and weeds. Thousands of cattle stood in huge, muddy corrals, waiting for food to automatically appear. Technicians sat in control towers, surrounded by screens, running whole operations in air conditioned comfort.

"These are but the tools of liberation. The best is yet to come."

The next slide showed an organizational chart. It showed an overall national agriculture control company, AgriCorp, at its top. At the bottom were not farms but "franchises."

"No more will individual families toil and worry, cut off from civilization. Individual franchises, owned by the corporation and run by corporate employees, will be the bedrock of production."

He leaned forward, frowning knowingly.

"I've been in this business for many years. I know how horrific it is to be tied to the land. You can't set your own schedule. You can't take trips. Entertainment and night life are out of the question. You are assailed, day and night, by forces, smells and sounds beyond your control. You worry, worry, worry about prices, weather, insects, machinery breakdowns, and a swarm of other pestilences.

He straightened, smiling broadly, and triumphantly raised his fists in the air.

"This is all changing! With a rational, overall business plan to consolidate all farms, no one need ever worry again! No one ever again needs to shoulder the burden of running a complex ag enterprise alone! Corporations, those mighty bastions of modern society, will do all the worrying. Their broad shoulders will bear the weight of decisions and troubles. Farms will be consolidated and automated, with hired caretakers stationed only where needed. These servants of corporate wisdom will have full benefits, including housing. They will only need to be isolated from society for limited stays on their posts, a few years at most. They will then be able to return to the cities to enjoy life, having endured hardships in the service of their fellow man. Those who work on farms will be heroes, like firemen and policemen."

Jody sat, silently aghast. The man actually meant what he was saying. He was a True Believer. Worse, he could make others live his dreams-even though they were nightmares to those who loved the prairie.

The question and answer period was also frightening. Several students, city-born and bred, came forward. They had clearly come to UMM for its good reputation, and had no intention of being contaminated by the hicks they dwelt among. How they could live on the prairie, breathing the air of freedom and open spaces, surrounded by magnificent natural beauty, and not "get it" was beyond Jody's comprehension. They asked questions about food supplies and prices. Erhart assured them that food would be more plentiful and cheaper than ever, under the AgriCorp plan.

They asked about job possibilities. He told them that the opportunities were great, and gave them the contact e-mail for the LaSalle Personnel Department.

Jody couldn't bear it. She got up and went to the questioners' microphone.

"But what about the history and values of rural people? What about personal responsibility and self-respect? What if we WANT to live here?"

Erhart smiled indulgently.

"I'm sure that some accommodation will need to be made for those few who can't enter Man's glorious future. But those primitives who want to keep grubbing in the dirt must not stop the wonderful emergence of Corporate Man."

A small group of stunned spectators gathered at Kate's after the address.

"Yes, that's what too much Science will do to a person!" declared Rachel Hunt, a Humanities professor.

Karl answered, "That's not Science's fault. It's the arrogance of small people with grandiose schemes."

"What do you mean?" asked Jody.

"Their values are screwed up," said Karl. "They take the spiritual ideal of nurturing the Earth as a garden, and turn it into a struggle for dominance and profit. I used to know Ed. He wasn't a bad sort, then, but guys like him have forgotten who they are, what Humanity's place is. For them, everything boils down to control, conflict and profit."

"What about the blasphemy of Genetically Modified Organisms?" said Rachel

"It's only blasphemy if you believe that the creation of Humans was a mistake in the first place," Karl said. "The people against GMOs don't realize that GMOs aren't the problem- it's the things that GMOs let the big guys get away with. GMOs could help repair ecological damage and feed humans better. However, they're often used as just another tool to strip-mine our soil, and to strengthen monopoly."

Whatever their differences, the Fat Tuesday bunch agreed that Erhart's vision was a nightmare born of shortsightedness and fear. The trouble was, people like him had been strengthening their hold on society for decades. They controlled the discussions and the media. The great masses only heard the story that the sterile, shallow control freaks wanted to be heard. If rural people didn't somehow raise another voice, they would lose all that they valued. Worse, the destroyers wouldn't even realize what they were destroying, or understand why anyone cared.

Jody was glad of the passive solar "hot box" that Andre had helped her build across the studio's south wall the fall before. It captured enough solar heat that she rarely had to fire up the corn-burning stove. Isis was sleeping in front of its inlet vent while Jody wove a wall hanging.

A knock came at the door, followed by Inge's "haloo."

"Come on in," Jody called.

As Inge stomped the snow from her boots, Jody asked, "So, how's Dad doing, then?"

Mike had suffered a mild heart attack the week before while blowing snow. In the midst of a very mild winter had come a storm that left a foot of snow over glare ice.

"Oh, as well as can be expected," said Inge. Jody could tell that something was on her mind.

"And…" Jody prompted. She sensed that something was on her mother's mind.

"I'm glad that you're getting so settled in, dear," said Inge.

"And…" Jody prompted.

Inge looked down…

"Your Dad had a close call, then, you know."

"Yes. Mom."

"If your friend Andre hadn't found him when he did, Who knows…"

"Yes, Mom. What else?"

Inge looked Jody in the face, tears in her eyes.

"You know that we love you. We've been talking…"

"Mom! What?"

"We've decided to move to Arizona."

The women rushed together to embrace.

"Oh, Mom," Jody said. "What could I do?"

"It's not you. It's not you. We're just old. There's nothing else here for us any more. With the weather changing, and everyone moving away or dying, we figured it was time."

"But what about the house and the land?"

"We're selling the farmland to the renter. We want you to have the rest- the woods, both houses, the outbuildings and the extra lots."

"But that's way more than I need!"

"Fine, but we sure don't need it any more, either. You can sell it, or maybe some of your college friends want to live up here. You have time to think. We won't be leaving for a few months, anyway."

Jody used the time. She asked her friends at UMM, especially the Fat Tuesday group, what they would do in her shoes.

Karl Mueller laughed. "You know what I'd do," he said. "I did it."

"You mean some kind of commune?" Jody said. "A bunch of people living together? They'd think we were freaky hippies or something!"

"Who are 'they' anyway?" said Karl, "And since when do they run your life?"

"They're my parents, friends, and everybody else in Asyl. And they don't run my life, but there are just things people don't do."

"Things people don't do?" said Karl. "Like having friends who aren't all straight whites? Like getting together with a bunch of troublemakers to defy accepted ideas every week?"

"But I, well…"

"Look, Jody," Kate chimed in. "If I'd listened to 'them' I'd've been just a good hausfrau. I'd still be in Asyl. I didn't go out of my way to challenge them OR to worry about what they said. I just did what I had to do."

So Jody did what she had to do.

By that summer, "The Old Neihaus Place" became "Jody's Place." Several UMM folks had come in to occupy the Big House. Andre had moved his shop to an outbuilding. Students who otherwise couldn't have afforded school received room and board for helping with maintenance and projects.

Isis basked in the attention.

POP began having meetings in the big garage, and storing produce in another shed. By bartering with them, and other local producers, Jody's "family" was able to keep living expenses very low, with cooperation and fellowship high.

The old frame house also served as a test bed for some of Phoenix's energy projects.

Jody and her friends often helped others in town, such as by giving older folks rides to Monte or Morris to shop. Interns often were available to help with odd jobs. Andre helped the local blacksmith through busy times.

Of course, it couldn't last.

Technically, Jody was in violation of zoning ordinances. Hill Avenue was zoned R-1, which meant that only single-family dwellings were allowed. There were no near neighbors to complain about increased traffic, so most people had just let it slide.

Frank Dryer was a man stuck in conventionality. That a bunch of "artist hippie dope fiend wackos" were operating right in town was intolerable. He forced the issue, haunting City Council meetings and threatening to complain to the State Zoning Commission. Finally, "the Neihaus matter" was considered at a City Council meeting.

The Council chambers were packed. The Mayor and four councilmen sat behind a massive table. Facing them, in folding chairs or standing close together, were nearly forty people. Karl Mueller and Jack Hanson were there to give moral support.

Once the meeting was called to order, Frank Dryer pressed his case.

"It isn't just the violation," he said. "We don't want their kind in town!"

"What kind?" said Jody. "Do you mean like Deb Johnson? Agnes Arvidson? Cathy Brown? They're all artists too!"

"But they've always lived here!"

"So has my family!" Jody said. "We were founders! When did you move here, Frank?"

"That doesn't matter! I'm a businessman!"

And so it continued until Mayor Klinger called for other witnesses. Frank produced a string of cronies who held that letting Jody "get away with murder" just wasn't right. Other residents spoke of the help they'd received from Jody's household. They affirmed that the people on the hill were good, quiet, helpful neighbors.

Finally, Al called a halt to testimony.

"Folks," he said. "This seems pretty clear cut. Everybody likes Jody's bunch except Frank. But Frank is right- she's breaking the zoning laws. Now, we can make Jody send everybody home, putting just one more vacant house on the 'For Sale' list. We don't need that kind of waste, so what else is there?"

"Point of information?" said a young woman. "What about a zoning variance?"

Mayor Klinger smiled.

"Now, how about that? As I recall, it requires a public hearing, with at least two weeks notice."

He pretended to suddenly notice the gathered crowd.

"Hey, this looks like a hearing to me? When did you all hear about this meeting?" he asked.

"Heck! Three, four weeks ago!" shouted a man in the back.

"And you've been testifying up a storm. I think that we can put this to a vote! Discussion is closed. Do I have a motion?"

"I so move that a variance be granted for Jody's extended family," said Councilman Dave Gruning.

"Now hold it!" shouted Frank.

Mayor Al banged his gavel, then pointed its handle at Frank.

"Hey, boyo, discussion is closed!" he said. "If you keep interrupting, I'm sure that we'll remember when your fuels permit comes up for renewal.

"All in favor? Any opposed? There being none, a variance is granted."

Jody learned that night that politics is the art of the possible, and that good will can make anything possible.

It had started with a phone call. Jack Hansen of POP was getting together a group to join a rally and lobbying day in St. Paul. The Minnesota Environmental Partnership had requested the help of allied groups from around the state to protest some upcoming legislation.

So Jody found herself in a minivan with half a dozen acquaintances, traveling across Minnesota. The trip was a great time to get to know folks who she'd only seen at meetings or concerts. Several were veterans of past activism. Some had been involved in the DC Tractorcade protests of the late 1970s. Others had marched with Dr. King in Alabama. Most knew much more than Jody did about the forces threatening rural folks. That day, she would learn how ominous those forces were.

The activists gathered with a few hundred others at the Science Museum of Minnesota in downtown St. Paul for training and coordination. Jody was shocked to learn of the bills that Twin Cities legislators had introduced. They would make rural areas powerless before the sort of corporate takeovers Ed Erhart had talked about. Some would strip townships, small municipalities and even urban neighborhoods of tools to resist big development. Others would redefine Family Farms and Sustainability in ways that left them wide open for absorption by corporations.

The rally in the Capitol rotunda was eye-opening for Jody. She found herself side-by-side with people from all around the state. She knew people from the Montevideo and Ortonville groups. The central lakes district, the North Shore, Grand Forks, Rochester and Mankato were represented by busloads. Many others had come, as she had, packed in cars and vans. Farmers, resort owners, fishermen, and inner city people had all come together to work against takeover by the growing neo-Fascist corporate system.

Jody's meetings with her legislators were pleasant, but scary. She was told that many well-meaning Senators and Representatives were making decisions based on bad information they'd been force-fed by wealthy corporate lobbyists. Urban legislators, the distinct majority, were especially unaware of the effects of the laws they enacted on rural areas.

Just by luck, a group of scientists was making a presentation for legislators that afternoon. She sat in while they described the devastating effects that Global Climate Change was going to have on Minnesota. They made it very clear that "business as usual" was doomed. It was necessary information, but depressing to hear.

Jody came home that evening feeling that at least she'd tried. She was glad to know people who were keeping an eye on these things. At the same time she felt almost helpless to fight the tide that was enveloping her home territory.

Asyl's 125th Anniversary was a great time. The Viking café turned out traditional Norwegian foods, twelve hours a day, for the three days of the festival. There were street dances, storytellers, and an open-mike

Oral History event. The parade of folks in traditional dress was gloriously colorful.

Asyl had much to be proud of. Its founders, Jody's own ancestors, had lifted their entire village from coastal Norway. They had endured the difficult ocean voyage across the North Atlantic. They had ridden in filthy, sooty train cars from New York to St. Paul. After all that, they had walked with their wagons the last 150 miles to their new homes. Their spirit and exploits were justly celebrated.

But all this made Jody think. What was she doing to be worthy of their heritage? They had fled a strict class system in the Old Country, a system that impoverished all but a lucky few. Now, that same sort of system was emerging in the United States. What would they have done?

She had no New World to flee to, but her connections showed her the kind of New World that could be built right in Asyl. She really just wanted to live her life quietly, teaching, doing Art and eating good local foods. She knew, though, that she'd never feel right letting others do the work of keeping that life safe and simple. The threats were too big, and most people didn't seem to grasp them.

It was an election year. She decided to run for City Council.

Frank Dryer wasn't above making a scene. Jody, Myra, and a few AVAS instructors had been eating in the Viking Café when he'd stomped in. Spotting them, he'd stormed over to their table.

"What's this crap about Jody running for Council?!" he fumed. "Myra, did you put her up to this?"

The redhead calmly laid her burger down and smiled at the big man.

"No, Frank," said Myra, calmly. "It was her own idea. Why? Is there a problem?"

"Damn right there's a problem!" he shouted. "We've got enough trouble without any funny new ideas on the council! We just need to keep what we've got!"

Jody knew that she'd have to face this, and worse, if she were to win the council seat. She stood and shook her finger at Frank.

"Hey! I don't hear you, Mister Gas Station Owner, making any good suggestions!"

"I'm busy enough running my business! This town needs my business!"

"Maybe we do," Jody said. "And maybe we need you to protest to your suppliers about the ridiculous price of gas. Have you ever done that?"

"No," he snorted. "Business is business. You take things as they come. You don't make waves."

71

"Make waves? Frank, Frank, don't you know that tidal waves are already on the way?"

Jody told the Fat Tuesday group about her decision.

"Jody, why do you bother?" said Karl. "They don't want to see what's happening! Asyl is doomed!"

"I don't think so, Karl, but we have to do something," Jody said. "I'm counting on the good horse sense of Asyl's people."

Karl scowled.

"Horse sense?" he said. "Jody, have you ever ridden a horse?"

"Sure. Lots of times, especially on trips."

"On trips. OK, remember how different it was from a car, slower, more sensual, a trusting, familiar relationship?"

"Right. The horse knew where to go. I just made suggestions."

"Right. You were following the known path- that's when horse sense applies. To you, building an economy on the Arts, self-sufficiency and such makes perfect sense, but to the other people around here, MOST people around here, it's downright bizarre. Horse sense fails. It's more like being on a runaway train for them than riding a horse; and you're that train's engineer, with your strange talk. You scare them."

"So you don't think I should try?"

Karl shrugged. "No, I think that you should. Gods know, this country needs more people trying. I just mean don't expect too much. You're riding the wave of historic change. History is an ocean, but some people are just naturally shoreline. You're going to crash into them. The sea always wins in the end, but it needs to wash away a helluva lot of sand, first."

Jody won by a slim margin. The voters were so astonished that someone beside a middle-aged white businessman was running that they voted for her just to see what would happen.

What happened was Jody, and many other things. Some would not have happened without her voice.

The town's economic base was eroded as more and more farms became corporate outposts. The caretaker "farmers" on these places got their food and goods from Central Supply, not local businesses. Asyl was in serious trouble.

At the same time, Jody's group made a point of buying locally. She also helped establish a "Business Incubator" in town. Local entrepreneurs could get help starting and nourishing new businesses. These included Internet-based sales of local artistic works, a greenhouse that supplied fresh vegetables through the winter, car and appliance repair shops, data processing services, and a regional publishing house.

Jody's vision was only part of what was happening in Western Minnesota. As the economy deteriorated, the climate changed, and eternal war loomed, people got imaginative.

AVAS became better known around the region. Soon, classes were running all day and every day. This brought a steady stream of students, instructors, and curious tourists. The museum gift shop, closed in 2001, was reopened. It sold thousands of dollars in local artist's works every month.

Many producers, some working through POP, aggressively marketed their goods. Some moved into niche markets, and experimented with unusual crops. Soon, many people around Asyl were eating only locally grown foods.

Recycling of wastes, always a good idea, got better. People in Asyl were diligent recyclers, but their recycled goods were sent far away for processing; much money was wasted in transport. Phoenix developed a system whereby the plastic, glass and metals collected could be processed locally, making fenceposts, building panels and other things for local use.

This intense local self-sufficiency led to developing a local currency. A more sophisticated version of "Holiday Bucks," the local currency allowed sellers and buyers to work out their prices independent of outside influences. Along with a thriving in-kind and barter system, people around Asyl could live good lives with very little cash income.

Of course, this did not sit well with some. Those who could not embrace the community-centered spirit felt increasingly poorer and left out. People like Frank Dryer, who were heavily invested in the old system, saw the changes as a threat.

"It just isn't our sort of town anymore," they said. "If we put normal people in charge and do what we used to, things will get better."

They tried whisper campaigns against Jody and her ideas. They ran their own candidates for Council. But "nothing succeeds like success."

When Mayor Al retired, Jody was his obvious successor.

Chapter Ten (2008)

If it's not one thing it's another

Jody

She'd picked a bad time to be Mayor. Following the pattern begun in 2001 to 2004, Spring became wetter, and Fall a time of drought. City resources were strained every year, first to handle tons of snow and millions of gallons of runoff, then to keep the water tower filled and the parks from becoming dust pits.

Storms and extreme weather took their toll on farming. Small operators simply couldn't handle the costs of both flood control and irrigation. This was on top of markets that didn't pay enough to make their crops worth growing. Seed and chemical companies exerted more pressure for farms to become "vertically integrated" parts of the monolithic agribusiness system. Many more farms simply failed. These were bought up by swelling corporate operations and absentee landlords.

The only farms to truly thrive were those already operating under sustainable, "Small is Beautiful" principles. Phoenix worked closely with these, supplying them with clever appropriate technologies.

The failures made an economic storm to match those from the skies. Many rural phone companies stopped offering service to customers outside of towns; there were just too few subscribers left to pay for even basic line maintenance. Many small businesses failed. Some, like the Viking Café, held on by becoming more locally oriented, dealing in goods and services created in and needed by their own communities.

Tax returns from rural areas plummeted. State legislators saw that the funding needs of rural areas had become much greater than the revenues they generated. They "solved" this imbalance by slashing state services to "outstate" regions. To be fair, they likewise eliminated most taxes in those areas, making them corporate-run tax free zones.

In Western Minnesota, many fire departments became members-only Mutual Aid Societies. Major roads and bridges began to charge tolls, hitting hard the people who could least afford to pay.

Jody could take some small comfort in the Local Powers Act. Mayors of small, rural towns were declared virtual dictators, and their towns effective city-states.

It was a very logical decision. Minnesota's State Universities had faced tighter budgets yearly, even as their curriculum was increasingly dictated by the needs of business. What was more sensible than for the cash-strapped State to simply sell the Universities to those very businesses?

After the Governor's press conference announcing the change, UMM buzzed with rumors. "Western Minnesota Business University" wouldn't hurt for money, but what would its priorities be?

The answer came just as spring semester began.

Jody was in her office, trying to prepare for the classes which would start in just a week. Chairman Sandte came to her door, looking devastated.

"Jody, the word has come down," he said. "Most of us are out."

She jumped up and took his hands in hers.

"No! Why?"

"This is to be an agribusiness school," he said. "It'll be for training middle managers. The only Art they'll need is for advertising. Andy Stockwell, the video instructor, will be taking my place."

"But when?" Jody said.

"We finish out this semester. Summer classes are cancelled. Next fall the new faculty and classes will be in place."

"But what about the students? What about all of us?"

"Students will have the option of transferring to the Twin Cities, Duluth or St. Cloud campuses. Some instructors may be offered jobs there."

"What about tenured people?"

"You can't have tenure in a school that has ceased to exist."

People at the last Fat Tuesday tried to be philosophical, but Kate was furious.

"These shortsighted little twits!" she shouted. "This has all happened before. When the needs of commerce become the needs of society, you're looking at civil war!"

"How's that?" said Jody.

"The Haves will lock in their power. The Have-Nots won't even be able to pretend that they aren't slaves. The rich will fear the poor, and the poor will hate the rich. Then something will set it all off, and BOOM."

"Jody's Place" grew that summer. Kate Mikkelson and several other former professors moved to Asyl, where many houses were available for the reclaiming. Some writers and artists continued their careers, using satellite internet to stay connected and to market their works.

Most had other useful skills, skills to contribute to the growing cooperative community around Asyl. They formed an ingenious bunch, carving a post-industrial lifestyle out of diminishing resources. In company with the others already there, they created a rich culture. It was a culture based not on the accumulation of stuff, but on community, self-sufficiency, learning, and love of the land.

Chapter Eleven (2009)

Reaping the whirlwind

Asyl

When the UN decided that US occupation of other countries was imperialism, it took over peacekeeping functions worldwide. All United States troops and administrators were sent home. The US was pressured to decommission most of its warships.

In Asyl this meant that the old Samuelson place would be reoccupied. The huge home stood just south of town. It had been vacant, except for an elderly caretaker couple, for many years. Now Colonel Ralph Samuelson, last heir to a family of grain magnates, was coming home.

Jody felt that she should welcome the adventurer. When she heard that a convoy of moving vans and a minibus were at the place, she waited for an hour, then walked up the long driveway.

She was met at the top of the hill by a small group of young people, who were clearly from all over the world. All were strong and determined looking. They smiled, but the smiles also held a warning not to underestimate them. Their leader was a tall African woman.

"I am Tina. I will speak for the Colonel in town. He values his privacy," she said. "He wishes to research the impact of America's military on the world in the last century. His studies will keep him very busy. He has told us to wish you well, but he will not speak with you. Do not come closer to the house. Please."

The United States

Social Security had been under increasing strain since the 1990s. Finally, the money it brought in could no longer match the benefits it paid out. Costs had to be cut. The Grey Lobby wouldn't stand for any cut in benefits. Something had to give.

After the United States had been forced to reduce its military, many bases had been closed. This left huge tracts of land, effectively whole small cities, unoccupied.

The two problems, put together, became a solution. The abandoned bases became retirement towns. Anyone drawing Social Security retirement or disability benefits had to move to a new Resettlement Village, or lose all present and future rights to Social Security or Medicare benefits. Those who went to these camps had to sign away their estates to the Federal government.

Following the principal, "When life gives you lemons, make lemonade," the residents of these new towns became well organized to enforce their will. They became ruthlessly conservative. Any district which hosted a Resettlement Village was soon dominated by that Village. This power was felt in both State legislatures and Congress. Security became the paramount value. Restrictive measures against anyone "different," anyone "unpatriotic," and all "potential terrorists" stormed into place. The United States became even more ingrown, fearful and restrictive.

In rural areas, where the appropriated homes of senior citizens had no resale value, they reverted to local governments. In small towns like Asyl, this meant that the city became the largest landlord. Farm houses, though, were mostly burned, and their yards plowed under.

The effects of this depopulation rippled through communities. Most rural churches, such as Asyl Lutheran, closed permanently for lack of funds. Small-town grocery stores followed. The Asyl Market was able to stay open because it had long since become mostly a brokerage for local products.

In the increasingly rigid urban atmosphere, many artists and non-conformists fled to rural areas. Some small towns were destroyed by the migration. Asyl, though, was ready. The already strong "Bohemian" element was organized to absorb the welcome influx. They were ready to discern the true counterculture people from the mere far-out slackers.

Bizarrely, Asyl's population grew and strengthened during the national disaster, while many other towns simply disappeared.

Asyl

If Asyl had not become a strong, cooperative community, more than just a town, it would never have survived. State and Federal aid had become non-existent. The city budget was increasingly strained to meet the costs of road repair, sewer and water services, and snow removal.

Even worse, when the flood of 2010 destroyed Montevideo, it destroyed the usual source of supply for a whole region. No more could someone jump in the car to go to Wal-Mart or the big supermarket. Those who couldn't find local sources for their needs learned to do without or improvise. Old sawmill, well drilling and other equipment was resurrected from barns. Blacksmithing changed from being a hobby to a vital skill. Canning jars and the equipment to use them became precious.

By 2010, the only people left in Asyl were the die-hard and imaginative ones. They lived a life more like that of the ton's founders than that of folks in 2000, and they lived it well.

Phoenix

After the "500 Year Flood" in the spring of 1997, many in the Midwest had hoped that the worst was over. That catastrophe had destroyed neighborhoods in the cities of Fargo, Grand Forks, Montevideo and many other towns. Cars, semis, even a train far from any river, had been swept from roads by overland waves of snowmelt and warm rain. From the air, it looked as though ancient Lake Agassiz had returned to reclaim chunks of Minnesota, North Dakota, and Manitoba. Then the clouds parted, the sun came out, and the waters receded. *At least THAT fluke can't happen again,* thought weary survivors as they waded through the muck of cleanup.

They were wrong.

In 2001, headlines read "Next 500 Year Flood Comes 496 Years Early." Of some comfort was the fact that many neighborhoods and farmsteads in its path hadn't been rebuilt since 1997. But for many who had rebuilt it was the last straw. As their brand-new homes and businesses floated downstream, they headed, permanently, for drier parts.

Insurance companies and governments followed their lead. Large areas of what had been towns were declared off limits to any further construction. Insurance companies refused to write policies of any kind, much less flood insurance, for even larger areas. The invasion of the prairie by Industrial Civilization ironically began its retreat at the hopeful dawn of the new millennium.

Fledgling Phoenix experienced the 2001 flood with trepidation. Would the strengthened riprap lake wall hold? How much of their land would be inundated? Fortunately, the waters covered only the campground, boat landing and parking area- this time. The Bait Shop and Big House had wet basements, but these were only nuisances.

Still, this was another "fluke" far too early for conventional prediction. Karl researched the projections of climatologists, even as the recalcitrant Bush Administration admitted that, "Gee, maybe there is something to this global warming thing." He realized that 500 Year Floods were likely to become common, soon to be followed by Millennial Floods- and worse.

Phoenix prepared. They dug in new housing hundreds of feet back from the shore. They built new, earth-sheltered shops and common buildings on the ridge above. The Bait Shop and Big House were still used, but with the knowledge that their time was limited; one year, likely soon, they would be lost.

Then came the winter of 2009-2010. It started off very warm and dry, but in February and March it got nasty. Record snowfall all across North America alternated with extremes of heat and cold. In Minneapolis, temperatures of 75 degrees above zero Fahrenheit in March followed readings of 30 degrees below in February. With each wave of heat and cold came heavy snowfalls. The freezing and thawing weakened bridges, roads, dams and levees from Virginia to Oregon. What Canada, Scandinavia and Siberia experienced didn't bear thinking about.

In Minnesota, the fastest thaw on record followed the worst snow season in history. In some areas, temperatures rose 40 degrees in an hour that March. Fields six feet deep in snow became flowing lakes in a day. These surged into ditches, which overflowed roads and washed out culverts. The water carried its debris to local bridges, battering them apart and adding their flotsam to the flow. Ten-foot walls of water hit valley towns. The Red, Minnesota and Mississippi rivers doubled their volumes, and then tripled, then squared them.

For Phoenix, this meant goodbye to the Bait Shop, the old cabins, the Big House, Ben and Marta's place, and hundreds of trees. Karl, Alec, Maria, Ben and the rest watched from the ridge as the dozen smaller cabins, and finally the larger buildings, groaned from their foundations. The cabins shattered and disappeared under the Asyl Bridge, but the house and shop joined the mass of debris tangled in the bridge's trusses. Sadly, the churning heap included many deer and cattle that had fled to high ground- but not high enough.

Then, slowly, like an elephant kneeling, the bridge slipped from its eastern pilings. It was an amazingly quiet process, but its subsonic groans gave the watchers chills. The bridge knelt, then tipped over, then disappeared.

The bridge and its causeway had held back a mountain of water thirty feet deep and a mile wide. The collapse opened a three-hundred-foot gate between the north and south lakes. As the North invaded the South, both headed for the Lac qui Parle dam, twelve miles below. That dam and its causeway had already been under twenty feet of water, forty feet above the usual water level. When the new wave hit them, they gave way. The hydraulic juggernaut sped, a mile a minute, for Montevideo, eight miles further along.

Like many Midwestern towns, Monte was built at a confluence of streams. When the Minnesota torrent merged with the smaller but equally swollen Chippewa, it was the city's death knell. Sandbaggers, toiling in freezing rain, heard the great aquatic predator's roar. They ran to escape to higher ground. Some of them made it. The rest joined the buildings of half of the town, cars from the railroad switchyard, and the contents of the sewage treatment plant as they rushed downstream.

As such scenes were repeated along most of the America's rivers, President Bush the Third declared that the Emergency War Status was now permanent. The United States ceased to exist as a representative republic.

For Jody, this was a two-edged pronouncement. Civil authorities, such as the mayors of isolated towns, were granted broad powers of immanent domain, and direct control over local law enforcement. But it also meant that State assistance became non-existent. Money, law enforcement personnel, infrastructure maintenance, and school funding became strictly local responsibilities. The attitude was: If you want to live in the sticks, figure it out for yourself. It's your own problem.

Earth, 2011 Ce

In August of the next year, the powerful el Niño spawned a tropical depression north of the Galapagos. Once it reached tropical storm status it was routinely labeled George. That was the last routine thing about what became known as Typhoon Godzilla.

By the time George was south of Hawai'i he had become a Category 3 storm, and was still growing. Residents of the western Pacific island nations became nervous, then frantic, as the atmospheric juggernaut bore down on them.

George meandered his way westward, a few degrees north of the equator. His low pressure occasionally triggered other storms near his path, but few became sizable, and none did any serious damage- except for Herbert.

Herbert brewed up just south of the equator. Paralleling his larger sibling's course, he plowed into the Phoenix Islands, then southwestward toward the Solomons and New Guinea. In any other year Herbert would have been big news, a Category 2 storm aimed at low-lying, highly populated islands. But George would not surrender the headlines for another two weeks.

As Herbert turned southward, George turned northwestward. He was at Category 4 and rising as he plowed over the Marshall Islands, stripping the smaller islands bare. Tens of thousands were evacuated to the Philippines and Japan. Those in the Philippines survived.

By now George had passed beyond all previous storm categories. As he strolled along the Marianas, feeding on the Japan Current, his destination became clear; he was headed on a direct line to Tokyo, largest city on earth. A pundit at the Hong Kong times dubbed him "Typhoon Godzilla,"

No one was laughing as Godzilla bore down on his namesake's favorite target. Every airplane, ship, cruise liner and fishing boat on Honshu was commandeered to clear people from the storm's path. Even a US Navy submarine, in port between tours, found its passages crammed with desperate humanity. No one knows how many tens of thousands died in the crush to evacuate the Home Island. Newly-reunited Korea accepted multitudes, as did China, the Philippines to the south and Russia to the North.

Not an inch of the main island was untouched by gale-force winds. Tornadoes scoured mountain valleys. Centuries of construction, of roads, dams, bridges, castles, shrines and terraces were lost. The cost of the losses was incalculable, and rebuilding impossible. Thus ended Japan as an industrial nation, and began the Japanese Diaspora.

But that was not the only ending. In the Middle East, a place of constant upheaval since Saladin's death, rising sea levels and dwindling fresh water pushed people to even greater extremes. Jordan moved to seize the last few hundred thousand acres of the Dead Sea. Israel rebuilt the drowned city of Haifa on Palestinian land, bulldozing refugee camps to clear the way; Syria and Egypt protested. The United Islamic Republic, the former Iran, Iraq, Afghanistan and Pakistan, threatened war if Israel did not retreat to pre-1967 borders. No one knew who launched the first missiles, or what warheads they had actually carried, but Israel soon unleashed her nuclear weapons. Then so did the UIR. India, taking revenge for the loss of Kashmir, joined in. After a twelve hour blizzard of strike and counterstrike, the entire region, from the Sinai to Mesopotamia, from the Persian Gulf to the Mediterranean, was uninhabitable. It was called the Masada War.

Asyl

The Kragero Hop had been a fixture of the local scene since the 1980s. For five days in late summer, musicians from across the country would gather on a farmstead near Asyl to play, listen, eat, and catch up on gossip. When the original barn had been destroyed by the tornado of 2009, a replacement had been found a mile away. Although the new place wasn't actually in Kragero Township, the original name had stuck. And although the long-distance guests could no longer come, and the festivities lasted only two days, the spirit of the Hop remained. It had become not just fun, but a vital pause in preparing for winter.

Jody's people particularly needed the break. Over the years, the City Council and the residents of Jody's place had become the same. Even with Phoenix's help keeping the klunky City truck and plow running, even with the new high-velocity windmills and partially restored phone net, running the town wasn't an easy task.

Jody, Andre and the rest had put on their sun clothes and glasses, fired up the antique dump truck, piled into the cab and bed, and groaned their way to the farm. Once there, they had parked it well away from the corral of horses.

As she wandered over the ten acre site, Jody saw many familiar faces. Deb Johnson's daughter, Barbi, was doing portraits by the Big Oak; she had made the paper and charcoal sticks herself. Billy Hotchkiss was giving fiddle lessons behind the Big House.

She stopped to talk with Jack Hansen, who was minding the roasters. Three huge metal drums held meat- a hog and calf on rotating spits, and innumerable chicken, geese and turkey parts on a grill.

"Hey, Jack," she said. "How's it going." She had to shout a bit to be heard over the music coming from the barn.

"Can't complain, can't complain," he said. "Well, I could, but it wouldn't help."

Jody pointed her chin at the trestle tables nearby. They were laden with bowls of fresh salad, bread, berries in cream, and roast potatoes. A cauldron of corn on the cob boiled close by, with crocks of fresh, white butter waiting to slather it.

"The veggie folks have done their part," she said. "I just wish we had some Coke or Mountain Dew to wash it down with."

"Hah! In your dreams, girl," said Jack, "We haven't seen any of that stuff for years! But hey, we got cider, tea, nectar, home brew and REAL mountain dew if you're thirsty."

She laughed,

"I think I'll start with tea."

The big electric flatbed from Phoenix pulled up. The people piling off were wearing odd, bright white robes. They looked like extras from Mel Gibson's "Maccabees." Jody wandered over to it as it emptied out.

"Hey, Karl, what's with the robes?"

"It's a surprise," he said "You know that we've been making spider silk for cording and such. A couple of months ago somebody realized that a medium tight weave would be light, breathable, and Ultraviolet-proof. So, white robes for 'The End of the World as We Know it.' Isn't that fine?"

Karl

"They've run smack up against the Law of Social Control," Karl said. "As Poul Anderson pointed out, the more control you exert on people, the more they rebel, You respond with more control, they rebel more, and so on until the society collapses. The crazies come out of the woodwork. Decent people give up on keeping the rules."

He was talking about the latest Homeland Security measures. Terrorists had been found making bombs and other weapons using instructions they'd found in library books. The Government's solution was to close all public libraries, and seriously restrict the holdings of school libraries, "for the duration." These changes would have the added economic bonus of increasing sales of "safe" books, such as romances, westerns, and inspirational bestsellers. The Market, with a little oversight, would keep people entertained without any uncomfortable or dangerous ideas getting loose.

There were riots over the closings. Angry library patrons picketed before the closed facilities, while others drove by, hurling "Geek!" "Traitor!" and worse epithets. The masses who wanted nothing more than their TV sets saw their chance to gain revenge on the readers who had annoyed them for so long. Rocks and bottles soon followed insults.

The police stayed out of the way. If a stray Molotov cocktail set a Library ablaze, the Fire Department made sure that the flames didn't spread to more valuable buildings.

The libraries were not the only targets of the "public safety" crusade. Internet Service Providers came under the regulation of Homeland Security. Not only was every user's net traffic logged, but filtering of dangerous, un-American or immoral materials was mandatory. Users could apply for permits to view restricted information, if they had a legitimate reason. Of course, they were then watched even more closely.

A hacking war ensued. Servers and hubs went down almost daily as government programmers battled with "outlaws" over the public's right to free speech and expression. Authorities saw more laws and regulations as the solution, but these only brought on more attacks.

Chapter Twelve (2012)

Boys will be boys

Asyl

As in most small towns, the Asyl American Legion Hall had been a favorite hangout for vets since the Korean War. The Emergency Government made sure that the clubs stayed in business; they were good for patriotic morale. The Feds had paid for a huge generator, satellite TV, and all the amenities for the Asyl post.

Frank Dryer's gas station had become part of the complex as well, since he considered himself a good, loyal patriot. After that, the Asyl Legion Club was the only game in town. It was the perfect loyalty enhancer.

In the Oughts, Zack Dryer and Pete Cole had been drafted and served in the Iraqi Occupation together. They were drinking beer and playing darts in the club one night. The television was blaring the latest civil unrest news. Zack's eyes lit on the poster of the Legion Pledge.

"Hah, lookit that," he slurringly shouted. "We're supposed ta 'promote one hunnert percent Murcanism.' Shoo, an we're putting up with foreigners and weirdoes right down by the lake! We need ta teach them Phoenix shits a lesson!"

"Zack," said Pete. "I don't think that's what it means. They're not hurting anything!"

"Hell, I lost two fingers ta ragheads in Eye-rack! An' now they even dress like em! Waddya mean they aren't hurtin' nothin?"

"Zack, you've had too much. Let's just go home."

"Damn right, I've had too much. I'm gonna go give 'em some back!"

"Lay off, Zack!" shouted Pete.

Pete tried to grab his friend, who slugged him in the gut, driving him against the pool table. While Pete lay, moaning, Zack ran out the door. Onlookers heard his huge four-wheeler roar to life and spray gravel a few seconds later.

"Oh, no," someone shouted. "That's his old volunteer fireman's truck! It'll do 120 easy, and he keeps his rifle and pistol in it! Call out there and warn them!"

"I can't," said Jolene the bartender. "The phones went out to stay two weeks ago."

The joint emptied out in less than a minute as the Asylites rushed to stop their buddy from getting himself killed- or worse. Someone grabbed Pete and brought him along, because he was the one most likely to get through to Zack. Three overloaded pickups roared off in vain pursuit.

Kate Mikkelson (b.1950, d.2012)

Most folks are decent enough, but the strains of eternal war and terrorism can break down the veneer of civilization.

Kate pondered this conundrum on her evening walk. She'd seen the phenomenon in her travels. Beirut had gone from playground to battleground almost overnight. Sarajevo, ancient home of arts and culture, had become a killing field. And now, she heard stories of the same pattern emerging in the larger US cities. She wondered how long Asyl would remain the refuge its Norwegian founders had named it.

Kate pulled her shawl, a gift from Jody, tighter against the evening chill. Deep in thought, the wise woman did not hear the commotion behind her.

Phoenix, 2012 Ce

The Phoenixites were sitting down to supper. Several suddenly stood up, alerted. They had all caught the same vibe.

"Storm drill!" Karl shouted. "Seal the windows and doors! Alec, go see what's happening! I'll supervise here"

Phoenix's half-dozen part-time security folks rushed out behind Alec, as the greenhouse and livestock keepers ran to secure their charges. From the direction of Asyl came engine roars, and the flashes of bouncing headlights in the mist.

"Damn!" shouted Alec. "Someone's been stirring the pot!"

A huge pickup stormed over the ridge and into the compound. It skidded to a stop where the Bait Shop had once been. A colorful knitted shawl fluttered from its front bumper. The driver waved a pistol out the window, firing a few wild shots, and then hollered, "We want you people out of here!"

"Now, Zack Dryer," Alec shouted back. "What the heck are you doing out here with your rig? We haven't got a fire!"

"Your kind have brought this disaster on us! Messing with Nature! Trying to play God! Encouraging foreigners!"

"Zack, you're tanked!"

"Fuckin' Alec-goodie-two shoes! You thought you were better than me in High School! You and your geek of an old man think you're better than everybody! It's payback time!"

Zack tried to aim at Alec. Alec concentrated on being invisible. Several more shots went wild as Phoenix Security moved into position.

"Forget it, Zack. Drop the gun and get out, or you'll regret it."

"Oh, and what are you dress-wearin' pansies gonna do?"

"Last chance. You don't want to find out, Zack."

"Up yours!" Zack yelled, and emptied his clip in Alec's general direction. When the hammer hit empty chambers, he looked into the barrel to see why.

"OK!" Alec shouted, and hit the dirt with his eyes tightly closed and his fingers in his ears.

From several points around the yard, loudspeakers began to blare a fingernails-on-chalkboard screech. Strobe lights flashed blindingly. Any pilot could tell you the disorientation which that combination brings. Zack screamed, fell out of his half-opened door, and writhed on the ground, retching. The noise and lights ceased. Alec stood up.

Pete and the others finally caught up. They stopped their pickups well clear of the battle zone. Pete got out, and walked toward Alec with his hands open at his sides.

"Alec, I just want to get Zack out of here," he said.

"You do that, Pete," Alec said. "You are welcome to come out and talk anytime. This foolishness, though, ISN'T welcome. Next time, somebody really gets hurt."

"Right," said Pete.

As he walked Zack to his truck, Pete wondered where the shawl on Zack's bumper had come from. Karl saw it and paled.

Jody

The trouble with being the Mayor of a town on its own is that everything is your problem. Jody wished for the days when she could call the Sheriff or the State Troopers. With Monte gone there was no Sheriff this far west any more, nor any courts.

She needed both, badly.

She'd been awakened before dawn by a pounding on her door. Shedpeeked out through the curtains to see Phoenix's old pickup in front of her house. Several people sat in the box, around a sheet-wrapped bundle. Karl was at her door, holding a familiar-looking bit of cloth. He was silently crying.

She threw open the door, and recognized what Karl held- Kate's shawl. Jody looked into Karl's eyes, and knew.

"Who? How?" she whispered.

Karl cleared his throat.

"Zack Dryer," Karl croaked. "He was driving drunk. It was quick."

The next few hours were a macabre blur of frantic activity, when all Jody wanted to do was hide. A posse had found Zack sleeping it off at Pete Cole's place. He was now locked in a closet in City Hall. His father was in Jody's office.

"What makes you artsy-farts think you've got the authority to hold MY son!?" shouted Frank Dryer.

Jody, red-eyed and bone tired, held her ground against his tirade.

"Who else is there, Frank? The State won't touch a case way out here. This is vehicular homicide, not the petty theft Zack's done before. The Phoenix guys are out recruiting a jury for a people's court. I wish you'd spend your time getting together witnesses and building a case, not yelling at me. The trial starts at Noon tomorrow. Zack is counting on you."

"He damn well is, you sanctimonious bitch! You'll see how I defend him!" Frank shouted as he stormed out.

The Fire Department garage had been cleared out for a courtroom. A platform had been hastily built at one end, with chairs for the jurors. Jody, who would act as judge, sat behind a massive oaken desk that they'd found in storage. The podium from the City Council chambers stood at center back, where it would serve as the witness stand.

Perhaps 350 people sat on folding chairs and boxes, or stood around, as the jury of twenty Asyl and Phoenix residents was seated. No one looked forward to this ordeal, but murder could not go unresolved.

Jody rapped her gavel, and called the court to order. She was surprised not to see Frank Dryer. She wondered what he was up to. Whatever it was, he had left his son alone and shackled.

The jurors had been sworn in, and the charge was being read, when a commotion began outside. Engines roared and tires squealed. Then came the sound of doors slamming and booted feet running. The hall door burst open. A squad of middle-aged men in badly-fitting military uniforms rushed in, brandishing shotguns. They spread out to bracket the room. Frank Dryer was at their head, and ran to Zack's side.

"I'm putting a stop to this!" he shouted.

Jody stood to face him.

"Now, everybody calm down!" she shouted. "By whose authority do you interrupt? Who are these people?"

"By the authority of those who've bled for this country! You people, you parasites, think you can judge a fighting man? He shall be judged by his peers, not a rabble of civilians. These are his fellow vets from Wilmar. We'll take him there for a FAIR trial."

He spat on the floor.

"OK, mister vigilante!" Jody answered. She knew that the Emergency Government would pander to just this sort of bravado.

"You can have the little shit. WE didn't want to soil our hands with him anyway."

She stepped down from the stand, and strode over to Frank.

She stood nose to nose with him as she said, "But don't let him show his face around here again. You've chosen for him. We take care of our own, and now that doesn't include him. Or you. You're both outlaws to us."

Phoenix

Alec gave Karl and the assembled chiefs his report. That their neighbors could turn on them was a sobering thought. They decided that it was time to take a step they'd avoided. They would build a fence around Phoenix, and set up armed patrols.

"But that isn't all," Alec said. "Things are likely just going to get worse. We need an overall security plan. We need advice. Dad, can you ask The Colonel?"

Karl sighed.

"All right, son. I'll ask him," he said. "I've met him a few times, but he's a reclusive sort. He may not want to talk about this."

The following day, Phoenix work crews began erecting a high chain link fence around the compound. Karl went to Asyl to try to talk to The Colonel.

As he drove up the long, exposed driveway, Karl knew that he was being watched. The feeling persisted as he climbed the wooden stairway of the huge log house, crossed the wide porch, and knocked on the door.

A voice spoke from the speaker grille beside the door.

"Eh? Who is bothering me?"

"Colonel Samuelson? I'm Karl Mueller, from Phoenix. I've come…"

"I know exactly why you've come, Mr. Mueller. It has begun, and you want to know what you can do."

"Yes. I read your memoirs before they went out of print. Your UN Peacekeeping experiences would be helpful to us."

"I should hope that they'd be helpful to somebody. God knows, they didn't help me much."

The door opened into a dimly lit room.

"Come in. Let's toss some ideas around."

Karl entered the living room. It had a dark hardwood floor and vaulted ceiling. The Colonel stood at a large table, on which were spread a map of the Phoenix area, some legal pads and markers, and a stack of military reference books.

He was a tall man, thin but not skinny. His short hair and handlebar mustache were speckled gray. His clothes were casual- khaki pants and a lumberjack shirt. Beside him stood a young African woman. She was sober and regal, even in bare feet and a simple purple wrap-around gown.

"Mueller, meet my student, Tina Dahingwa. Tina, please fetch us some tea and cookies. We have work to do."

She smiled and padded out to the kitchen.

"Now, don't get any ideas, Mueller. She's a student, not a concubine. A good student, too- any man who tried to have his way with her would shortly be minus some prized body parts.

"You need a security plan. I've had to rescue idealists from Reality before. At least you came to your senses sooner than some."

Tina returned with a tray of snacks. The Colonel pointed out weak points in the Phoenix perimeter. In some places, gullies gave cover, or could be used to jump fences.

After some tactical summaries, the Colonel said to Alec, "Youngster, you have base security training, yes? Military Police ops and such?"

"Yes, sir," Alec answered.

"But no special ops work, guerilla, commando school, that sort of thing?"

"No. I was always in secured zones."

"So, you're the sheriff. Sheriff, you need a Marshall."

"You, sir?"

"No, I'm content to be the weird old guy in his castle on the hill. I mean this lady here."

He turned to the African woman.

"How about it, Tina? Ready to go help the peaceniks keep from getting blown up?"

She smiled the smile of a stalking cat.

"I would enjoy that, sir."

Chapter Thirteen (2019)

Committing suicide as a national sport

Phoenix

The few televisions left around Asyl were all tuned in that afternoon; the Great Leader of the Emergency Government was to address the nation on matters of "supreme importance." The dining hall at Phoenix had been transformed into a TV theater, with a huge screen erected at one end. The address coincided with supper time. It was the best-attended meal in Phoenix history. As people gathered their meals, there was much loud discussion about what could be coming.

The Presidential seal appeared on the screen. The Phoenixites quieted down. Most looked anxious. Many held hands across tables.

"Ladies and Gentlemen, the President of the United States"

"My fellow Americans," President Bush the Third began. "Our nation and our world are sad and wounded. Events far beyond our control have stripped hundreds of thousands of our fellow citizens, and over a billion souls worldwide, of their homes and livelihood. Our nation of wise, broad-shouldered people has stood strong in these tribulations. We have paid the war reparations demanded by a vindictive UN. We lead the way in helping the victims of disaster, even as we fight the forces of terrorism and subversion from within. Nevertheless, our best, hamstrung by antiquated structures, is not enough.

"My father, during his presidency, wisely saw that economic recovery was not possible without unleashing the genius of American business. Accordingly, he declared our Federal Lands to be Long Term Outlook Zones, to be wisely administered for the benefit of ALL Americans, not just a few outdoorsmen and animal lovers. From the great forests thus liberated for development, millions of board feet of lumber flowed. From newly opened oil fields, an abundance of fuel gushed to increase our national security.

"But even that bounty is not enough for our new challenges.

"America now, more than every in its history, feeds the world. Much of that world has been forced upon us as refugees, and many more depend upon our exports of grain. Because of this, I have decided, after deliberation with my Emergency Cabinet, our 65 Governors, and prominent business leaders, to turn all food production over to a new conglomerate, AgriCorp. Just as vertically integrated retail corporations changed inefficient, high-priced, small-scale stores and restaurants into the efficient, consistent chains we know today, AgriCorp shall revolutionize agriculture. From the field to the table, all facets of food creation will be part of a balanced, manageable whole. Productivity, quality and uniformity of product will rise to unequalled levels.

"Some small towns which now serve agribusiness will be retained, although most will be consolidated with others, or eliminated. AgriCorp shall administer all settlements outside of the Metros as company towns.

"Small, privately held farms will be united under AgriCorp. Their current owners will be compensated by giving them apartments in metropolitan areas, along with whatever retraining they need to become productive members of Corporate Society.

"As always, the United States of America has room for the non-conformist and free-thinker. But in these times, such people can easily become pawns of terrorists; Therefore, I am empowering the states to create within their borders Local Outlook Opportunity Zones, places where these people can pursue their ways with no government interference or aid. From the acronym, these shall be known as LOOZes, and their inhabitants as LOOZers.

"Security needs must be served. Once people are in the Zones, they may not leave, except temporarily and as per the needs of commerce, subject to their Administrator's policies.

"Time is of the essence. All of these changes shall be implemented by June 1st, Two Thousand and Twenty. To this end, I am invoking emergency powers of eminent domain and travel regulation. We must move quickly to meet the threats which, uh, threaten us.

"These are troubling times, but we of the United States are a tough and proud people. Together, we shall weather this storm, preserving our sacred values and rights. God be with us all."

Karl thumbed off the television. The Phoenix people looked around the room. Many were crying. All knew that this was a decisive moment.

"OK," Karl began. "This follows. The Metros have cut us off more every year. Everywhere 'outstate' is just a colony to be milked.

"The question is, what do we do? Do we become an AgriCorp subsidiary, or try to get one of those Zones set up here? Ideas? Ben?"

"I fought these bastards for my farm for twenty-five years," said the old farmer. "They won that one in the end. I'll be damned if they'll win this one! I'm for the Zone. We can take care of ourselves. Hell, my great-grandparents did when they homesteaded here!"

"I'm with you, Ben," said Karl. "But we're a couple of set in our ways old farts. We'd never be able to do this without young blood. Let's discuss this. I don't want anybody to make any decisions tonight, but let's see where things lie. Maria?"

"I gave up my country for this place," said the Brazilian expatriate. "I let your Homeland Security put their tracker chip in my body so I could stay here. Why should I resign now?"

Steve, a web designer, said, "I climbed out of the inner city by my fingernails. I'm not going back."

"But can we make it on our own without turning weird?" asked someone.

"That's a good question," Karl said. "I submit that we can, but not alone. Supplies won't be a problem, but we need our neighbors to keep us sane. The LOOZ must include our whole area."

"But what about the children?"

"Better they grow up here than in The Cities!" shouted a father.

The group discussion lasted through the night, and continued individually for months. All were game to try the LOOZ. After all, they hadn't come here to play by the rules of corporate society, but to develop ways to make people free of it.

Jody

In the Milan City Hall, the direct line phone to Phoenix rang.

"Jody? It's Karl Mueller. We need to talk about this LOOZ thing, right?"

"Hell, yes, we can try for a LOOZ!" Jody said. "To get plowed under would be a tragic end for this town. All that's left are a bunch of artists and old people, but we can make it. Let's go tilt at some windmills!"

Karl outlined a strategy that could work. It was risky, but it was that or be swallowed up by the neo-Fascists. She told him to count her in, whatever it took.

Jody hung up, wondering what to do next. Skippering her town through stormy times was one thing, but going up against an outfit that could literally buy the whole place was another. At least Karl knew how to play that game. She hoped that he knew how to play rough.

She had no doubt that they could make it on their own. With Phoenix's technical expertise, the local growers' skills, and their strong sense of community, they'd be fine, IF they could break free once and for all.

Karl

After Jody agreed with the LOOZ idea, Karl sounded out other leaders in the area.

Headman Kee Punan of Western Dawn, the Hmong village north of Asyl, was eloquent.

"We are a proud people," he said. "I was a youth when my family sailed away from Cambodia in a tiny boat. We would not be told what to do. We would not live in stinking cities. We would not live where the spirits could not be heard.

"My father led our people here. He helped us find a way back to the land. The spirits of those others who lived here before us are in this land. They were not so different from us- we get along with them.

"Now I am an old man. My wife's body lies within this land. Her spirit dwells here. I want my spirit to dwell here, too. We shall stay. If we must fight, we have fought before."

"I hope that it will not come to fighting, old man," Karl said. "Grant me your wisdom. Join your voice to mine when we go to plead our case."

"I shall come. My people shall live, as shall yours."

Tommy Jensen shrugged. "Hey, it's no surprise," he said. "The Metros have been sucking us dry for decades. This land has been my family's for over a century, and we were just getting it back into shape. We bucked the System to get it this way. It'd be pretty stupid to give up now."

Two weeks later, Karl, Jody, Punan and Tommy headed for the Twin Cities. Their travel permits only allowed them to visit the growing AgriCorp complex. They would speak with the Minnesota LOOZ Administrator. They drove Phoenix's ethanol-burning minivan, with its extra tank, so they would need no fuel stops or gasoline ration cards.

Approaching the Metro, they encountered several checkpoints, and passed miles of refugee camps. The President hadn't overstated the magnitude of the disaster.

"It didn't have to come to this," Karl grumbled.

Their destination was a former business campus in the western Twin City suburb of Golden Valley. This was the temporary headquarters of AgriCorp administration, until its vast new complex could be erected. That future structure was already beginning to take shape, in a termite mound of feverish activity, on adjacent land.

The LOOZers-to-be passed through the razor wire gate after showing their pass to a guard. He was an odd-looking man, huge and hunchbacked under his body armor, with a large red scanner-crystal grafted into his forehead.

"Damn," said Karl. "I'd heard that they were working on those. They wire people up with extra senses and strength, and reprogram them as super-soldiers. They call them 'Augments.' There's no telling how far the corpos might go with them. I wonder how much free will they have left, and where the 'volunteers' came from."

They parked the car in the visitor's parking area. At the building's entrance they were again met by an Augment. He checked their pass by holding it in front of his forehead scanner. He nodded approval, and the high glass doors slid open.

A guide was waiting for them, a sparklingly clean-cut, anonymous young man.

"The Administrator is expecting you," he said.

The guide led the representatives through a maze of hallways, and on three elevator rides, down, up, and down. They emerged into a windowless hallway. Karl could tell that they were far underground, and that many eyes were watching them. *Whoever this guy is,* he thought, *he's big on security.*

The hallway ended in an ordinary waiting room. Chrome chairs sat on maroon carpeting around a glass-topped coffee table. Animated posters of smiling young people, American flags fluttering behind them, touted the marvelous future AgriCorp would bring.

As the LOOZ delegation entered the room, double doors opened on the opposite end. Three dark-skinned men emerged. Two wore business suits and carried briefcases. The third, a much older man with long, braided hair, was dressed in blue jeans, moccasins, and a buckskin jacket decorated with bead- and quill-work. In his arms, he carried a long leather bag with feathers dangling from its end. Karl recognized it as a sacred pipe bag. He had heard that the Ojibwe Nations of northern Minnesota were asking for their own autonomous region; this must be their delegation.

None of them looked happy. The old man looked at Karl, recognized a peer, then sent silently- *Do not trust this thief, cousin*. They exited, grim and silent.

It was the Chippewa LOOZ delegation's turn. They were ushered into a large, but surprisingly bare, office. Its concrete floor was covered in gray, utilitarian carpet. On the blue-painted concrete walls were large flatscreens, showing various AgriCorp operations. Behind the steel desk sat... Ed Erhart.

He stood and offered his hand.

"Ah, Karl, good to see you," he said. "It looks like the shoe is on the other foot today; you're on my turf for a change."

Kharma with a vengeance, thought Karl as foggy memories of long-ago meetings drifted to mind. *This scenario again.*

"You know why we're here, Ed," he said. "Let's talk deals."

Erhart leaned back, steepling his hands.

"Deals? What can you offer me?"

Karl crossed his arms.

"Phoenix. In working order," he declared.

Erhart laughed.

"Phoenix? I OWN Phoenix in nine months, Karl! How can you offer me what I already have?"

"But you can't make it WORK, Ed," Karl said. "You've been there. You've seen how we do things. You never understood how we thought, so you couldn't possibly keep that attitude and atmosphere going. Neither could some hireling manager. Slaves make poor inventors."

"So, I suppose you want Phoenix to be a LOOZ."

"No. I want it to be part of one. We're a community."

Karl gestured to his companions.

"We want a five mile strip around Lac qui Parle, Montevideo to Appleton, as a LOOZ."

"Ten by twenty five miles! That's a lot of cropland!"

"Compared to the biggest innovative gold mine since 3M? Get your priorities straight, Ed."

"Make it just the eastern side of the lake, and it might be a deal," said Erhart, "IF- if you can get the residents to sign a governing Compact. I can't justify turning over thousands of acres to a rabble."

Asyl

Karl remembered the sarcastic old quip about "herding ferrets." The Asyl Fire Hall was filled with delegates from around the coming LOOZ, both from the communes and the family steadings. They agreed that they must band together, but the needed structure eluded them. Many questions needed answering:

How can a few thousand people, raised in a global society, become an island to themselves?

How much central authority should there be, and how chosen?

What kind of technology should be preserved?

Can we actually be completely self-sufficient?

What are the rules of conduct?

How are rules to be enforced?

Karl suggested that the Great Law of the Iroquois was a good model. It provided for a loose, clan-based federation. The Hmong brought similar ideas from their own mountain communities.

A few people suggested a kind of theocracy, but this idea was quickly shouted down as "Un-American."

Even the area's lifestyle came up for debate.

A young woman said, "We can learn to do without phones, computers, and electricity. The people who first settled here did."

Karl shook his head. "Not necessarily 'without.' We'll need to rethink priorities, sure, but Phoenix can produce and maintain the equipment. How many people we can spare to keep things running, and how much is enough, will be the questions."

The debates, proposals and counterproposals lasted for months. A few weeks before Sealing Day, when the gates would be closed upon them, a compromise was reached. The full Compact was a twenty-page document. A summary version was also devised, printed on blue paper, and distributed throughout the area.

Part Two: Ashes

2020-2022 AD

Chapter Fourteen (2020)

Mournings and Mornings

Jimmie Olson

The apartment purred in a seductive voice: "Jimmie! Time to get up! Wake up now!"

"Mrrrpph. Ya, I'm up, Marilyn. I'm up."

"Good morning, Jimmie. You're due to start your trip to Phoenix today."

"Yeah, OK. I'm up."

I sat up. The security camera in the light fixture was glowing blue; another human being was checking up on me, not just the ComputerEye.

"Marilyn, who's watching?"

"Lois Nesmith from room 1512 is Citizen Proctor today."

I wriggled my fingers at my neighbor, imagining her curly blonde hair and nicely padded body, and climbed out of bed. *Maybe I should make a move on her,* I thought. *But carefully; the self-appointed Moral Guardians are everywhere. I don't need their hassles.*

It was May 15th. From my windowless, fifth-floor, one-room South Minneapolis apartment it could have been July or August. I didn't complain; at only $3500 a month, I was lucky to have it.

A couple of weeks before, I'd received a message from Karl Mueller. He wondered whether I'd like to see Phoenix before access became restricted. I managed to wrangle a travel permit from AgriCorp, on the condition that I'd write an exposé of the place when I returned.

I thought about it while I hunched in the tiny shower cubicle, trying to finish before my water ration ran out. Karl Mueller! Phoenix! The eccentric genius and his mysterious commune! The man who brought the world scrubberbushes, those indispensable tools for toxic cleanup! Mueller could have taken his place in Corporate America as a multi-billionaire, but chose to remain in the virtual concentration camp of the Chippewa Local Outlook Opportunity Zone, the LOOZ.

I'd been out that way once as a boy, on a fishing trip. I'd heard that Phoenix had bought the resort that I'd visited as a boy in the '90s, only to have it washed away in the Flood of 2010. After that they'd become much more secretive. Now they dealt with people in the area, and shipped out marvelous inventions, but rarely admitted strangers. With the LOOZ Sealing Day coming in two weeks, they'd soon be inaccessible. A freelance writer like me couldn't pass this up!

Into my electric two-seater car went my ComComp and recorder, a duffel bag and a couple of pairs of shoes. My travel passes, and the all-important AgriCorp LOOZ Entry Permit went in the glove box. I stuffed my Aussie bush hat on my head- no sane person went out without a hat and sunglasses any more. I threw on my silvery sun poncho and glasses, and was ready to rough it in the wilds of Western Minnesota.

Getting through the suburbs and the refugee camps, the "Kyotos," took several hours. Traffic was also thick around the Social Security retirement camp. Besides the usual traffic snarls and checkpoints at every town's border, I had to pull over three times for convoys headed in. These were groups of about a dozen busses and semis, painted a cheery red, white and blue, with signs reading RELOCATION. A guard with a shotgun stood next to each driver. The bus side windows were barred and hard to see through. The faces I glimpsed looked tired and afraid. I wondered why; they were being evacuated from the deserted boondocks, to be given jobs and apartments in the Twin Cities. It was their own choice; they could have stayed on their farms as AgriCorp employees, or tried their luck in the free zone of the LOOZ. At least they'd been patriots, and hadn't gone renegade.

Tina Dahingwa

Tina's inner clock woke her precisely one half hour before dawn. She eased out from beneath the light covers. Long, puckered scars were visible on her well-muscled back and legs. She went to her corner shrine- a carved ebony goddess under photos of Nelson Mandela, Desmond Tutu, and other great Africans. Lighting an incense cone, she prayed.

"Mother of Life and Death, guide me in Honor and Strength this day, that my people shall live."

Brushing long dreadlocks back from her face, Tina padded to the bathroom alcove. When she emerged, she took a fighting stance in the middle of the room. Her morning kata routine consisted of 35 minutes of Ta'i chi', Aikido, Savat and lesser-known African variations.

Warmed up, and sweating lightly, Tina pulled on a pair of white shorts and a tee shirt. The sun was just rising, and her dark skin was resistant to burning, so she wouldn't need protective gear or sunscreen yet. She pushed aside the doorway curtain of her room, passed through Walker House's common area, and jogged up the sloping tunnel into the new day.

Tina's bobbing hair and ready smile were a familiar early-morning sight as she ran the full three-mile circuit of the Phoenix compound. The trip past greenhouses and through pine copses and prairie grasses not only kept her body fit, the run also gave her a chance to see how everything was progressing, and to plan for the day.

She waved to some children who were moving goats to a new field. She slowed to watch workers adjust a blade on a power windmill. She passed a few other runners on the same circuit, including her boss, Security Chief Alec Mueller.

Half an hour later, Tina entered the Community Center and headed for the showers. She emerged in a clean tee shirt and shorts, shaking the wetness from her hair. She carried a thin, voluminous white robe, a pair of sunglasses, and a colorfully decorated straw hat. She stopped at the serving window to grab a glass of tea, an apple, and a pita sandwich. Helen Tomkins, the Kitchen Chief, talked with her for a bit about how much work the welcome surge of new residents put on them.

Tina sat at a table in the Dining Hall, and was soon joined by Alec, and Jules, the Logistics Chief.

"I will mind the gate most of today," she said. "For what should I be ready?"

Jules looked through papers on his omnipresent clipboard.

"Two truck convoys are expected, one in a couple of hours, and the other by mid-afternoon," Jules said. "And that Jimmie writer guy should show up at about the same time."

Jimmie

West of Wilmar, traffic diminished. I remembered the drive through there years before, when you could see for miles and miles over the prairie. It was unnervingly vast back then. The woodlots around farmsteads had looked like islands in a vast green sea. Now, that view was blurred. High chain-link fences stretched along both sides of the road. Occasionally I saw a gap where a driveway or gravel road joined Highway 40; beside every one lay a pile of fencing parts to close the gap. In only a week, the fences would be unbroken. All agricultural lands in Minnesota had been seized via Eminent Domain. AgriCorp had been given control, to "secure and protect our vital food resources from terrorists." Only a few small towns and three LOOZes would remain un-appropriated in Minnesota. The all-generous AgriCorp would administer these.

Here and there a column of smoke rose. Each pointed to a farmstead, like an accusing finger from Heaven. Red, white and blue AgriCorp vans and bulldozers were parked beside some. At one just beside the highway a family stood, watching the flames. Lumpy bundles covered in orange tarps and ropes were piled on their pickup and a flatbed trailer. I'd read about "Oakies" from the Dust Bowl era: here was History repeating right in front of me. I pulled up to ask what was happening, ready to hit the accelerator if things looked ugly.

The father, a classic weather-toughened farmer, came up to my car. His kids, in team jackets and backward baseball caps, stayed close to their mother. The man bent down to talk to me.

"Hello! What's happening here?" I asked.

A stoic, resigned smile was on his face. "The end of a family."

"But I see you all here." I replied.

"That's the point. HERE. This place has been my family's land for 125 years. Now it isn't. Now the family isn't."

"Are you going to Relocate?"

He stretched up, proud and scowling at the AgriCorp truck nearby. "We'll not go where those fascist thieves tell us to! We'll find our own way!"

"But they're offering good apartments and jobs in The Cities."

The scowl deepened. "Move on, city rat."

I moved.

Forty-five miles west of Wilmar on old MN 40 I finally came to Asyl, the town at the center of the new Chippewa LOOZ. The fences ended at the top of a slope just east of the town. There I could see a work crew of homeless conscripts and captured terrorists with implanted security devices laboring to build a massive concrete gate and guardhouse.

I pulled up behind several yellow rental trucks that waited in line to go through the security check. An Augment guard questioned each driver. Some answer didn't please him; he forced the driver to open the back gate of the truck. After stomping aboard, sniffing at wall joints, slashing open some boxes and ripping loose a few boards with his metal-clawed fingers, he jumped down.

"Go on in you stinking traitor!" he shouted.

Finally, it was my turn. The guard waved for me to stop. His blood-red third eye glittered in the sunlight above his goggles. On one hip hung a heavy IM projector, which could disable my car with one blast. On the other hip he carried an old-fashioned .45 pistol, which could blow a hole in me the size of a dinner plate.

"Pass!" he demanded, stone-faced, hand extended.

He scanned my card with his third eye, pointed his ID wand at my chest, then waved me through with a sneer. I was officially in the about-to-be No Man's Land of the LOOZ.

Once through the gate I found myself on the edge of a wide, shallow valley. An abandoned rail line, highway, and small stream flowed along its bottom. The far ends of the valley weren't visible. There were no fences other than the one I'd just crossed. There was a spookier sense of open space here than I'd had on the prairie. The few dozen buildings of the town looked a bit forlorn as they climbed the opposite slope.

Asyl, Minnesota had surely seen better days. Why had anyone ever wanted to build a town in such a godforsaken place, hundreds of miles from the only decent city in the region? Most houses were empty. Some had had their windows and doors salvaged, leaving raw, ripped openings. Others had been burned to shells or sooty pits. As I crossed Main Street, I could see corporate crews erecting the new Farmers Market stalls in the old downtown. AgriCorp wasn't entirely heartless; every stall would have its own free TV, tuned to the corporate channel 24/7, so these misfits would be reminded of what they'd rejected.

I crossed old US 59, and was through town in less than two minutes. Phoenix was only a few miles farther west on this road. Driving had been a hot business; May didn't used to be like this. I hoped they had air conditioning and a cold drink ready!

Again I felt the overwhelming sensation of vast space. Green rolling prairie lay around me on all sides, the fences just a memory. I began to see how this land could grow on a person, once they got over the feeling of being a bug crawling on a plate.

Over a few ridges I came to a high, arched gate, standing on the lip of another broad valley. The gate was milky green and shiny, like an enormous jade carving. Flowering vines covered the guardhouse, in which I could glimpse a desk with flatscreen and keyboard.

A young woman with deep black skin was talking to the driver of the same truck that the Augment guard had hassled. She wore a vaguely Arabic-looking sun robe, a huge colorful straw hat, and green-tinted sunglasses. The robe was of a brilliant, almost iridescent, white fabric.

She pointed to a spot where the truck could park. She waved me forward, and then actually offered me her hand with her bright smile.

"Good afternoon!" she said with an African-sounding accent. "I'm Tina Dahingwa. You are Jimmy? Good. Karl's waiting for you. Please park over there, just past the trucks. There is a recharge stanchion for your car, there. Follow the main walking path, then take the left-hand turn by the river."

Part of old Minnesota 40 was now Phoenix's main access road. The highway had formerly crossed the Minnesota River/Lac qui Parle here on its way west. Floods had ripped away the highway bridge, which the state had never rebuilt. The Phoenix-ites had replaced with an arching green footbridge. A heavily eroded old causeway continued through the mud flats beyond the new river channel. At its end, above the far shore, loomed the security fences of the LOOZ's western border.

Tina

So, he is here, Tina thought. *Will he harm or help my people? Karl thinks help, but I've heard promises before.*

She called to a boy who was passing.

"Erik, please find Alec and tell him our writer guest is here."

The boy nodded and ran off, his white robe flapping behind him.

Tina returned to the guardhouse. She checked off the new arrivals' names from the EXPECTED list. A couple of unexpected RVs full of old interns and their families had arrived, too. She knew that Jules and the other organizers would find places for them, since any compatible and skilled people were priceless. She sighed. *They will keep trickling in right until Sealing Day,* she mused.

Erik arrived with Alec in tow. Tina pointed to where Jimmie was just climbing out of his car.

"So, our reporter got here on schedule," he said. "You sent him down by the river to see Dad, right?"

"Yes I did. Will you need me more today?" Tina asked.

"Nope. I'll give him the tour. I'll get a feel for his vibes, and then pass him to you tomorrow."

"That is fine."

Jimmie

My first impression of Phoenix was of plants gone riot. Red clover covered the ground. Mounds of tiny white flowers bordered the road. Trees were everywhere, mostly pines. The few leafy trees carried festoons of vines; many of the trees and vines had dark purple leaves. A sweet, spicy smell permeated the air.

My second impression was of calm activity. There was an unhurried bustle of people, some toting furniture or boxes on bike-wheeled carts. Most wore robes like Tina's, but their headgear varied wildly. Some wore elaborate constructions of feathers and beads, while others had simple straw or cloth hats.

Just to the left of the rounded stub of the old bridge approach, someone knelt on a large platform, perched near the water's edge. He wore a hooded robe of the same brilliant white material as Tina's. The hood was pulled far forward over his head. He faced the water, hands cupped together, meditating. He heard me, pushed his hood back, and turned to wave me on. He was Karl Mueller.

"Come have a seat. Well, a plank, anyway." he called.

Mueller offered his hand. His grip was firm. His gray beard and hair were long, with golden highlights. I sat cross-legged beside him. He gazed outward again.

"So Grasshopper," he said. "Look at the stream. Tell me what you see."

I'm sure that my face flushed when I answered him. I was tired and tense from the long drive.

"I'm a writer, come to get a story," I said. "Not a child or a character in an old TV show!"

His eyes met mine. His bushy gray eyebrows rose, and he broke into a puckish smile.

"Well, 'Jimmie Olson'," he said. "I know the images you saw on the way out here. Think about them, and then try to tell me we aren't all characters in some absurd drama. As far as being a child, we are ALL children in the face of this Universe. Out here, you are especially so. Try to remember that.

"Now, sit a bit. Breathe deeply. Look at the stream. When you're ready, tell me what you see."

OK, "When in Rome" and all that, I thought

After maybe two minutes I said, "It's the Minnesota River. It's wet. It flows into the Mississippi by the old airport in The Cities. Nobody lives by its banks anymore- except for you."

He sighed like someone who'd gotten a disappointing e-mail, and stood.

"That's all for now. Let's go get you started."

Karl walked me back up to the gate so I could grab my bags. A thirty-something man was talking with Tina. He had close-cropped blond hair and beard. He was tall, perhaps six feet four inches.

"Howdy." He said. "I'm Alec Mueller. I'm Security Chief. Dad asked me to give you the grand tour."

Alec took me toward an odd structure built into the hillside. It was made of smooth, gray concrete, with no square edges. Between its two large, round doors was a line of oval windows. It bulged outward, looking like a misplaced airliner's wall. Round skylight shafts sprouted from the hill above it.

"This was our Transients' Dorm," Alec explained. "Now it's singles' quarters. You'll be staying in one of the rooms here. Your neighbors are all new arrivals. They'll respect your privacy."

The place had clearly been modeled on an old motel. A wide common hallway, a bit crowded with people carrying bundles and boxes, ran the length of the front. Several rooms had large, curtained windows opening into the hall. The air carried a grassy, clean incense scent. It was a bit unsettling at first; the theme of rounded curves was repeated everywhere, like being in an underwater cavern.

As we entered my room, I realized that the entry didn't open directly into the main space, but went through a small, L-shaped alcove. There were no solid doors, but thick curtains hung across the oval doorways. We stopped to leave our outer garments on hooks, and our sunglasses on a shelf. I was surprised to see that Alec wore only shorts and sandals; later I realized that this was standard Phoenix garb.

The window and a skylight let a dim light into the room. It was larger than my apartment, and Spartan in a pleasant way. A wooden bedstead, with a quilted cover based on the ubiquitous white cloth, occupied one wall. Some shelves and a desk with built-in flatscreen and keyboard stood next to them. An oval, braided rug softened the concrete floor. Two wicker chairs sat in front of the window.

Alec showed me the toilet alcove in the back. The composting commode used no water. The sink was small, clearly only for washing hands or getting a drink. A wooden cup sat on its rim. A towel of some kind of homespun hung beside it.

On the desk-side shelves were several white sun robes in about my size. Alec explained that these were available to all residents and guests from central stores.

He said, "You can wear them or not, whatever you like, but you might get better interviews if you 'go native' a little."

I agreed with him. Excusing myself, I grabbed one and retreated to the back alcove to change. Topped off with my bush hat I thought I cut a dashing figure.

When I started to strap on my headband recorder, Alec stopped me.

"We're not afraid of tech," he explained, "but it's very rude to record anyone without permission. Bring your handhelds only. Never turn them on without asking the people you're with. You don't have any implants, do you?"

I shook my head.

"OK, let's go."

As we exited the tunnel, Alec said, "We'll get you something to eat and drink while you get your bearings."

The entire LOOZ took hospitality seriously; I think I gained five pounds in those few days.

Our first stop was the Community Hall. It was a long, low, half-underground building. We entered through its Dining Hall doors. The room reminded me of the student lounge at a small college, but with a spicy aroma of baking. Several people wandered through, looking lost; others pointed their way for them. A few had gathered around the two computer kiosks in one corner.

Functional tables, some for two, others for as many as eight, were scattered around the big room. The chairs were a mix of bentwood, wicker, and the same green plastic as the gate. Tapestries and paintings hung on most walls. People bustled in and out, setting up for the evening meal or guiding newcomers.

"Our people made the furniture," Alec said, caressing a finely finished tabletop, "and all the artwork. Creativity tends to pop out in all kinds of ways."

The only odd note was the display between the kitchen door and the serving window. Before a large golden sunburst on the wall stood a small table. On the table was a sculpture based on DaVinci's "Universal Man," the one with arms and legs transcribing a circle and square. In front of the statue was a slim green candle in a carved red stone holder. As we picked up a water pitcher, glasses, and a plate of cut vegetables and cheese, I asked Alec about it.

"It's a symbol of what we're doing here, a focal point and reminder. It embodies our concept of what Humanity is." he said.

"So Phoenix is a religious community?" I asked.

"Sort of, but not in the usual sense. We don't have doctrines or restrictions, although our general outlook is Pagan. For us, all spirituality comes from nature, the seasons, birth and death, real life. What mythology you clothe it in is your own business. You'll find people here who profess Christianity, Wicca, even Buddhism. Some go to church in town, or used to. Others have altars at home, or shrines in the woods. Whatever our outward practices, all of us believe that Humankind is still evolving. As a species, we aren't quite ready to assume our full role as co-creators. 'We stand between the Candle and the Star.'"

We took a table at the far end from the kitchen, to stay out of the way of the workers. I turned on my recorder, and began my first interview.

JO: So, Alec, you've lived here all your life?

AM: No, we moved here when I was eleven. After I finished High School, I went to the old U of M in Morris, and then spent four years in the Air Force.

JO: Did you ever wonder what you were missing out here?

AM: I never had time. There was a lake to canoe and fish in. I spent days tramping around the woods. There were always interesting people from all over the world passing through Phoenix. Local people came out for music festivals and potlucks. We had DSL Internet and full satellite TV. If we really wanted urban things there were several big towns in driving distance, and The Cities were only three hours away.

JO: Did you miss your relatives?

AM: Sometimes, yeah. My brother James went back to live with Mom in St. Paul. We went to visit them sometimes, and there were always phone calls and e-mail. We've kept in touch, but our worlds grew apart. Now the LOOZ restrictions are going to make the wall between us higher.

Alec then took me through the Community Center. There were classrooms, a small lounge with a video wall, shower rooms, and a large Japanese-style barrel bath.

In one of the classrooms, about a dozen teenagers were having an animated discussion. In front of the room stood a whiteboard, covered with Ps, Qs, parentheses and arrows. An older woman gently nudged the discussion from time to time.

"What are they doing?" I asked Alec. "I can't tell what they're talking about."

"It's a class on Symbolic Logic," he said. "Most people's minds are like old attics, messy and dusty. Everyone here meditates, to clear out the cobwebs. We also teach Logic, to build healthy, orderly thinking."

At the far end was another large room. A tool storage area was in the middle. Around the outside were partitioned areas, which held potter's wheels, painters' easels and other art supplies. There were also a couple of pianos, in rooms with closable doors. A few people worked at projects: they all wore shorts and tops of the white cloth. Robes, hats and sun goggles hung on wall hooks.

Alec remarked, "Phoenix is a research center, not a dropouts' commune. Everyone here is a creative expert in some field. We're also all fiercely nonconformist. The Community provides its members with a variety of stimulating challenges."

We continued through the art wing, emerging on the far side of the Center, away from the main road. This was clearly the "village commons" of Phoenix. Red clover grew thickly all over the park-like area. Sturdy benches and platforms were scattered about, or grouped around fire pits and under organic-looking pavilions of green plastic. It seemed like a fine place, but no one was out using it.

"Why is the park so empty?" I asked Alec.

He looked at me with surprise.

"We avoid full sun, just like anyone else, and we're all busy getting ready for the LOOZ Sealing. Fifty old acquaintances asked to join us at the last minute. More keep showing up unannounced. It takes a lot getting them moved in. You'll see more action by Sealing Day."

He gestured to the amphitheater carved out of the hillside above the commons. It was of classic proportions, with a low, concrete stage at the bottom. Behind the stage was a large, skeletal, metal tetrahedron on a pedestal of girders.

"More symbolism?" I asked.

113

"Yup. A whole human being is a balancing between four main factors. We call them Knowledge, Wisdom, Compassion and Flow. I'll spare you the whole lecture, but one who seeks a Higher Good needs all of them, or the structure falls apart."

We climbed the gravel path beside the amphitheater, and emerged among low, stair-stepped buildings. The greenhouses were set into the hillside, with only their glazed, south-facing walls fully exposed. Everywhere were plants along foundations and paths. A gray-haired man crouched before a flowerbed, weeding.

"Hey, Ben!" Alec called. "I want you to meet our visitor!"

Standing, Ben was of average height, and heavily muscled. Clearly, he'd been a farmer or laborer all his life. An improbable black Stetson set off his white robes. When we shook hands, I felt that his were large and calloused.

"Ben Guthrie." He said, smiling broadly. "And you are?"

"Jimmy Olson. I'm a freelance writer."

Ben guffawed. "Jimmy Olson? No, really!?"

"Yes, really. I changed my name after the Superman revival a few years back. I thought it would help my career."

"OK, at least you've got the hair for it," he chuckled.

"That's what started it. People were calling me Jimmy after the movies came out, and I figured 'Why the heck not?'"

Alec said, "Dad asked Jimmy to visit us before the LOOZ closed up. One last publicity hurrah, I guess."

"Hey!" Ben said. "Maybe he'd like to go scouting with us tomorrow? We could show him around."

"Scouting?" I asked.

Alec answered, "Not everyone in the LOOZ understands what it's about, Jimmy. They don't know about the community we've built. Some just moved into vacated buildings, expecting some kind of free ride. Others are lowlifes on the run. We've heard about some possibly hostile squatters we need to check out. We don't need some old survivalists with shotguns or something."

"Right!" Ben agreed. "So, OK, ya in?"

I wasn't sure what they were getting me into. Alec seemed to think it was all right, and I couldn't imagine Phoenix endangering its guests. Then I had a thought.

"Guys with shotguns? You mean like hillbillies and hermits? We could get shot!"

Ben laughed. "I've lived here all my life," he said. "I can handle a first encounter. Besides, these robes of ours are of spider silk. No shotgun made can penetrate them."

They promised to wake me at Dawn the next day. I was to dress lightly, but with stout shoes, and bring my recorder.

We let Ben return to his weeding. Before we entered the main greenhouse, Alec asked whether I was a smoker; I was surprised to learn that tobacco carries viruses, which are harmful to tomatoes and some other plants. If I'd been a smoker, I would have needed to take a shower and put on freshly washed clothes to go in among the plants.

"We need to be certain of all kinds of details," he said. "Once we're on our own it'll be grow or starve."

As we descended a short stairway, we passed through a series of three thermal strip curtains. The greenhouse was enormous, running along hundreds of feet of hillside. Thousands of purple and red seedlings stood in peat pots on many-layered racks.

"Tami! Are you here?" called Alec. "You should meet Jimmie."

A middle-aged woman with long, curly blond hair was watering the seedlings. Her hair was held back with a large carved barrette, and she wore a long, rather grubby denim coat with many pockets. Shears, trowels, a calculator and other tools swayed in them as she walked toward us.

She brushed off her hands, and then offered her right one.

"I'm pleased to meet you. I'm Tami Soulé. I get to play in the dirt all day."

"Don't let her fool you. Tami has a doctorate in Horticulture, with emphasis on Greenhouse Production. She developed most of our methods here, and wrote a textbook which is the standard in the field."

She shrugged.

"Whatever," she said. "You do what you can. OK, Jimmie, what you see here is most of our future food supply. We start them in this greenhouse, and then transplant them to the others in batches. There's a continual year-round cycle of planting and harvests, with a big push every few weeks. We'd been self-sufficient in food until the recent influx. Until the new greenhouse crops come in we've made arrangements with other farms to trade gadgets and help for food. Eventually the whole LOOZ will need greenhouses like these, because of the weather and AgriCorp's chemical spraying on our borders."

We walked between the rows of plants. The air smelled thick with moisture and humus, like breathing a rich soup. Through glass walls I saw that some of the back corners held pens of rabbits and chickens.

"Those are our portable heaters," she joked. "A goodly part of our winter heating comes from them. They use up wastes, such as cuttings, and create excellent fertilizer. Working with critters is good for your health, too. Eggs, meat, feathers and fur are almost by-products after all the other good they do."

As we walked away, she called after Alec.

"I'm planning to call a meeting of production chiefs to see whether we can push up construction on the aquaculture tanks. I thought that you'd like to know."

At the far end of the starting room, we came to a heavy door with a rubber gasket around it.

Alec said, "This is the Botany Lab. It's where we develop new strains, tweak for UV tolerance, that sort of thing. The scrubberbushes came from here. The seal keeps stray pollen out."

It was a standard-looking lab, with glass beakers and tubes on racks, microscopes, computerized whatzits, and a large refrigerator. Several people were at work. Bending over a microscope was a tall, red-haired woman. Alec walked up to her and hugged her. He stood with his arm around her as he introduced us.

"Connie Winston, Botanist, meet Jimmy Olson, Cub Reporter."

She had *that look* on her face. I raised my hand, and said, "No, don't say it."

She laughed. Alec told me that she was his fiancée. We agreed to get together for an interview later.

Alec and I walked back out through the greenhouse. Ben waved at us as we reappeared. We turned the other direction, and walked toward a group of four large windmills. From them ran cables, converging on a garage-sized shed standing between them. A hint of ozone tang spiced the air.

"We live in the 'Saudi Arabia of Wind'" Alec said. "We get a good bit of power from these."

"But what about when it isn't windy?" I asked.

"We have batteries, kinetic storage, and backup systems that use biomass. Up 'till now we've sold excess power to the power company. We'll find other things to do after next week. Maybe we'll re-energize part of the local grid after it's abandoned."

"But what if something breaks?"

"Ah, and of course it will. Come!"

Alec was clearly proud as we approached the next building. Beside it were racks of windmill components. On one side were large, open overhead doors. We didn't enter, for the noise and bustle were intense.

It was clearly a substantial machine shop, reeking of sour oil and acrid welding fumes.

"Most anything we need, we can make." Alec said. "We're adept at salvage work for raw materials. People are leaving a lot behind in the Zone. And here's something else…"

Around the back of the Machine Shop stood a stout concrete building with a biohazard symbol on its steel, gasketed door. Inside, complex controls and screens stood before a wall of thick glass windows. The place clearly wasn't operating yet; workers in white coveralls were connecting wires and tubing both in the control room and beyond the glass.

Beyond the windows were several tanks, each in its own glass room. The tanks ranged from the size of small aquariums to something that would hold a large truck. Overhead cranes and waldoes hung from ceiling rails.

"This is our new nanotech lab," Alec said. "We'll be able to make all kinds of things here once it's running. We'll just need assembly programs and raw materials."

"But isn't this stuff dangerous?"

"Of course it is! So's our machine shop. So's a sewage treatment plant. So's a campfire. Jimmy, LIFE is dangerous!"

This attitude was the opposite of what I'd grown up with. For most people, Safety and Security were everything.

To describe the entire "Industrial Zone" of Phoenix would take a volume in itself. These people, with a philosophy of "living lightly on the Earth," cleverly used every technology they could think of to achieve that goal. Even the woodworking shop used lasers for some kinds of joinery and engraving- right alongside folks using antique draw-planes.

The best example was the Recycling Center. These people recycled EVERYTHING. They "bio-refined" all kinds of organic materials to produce fuels, foodstuffs and plastic. Even the scrubberbush berries, with their loads of toxic metals and compounds, were cracked and reclaimed.

"Waste is Food," Alec said. "Pretty much anything that's useless to one process is a resource for some other. If you can't reclaim and reuse something, you designed the process that creates it wrong. That's not just inefficient, it's immoral."

I learned that microbes in a vat produced the spider silk proteins. The technique was adapted from penicillin and insulin production. All they needed was heat, wood fiber, and some trace elements. The wood was abundant, as most of the trees in the LOOZ were dying. The trace elements were easily provided by dredged up and purified lake bottom ooze- with the side benefit of helping to clean decades of contamination from the lake.

The main residential area was beyond the amphitheater. A high hedge and gate shielded it from the Commons. Through the open gate I saw that none of the dwellings showed more than doors, windows and skylights above ground. In two places, workers were spraying concrete over inflated dome forms, with piles of dirt ready to be replaced over them. People trundled carts of belongings from the moving trucks. Alec warned me not to enter that area without permission.

Just on the "public" side of the hedge was a dojo straight out of an old kung fu movie. It was made of lacquered wood beams and panels, with a roof of curved tiles. Several panels had been slid aside, making the building almost a large gazebo. Thick straw mats covered the floor. At one end stood a small table, with another version of the Candle and Star emblem.

"We use the dojo for many things; Ta'i Chi, Tae Kwon Do, meditation, and small gatherings," Alec explained

Our quick once-over finished, Alec walked me back to my room.

"You'll want to get some rest before supper," he said. "I'll come get you in about two hours."

I lay on the bed, stripped down to boxers, and pondered. The people I'd met seemed genuinely happy with what they were doing, even though they lacked many of Civilization's benefits, including citizenship. They did many things communally, yet had intensely personal styles. They "did without," but did far more for themselves than anyone I knew. Without a word of criticism, they made me feel like a greedy primitive. I must have dozed off, for it seemed only minutes before Alec's "Haloo" sounded in my door.

Chapter Fifteen (2020)

Community is what you make it

Jimmie

"Hey Jimmie!" Alec called as he came in. "We usually dress up a bit for dinner, so put on something that says 'you.'"

Alec was wearing an electric blue tunic with embroidered silver trim, over black pants and boots. I couldn't match him; a regular office shirt and slacks would have to do. Maybe that said 'me;' not exactly a pleasant thought.

Alex explained on our way to the hall that residents were free to "raid the icebox" at any time. Still, Phoenix scheduled three sit-down meals each day, at hours varying according to the seasons. Attendance was optional, via a signup list. Time shared with the community was valued, so few missed the evening meal.

Tonight's supper was at 8:00. As we walked toward the Community Center, a high, clear bell began sounding.

"It's like summer camp!" I said to Alec, who grinned and shrugged.

Gaily-colored tablecloths now covered the dining hall tables. Families and individuals had their own cloths, which they spread on the tables they'd claimed for the meal. The colors and patterns varied wildly. Some were of plain, white spider silk, others were colorful patchworks, and others were classic red checks. Some smaller tables had been pulled together, and held two or three different cloths.

Each table also held a single candle in a simple stand, like that of the "candle and star" display.

People's clothing varied as wildly as their tablecloths. Many chose costumes reflecting their ethnicity. I also saw several wearing simple one-piece swimsuit-like garments in shimmering colors, with flowing capes.

Connie had already claimed a table for us. She wore basic green hospital scrubs, made festive with embroidered flowers and leaves, and jewel-like beadwork. Alec hugged her, and then we got in line to fill our trays. Although not all Phoenix-ites were vegetarians, shared meals were meatless out of respect for those who were. This was also a practical point, he added, since large-scale meat production was wasteful of resources. Tonight's menu featured big bowls of tabouli- a salad of wheat berries, tomatoes, cheese and greens, and vegetable sausage links. There were also pots of herbal tea, pitchers of water and fruit juice, and bowls of cut fruit. Everything had been produced within a few miles of Phoenix.

When everyone was seated with their food, a mother and daughter approached the Candle and Star display. They stood beside it until the room quieted. The girl lit the candle, as did people at each table. Then the mother and daughter began to sing. The crowd joined in, many rising to their feet. It was a song about Humanity's journey from pre-humanity, with visions of where we will go in the future. The refrain was:

We stand between the candle and the star,
What we were, and what we are,
Are only hints of what we'll be
Through Eternity.

After the song, a thin, red-haired and bearded man came forward. He wore a yellow and maroon batiked dashiki over black shorts, and held a clipboard.

"Ok- some announcements." He said. "Tammi needs more volunteers for the planting push in three weeks. We'll need to get several greenhouse loads in the ground all at once. Anyone willing to put in some extra community work hours, please talk with her. Tammi, please stand up so the newcomers know who you are."

"OK, thanks. Her office is on the other side of the greenhouses. Please sign up ASAP. With all the new folks and security changes, food could become a problem next fall if we don't jump on this.

"Congratulations to Danny Iverson. For the third week, he has the record scrubberbush berry harvest. Danny, take a bow. Folks, we're all going to need the kind of diligence this boy has shown. Good job."

He paged through the sheets on his clipboard. He smiled when he came to one.

"There's some talk from Western Dawn about having a get-together once the crops are in the ground. For you new folks, that's the Hmong village a couple of miles northeast of here. They DO know how to throw a party. Keep your ears open for this one.

"That's all for now." He said. "I'm Jules. If anyone has announcements, bring them to my office down that hall and on the left." He pointed to a door. "Don't forget to check the 'Net postings every day, too. Thanks."

Karl stood and moved over near Jules.

"Thanks, Jules, and thank you all for keeping him busy," Karl said.

"Alright, pep talk time. Most of you were interns or guests here before, and the rest were admitted on their recommendation, so you know what to expect.

"One person, Jimmy Olson there, is an outside observer. He doesn't realize it yet, but he's been given the job of Historian." He smiled, spreading his hands. "Be careful what you say to him; he's taking notes for posterity. Don't hold back, just think and be honest.

"Here's how I see our situation. In a few days, American society will commit the ultimate denial, a major step in its destruction. It will shut away our embarrassing, troubling ideas with fences and armed guards. They will shut us out, and we'll be on our own. We will survive and thrive alone, with only our commitment to each other, our resolve, and our abiding consciousness of our place as part of The All.

"This is the real deal, folks. We've all wanted to show what we could do on our own; now we've got it. We've won.

"OK, that's enough of me. Enjoy your meal."

While we ate I had my first interview with Connie.

JO: How did you come to be at Phoenix?

CW: I heard that Phoenix was looking for interns when I was doing my Grad work in Horticultural Genetics at the University of Minnesota. They were interested in my specialty, gene-tweaking food plants to grow in the new UV conditions. I could have gone for an internship with ADM or Cargil, but I was beginning to have my doubts about what the corporate mentality was doing with Bioengineering.

JO: So, you've been here ever since?

CW: No, that was just a one-year program. I loved it; I didn't have to worry about funding or being orthodox. I did some good, solid research here, most of it applying to the scrubberbushes. It was a sound underpinning for my thesis. I also spent time living outdoors with people who thought outside the box. I came to realize why I was uncomfortable with the corporate mentality: Everything hinged on the bottom line, on getting all possible profits from the Earth regardless of the wider, long-term costs. I couldn't live that shallow life any more.

JO: So, you gave up on having a professional career?

CW: (Laughing) No, I gave up on pretending that all I was doing was manipulating molecules. I understood that I was manipulating Life itself, which is a sacred thing. That's when science and spirituality merged for me; I became a Techno-Pagan. Going back to finish my degree was difficult. They couldn't fault my experimental work, and my thesis was tight. I nearly failed my orals, though. After living at Phoenix I had a hard time not showing my contempt for the hidebound, system-educated academics who questioned me. Karl had told me that if I got through that gauntlet I was welcome back here. So, I came.

JO: Of course, having Alec here was an attraction.

CW: Actually, I barely got to know him the first year I was here; I was putting too much time into getting to know myself. I thought that I'd be forever partnerless, married to science. Connecting with him after a few years here was a wonderful bonus.

JO: To go back a bit, you called yourself a "techno-pagan." What is that?

CW: It's a hard to define. In general, a Pagan is someone who knows that true spirituality and meaning come from Nature. Techno-Pagans see that service to and worship of Mother Earth are inseparable from technology. I can marvel at a sunset and commune with trees, but my rituals, prayers and spells happen in my lab. My work is improved by the insights and focus a Pagan outlook gives me; I'm not sure that we'd have managed the scrubberbushes without it.

By that time most folks were finished eating. Some had begun to mill around our table, wondering exactly who I was, and what I was up to. I think that some were disappointed that I didn't turn out to be some kind of spy.

My biggest surprise was when I found out who the "old acquaintances" were who had just moved in. I'd pictured college-aged people with no roots to pull up, but I was wrong. Several were middle-aged folks, who had brought their whole families. There was even, most welcome, an old intern who was now a doctor.

One woman with a southeastern accent told me: "I was here at the beginning, then I left to be a High School Science teacher. You'd think that Science would be straightforward, eh? It wasn't. I got tired of fighting one kind of crazies or another. No one wanted me to teach anything uncomfortable for them. The textbooks were a joke. Half the class time was spent watching propaganda TV. The kids had no vision or ambition beyond getting the latest clothes or tunes. Most of the other teachers weren't much better than the kids. It's crazy, but our fenced-in world here is actually bigger in some ways than the one I left out there."

Most people had work to do the next day, but we talked for an hour or so. I met folks I'd want to interview, and received invitations to visit their homes.

Tina was one of them. She told me that I could wander freely in Phoenix, but should really have a guide when I went outside of it. She had volunteered to be that guide, and had cleared her duties to be available whenever I needed her.

We eventually drifted outside. A few people were sitting around the park, some playing musical instruments. We wandered among them, Tina making brief introductions, before I headed back to my room. There, I dictated a few notes, washed up, and went to bed earlier than was usual for me.

I was awakened early the next morning by Ben calling at my doorway.

"Hey, Jimmie! Time's wasting! It's almost seven o'clock!"

"Come on in. I'll just be a minute."

Ben came in wearing a denim-colored sun robe. He tossed another to me.

"Here, wear this today," he said. "It's still spider silk, but less stark than those white jobbies. We'll be talking to folks who might react badly to white robes."

In a few minutes we were sitting in an ancient International Harvester Crew Cab pickup. Alec drove. Tina rode shotgun. Although the truck appeared old and battered, it was heavily modified under the skin. A sort of sunroof hatch comprised much of the roof. The window glass was unusually thick. A softball-sized black scanner bulge protruded from each corner of the roof. The back was loaded with boxes. Under and behind the seats were bags of sandwiches, bottles of tea- and guns.

"Is this a scouting trip, or a commando raid?" I asked.

123

Alec answered, "Mostly it's a supply run, and a chance to show you around. We do need to check out those squatters, though. Better safe than sorry. This is hunting territory, so pretty much everyone carries a gun."

"So it's Phoenix's job to check on squatters?"

"Yep. The folks who are staying in the LOOZ got together to write up a Compact. Our job is to be the tech suppliers and general troubleshooters."

We headed back up old Minnesota 40 to Asyl. As we topped the last ridge to the west of town, I could see the opposite side of the valley. A lot of progress had been made on the Security post that I'd come through the day before.

We saw few people among the ruined houses of Asyl until we neared Main Street. A block from the bustle of corporate workers building the market stalls stood a classic old red schoolhouse, which had the odd addition of Viking-style dragons at the ends of its roof beams. Across the street from it, several people in bright tie-dye and batik robes were hoeing a large garden.

"This was the Asyl Village Arts School." Alec explained. "It started as a place to teach Norwegian traditional crafts. Now it's an artists' colony, and effectively City Hall."

As the ancient truck wheezed to a stop, a tall, thin woman with streaked gray and blond hair approached. She nodded to my companions, and then cast an appraising gaze at me.

"Alec. Ben. Who's your friend here?" she said.

Ben introduced us. "Mayor Jody Ellis, I present Jimmy Olson, writer and last tourist."

She shook my hand, almost violently.

"Tourist, eh? Well, maybe if we'd had a few more of those we wouldn't be in this fix. What brings you out here in our moment of glory, eh?"

We chatted for a bit while several people put down their hoes and unloaded the boxes.

"So, do ya plan to stop by the Colonel's on the way out?" Jody asked.

"Of course," Alec answered. "We'd like him to come along if he will."

She snorted.

"I doubt that you'll be able to pry him loose from his research long enough," she said.

Jody agreed that I could interview her in the next few days, before the get-together on Sealing Day. Once the boxes were off loaded, we headed across town.

We detoured around the Implant work crews and their Augment supervisors on Main Street. We rejoined Main Street past downtown. In a few blocks it became a long, paved driveway; at its end, on the lip of the valley, stood a huge log house. Two house-type windmills stood behind the house. There were no obvious fences, but a small yellow sign warned ELECTRONIC SECURITY IN OPERATION. A pager-like device on the truck's dash began buzzing.

"OK," said Alec. "We've rung the doorbell. Let's go say howdy."

Alec pulled up in front of the massive porch.

"Now," he warned." Everybody out, one at a time. NOBODY carries anything. Keep your hands outside your robes."

"Who IS this guy?" I asked.

Tina turned to me, more serious than her usual sunny self.

"He's an old friend of Karl's, and my teacher." She answered. "Whatever you do, don't ask for an interview!"

Once we were all standing in front of the truck, the front door opened. A lean, powerful looking man came out. He had short, thinning iron gray hair, bushy sideburns, and a handlebar moustache. He was dressed casually in green slacks and a dark-red plaid cotton shirt. His expression and bearing were those of a professor toward favorite students, or a baron toward his loyal servants. He nodded at us in turn.

"Ben. Tina. Alec. I see you drove The Tank. Good." he said.

He smiled wryly as he turned to me. "Jimmy Olson. I wondered whether that old scoundrel would entice you out here."

I wasn't sure that I liked him knowing about me; but I wasn't sure I didn't, either.

He waved us up onto the porch.

"You may as well sit up here out of the sun," he said.

We climbed the broad steps. To one side of the deck were several Adirondack chairs. On the other was a large trestle table with four straight-backed wooden chairs. On the table were a glass pitcher of lemonade, a plate of fry bread, and a laminated USGS map.

We sat. The Colonel began pointing at the map while we helped ourselves.

"Some folks from out on the Sag Bypass brought news. A band of stragglers have appropriated the abandoned doll factory near Watson." he said. "There look to be about thirty of them, all ages. They're well-organized, in a civilian way. They don't seem aggressive, but they're damn crotchety about anyone approaching them.

"The highway runs along the ridge above them. The rail line and spur run between them and the river. It's got a couple of nice buildings. It's in a great spot for light industry, but it's completely undefendable. If they get nasty, we can evict them pretty easily. I advise that you not buy trouble yet, just look them over."

Ben agreed. "We're not looking for a fight." He said. "I'm just going to tell them how things are: give them a copy of the Compact, jawbone a little."

"We may not like them," Alec said to me. "But the Compact values diversity. If they're a problem, there's still time to kick them out. If they're OK, even if they're a bit peculiar, they can stay."

We were there for nearly an hour as the others discussed the scouting mission and the future security of the LOOZ. I watched quietly; I knew better than to ask any questions. It became clear that Ben was a born diplomat. Tina became more of a mystery; she seemed too young and sweet, but obviously had training in guerilla operations. Alec, I knew, had been in Air Force Security. This Colonel, though; what was he?

We said our goodbyes to the Colonel, and then left Asyl. Old US 59 headed south down a broad, shallow valley. On its eastern crest loomed the border fence. A long curve led into a sort of valley-in-the-valley, a rich-looking wetland.

"This is the Watson Sag." Alec explained. "It's an arm of Lac qui Parle. A long time ago the Corps of Engineers dredged a connection between it and the Chippewa River. That diversion flows past the doll factory."

He became serious.

"OK. We're about a mile out. Be alert; we don't know how nervous these people are."

A gravel driveway split off to the left just as the road began to climb again. A wooden sign beside the broken gate proclaimed;

LIVING WATERS
This land is the Lord's!

"Uh, oh," Ben said. "Religious communes can get paranoid. Let's hope this isn't one of those."

As we came within sight of a whitewashed old concrete factory building, a horn sounded three long notes. People who'd been in the fields ran for the main building, like English peasants fleeing to a castle during a Viking raid.

We stopped on the rise overlooking the site. Alec and Tina readied their weapons, just in case, but kept them out of sight. She also flipped open the glove box, revealing a computer keyboard and screen. All through the confrontation, she kept one hand on her gun and one eye on Ben; the other hand and eye were using sensors to scan the area.

Soon three men came through an iron door in the main building. Two were hulking young guys. In the lead was a lean, old, bearded man, who stalked along as though he himself were The Lord. I felt like a marauding barbarian under his gaze.

Ben jumped out to meet them, keeping his hands out at his sides.

"Hey neighbors!" he shouted. "We came to pay a friendly call!"

"We do not treat with apostates!" thundered the Leader.

Ben chuckled a bit as he answered. "Maybe not," he said. "But Jesus was pretty clear on how to treat neighbors, even if none of us is Samaritan."

The Leader looked skeptical. "Are you a student of the Holy Word?"

"I've been known to crack open a Bible from time to time. Maybe we can have a good discussion one of these days."

"Perhaps. But why are you here now?"

"We just want to get acquainted," said Ben. "Folks around here are organized. We're the welcoming committee."

"You represent the central authority? Who is it? Do they acknowledge The Lord?"

"We're Americans- everybody is the authority. We look out for each other around here."

He pointed to our truck with his chin.

"These folks are from Phoenix, the biggest group around here. The Mayor of Asyl sends her greetings, too. Nobody's looking to bother you folks if you're peaceable."

The Leader relaxed a fraction.

"All right then. What have you to say?"

Ben stepped forward, offering his hand.

"I'm Ben Guthrie. You are?"

The Leader shook hands reluctantly.

"I am Bishop Phelps. We are a remnant of Christ's flock, awaiting His return."

Ben reached inside the neck of his robe. He drew out a few sheets of blue paper, which he held out to Phelps.

"These are the main rules of the Compact. Basically, nobody can tell you what to do on your own land. You can trade with anybody who wants to. You can have a stall at the Asyl Farmers' Market: market day is

Tuesday. But there is NO religious proselytizing allowed. That, or any sort of brigandage or endangering the common good, is grounds for shunning. OK?"

Phelps took the papers between thumb and forefinger, and passed them to one of the boys.

"I will examine this document when I have time. If it is in accordance with Scripture, we will honor it. Go now!"

Ben smiled at him.

"Thanks again, Bishop Phelps. God Bless!"

As Ben walked back to The Tank, the three glared at his back.

"OK, get us out of here," he told Alec as he got in.

Alec revved the engine and backed out to the highway.

Once we were safely on the road, Alec asked Tina what she'd read.

"We'll need to do a reprocessing for details," she answered. "But right now it looks like forty or fifty people were in the area. They have a small amount of weaponry in the big building. I don't think they're equipped to be a major problem."

At the top of the ridge we were back on the prairie. We could see for ten or fifteen miles in all directions. From the east and west the fences crept together, headed for a point at Montevideo.

In a few miles we passed through the remains of another town. Empty grain elevators, a bar, and a double handful of houses stood silently beside the road. Rusted FOR SALE signs sprouted everywhere, some before blackened pits.

Ben said, "This was Watson. It held just a couple of hundred people. The folks had spirit, but no economic base; when Montevideo went under, they did too."

Where had these people had gone. I wondered. Why had they come in the first place? What had happened to their history?

But right in the middle of town, next to a burned-out convenience store, stood a church-like hall. It actually had a fresh coat of paint. A sign above its door proudly proclaimed "1897."

"Woah! Ben, what's with that building?" I asked.

"That's the old Watson Town Hall," he said. "People have put a lot of love into it over the years. There's still a committee that keeps it in shape for concerts and such."

A couple of miles past Watson another broad valley opened up on our left. It was cluttered with piles of trees, cars, walls of buildings and other flotsam. Down the middle ran the Chippewa River; on its opposite bank the security fence loomed.

Ben pointed at the ruins. "We're coming into the outskirts of Montevideo," he said. "It was the 'big town' in the area, with a Wal-Mart, two supermarkets, a hospital, airport, courthouse- all that important stuff. The floods were especially bad here where the Minnesota and Chippewa rivers come together. They wiped out close to half the town, including the sewage treatment plant, most of downtown, and City Hall. What're left are a few dozen corporate people who watch the southern gate and the east-west highway."

Our road took us into the edge of town. On the last long run down into the valley, I could see that old 59 was completely washed away half a mile further on. We turned back northward onto an old county road. It was a pleasant drive, halfway down the valley wall, paralleling the Minnesota River. The river bottom was a labyrinth of greenery. I could almost ignore the Security fence on the far side ridge.

We descended lower into the valley, where the road became more the memory of a road. We jounced along, thankful for The Tank's heavy-duty suspension and high clearance. We passed foundations of houses, and a pile of lumber that had been a barn.

After a couple of miles we came to a narrow, overgrown side valley. We followed a rude path back between huge trees. Just where it reached the prairie stood a shack. I recognized a small windmill of Phoenix make on its roof. On the porch sat a powerful-looking, deeply tanned man with a grizzled, forked beard. A rifle lay across his lap. Two huge cats sat beside him.

He rose to greet us, setting his gun down. The cats stayed- sitting, watching, watching.

Ben jumped out.

"Hey, you old so and so!" He shouted. "What's up?"

The big man pounded Ben on the back.

"Endeavoring to persevere," he said. "Endeavoring to persevere. So, who have you got into what sort of trouble today?"

"Jacko Stavanger, you know Alec and Tina. This carrot top is Jimmy Olson, a writer. Jimmie is our guest until Sealing Day."

He shook my hand, adopting a mock-serious pose.

"In my travels I have met Napoleons and Caesars, Brick Reeds and Bruce Waynes, innumerable Darth This-And-Thats, but never before the famed cub reporter! I salute you!"

Ben said, grinning, "Now, don't take this fellow seriously. He's traded tall tales from Barrow to Tierra del Fuego. He's got a good sense of humor for a hermit."

"What? Hermit?" Jacko snorted. "Please! EX-hermit! Young man, these people won't let a body change!"

I liked this character.

"So," I asked, "Why did you change?"

"Because Life wouldn't give up on me. She's a tenacious old broad. She sent a couple of bad-ass warriors to knock some sense into me."

The others had the look of people expecting a familiar scene to play out.

"You don't know? These lightweights didn't tell you?"

Ben protested. "We've only got time for introductions today, Jacko. Jimmie will be around until Sealing Day, though."

Jacko smiled at me. "Then you'll have to come back and talk about it. Right?"

"We'll see to it." Alec answered.

"All right, then. I'll expect you, Mr. Writer!"

After the interminable leave-taking of the "Minnesota Goodbye," we piled back into The Tank and headed up past Jacko's shack onto the prairie. I looked forward to returning.

In a few hundred feet, we caught an old gravel road, which ran straight to the North. After crossing several identical roads at right angles, we took a left, then another right. I wondered how Alec could tell one dusty crossroad from another.

As the sun was setting, we came upon a stand of trees many blocks across. The road ran right through it, past a huge old house and several outbuildings. It was the most bustling place I'd seen since Phoenix; people in bib overalls, tie-dyes, even some Phoenix robes, were erecting greenhouses and putting up fences. Children chased chickens and geese. Riders on horseback drove a herd of dark-red cattle across the road.

A Clint Eastwood clone rode up beside us, and waved his hat in greeting.

"Hey, Alec! What brings you guys out here?" he called.

He ducked his head and peered through the window. "Hiya," he said.

Alec told him who I was.

"I'm Tommy Jensen." The cowboy said. "Pleased ta meet ya. Come back when I'm not so busy, and we'll talk."

Tina asked "How about late tomorrow?"

"You're on."

With that he nickered to his horse and rode after the cattle.

"What is going on here?" I asked Alec.

He explained that this place, called Magic Pumpkin, was the merger of three organic farms. Various family members had run a beef operation, a vegetable farm, and a horse ranch on different plots. The vegetable farm was now outside the LOOZ boundaries, so they'd trucked in its greenhouses and equipment to create the new cooperative farm. They'd had to reorganize EVERYTHING.

"These folks were some of my Dad's first friends out here." Alec added. "They stayed 'Liberal' and 'Environmentalist' even when the early Corporates made those swear words. They're pleasant, gentle people. They can seem goofy, but they're tough."

We went on through the woods. Where the road reached the valley rim again, we turned northwestward to parallel the river. A few miles west of the ruins of Watson, we passed the jagged concrete and steel remnants of the old Lac qui Parle dam. The millions of tons of water its collapse released in 2010 were what had scoured Montevideo from the map.

Folks at a few other farmsteads waved to us from a distance, but none gestured for us to stop. We got back to Phoenix after Supper, but the kitchen had stayed open for us. We picked up some sandwiches and rolls, and tea to wash them down. We about the day's events, and then Tina warned me:

"Tomorrow we'll go interviewing. Get your rest. I'll see you for breakfast."

Chapter Sixteen (2020)

"Everyone has their story"

Jimmie

After a sounder sleep than I'd had in years, I awoke at the sound of the breakfast bell. I hustled over to the Dining Hall so Tina and I could get an early start.

Tina was waiting for me, holding a table. She was dressed colorfully, in a long, gaily African printed skirt and top. When I asked what the occasion was, she said that she'd just felt like wearing something to remind her of home.

Breakfast was informal, with no ceremonies or announcements. After getting a tray of fruit, huevos rancheros and juice, we sat down to plan the day. I told her that since we'd be working together, hers should be the first interview of the day.

JO: Tina, your accent marks you as someone "not from around here." Where are you from, and how did you end up in Phoenix?

TD: You are perceptive. I was originally from Rwanda. You know about the massacres there in the '90s.

JO: No, I'm sorry, I don't.

TD: What a blessed life you have had! I was a happy little girl who sang and made up stories. Then all the rest of my family was killed for being of the wrong clan. Thousands of us were hacked apart with machetes, or burned alive in their homes.

I fled to the forests. Marxist guerillas took me in. I stayed with them for many years. I learned to fight, but didn't like it. I learned to stand watch, and had to like it. I learned to hate, which held less shame than fear did. I didn't sing any more.

I was sixteen when the UN soldiers captured me. I met the Colonel. He rather adopted me. He gave me to hope again, and showed me how to use my skills for helping. Then he came back to Asyl, his home, and I joined Phoenix.

JO: I'm sorry to hear about your troubles. Are the memories still painful to you?

TD: Of course! But life isn't about comfort. It's about living. You live. You help others to live. You cherish the life of Mother Earth. People have always been cruel and stupid. These people are less cruel and stupid than any I've known. Here, I can live.

After breakfast, we went out "to see what there was to see." At the river's edge we came upon Francie, the teacher who'd introduced herself after supper that first night. She was showing a group of teenagers how to use a water-sampling scoop. We watched from a short distance.

"The Minnesota has long been one of the most polluted rivers in North America," she explained. "Some progress at cleaning it up was being made around the turn of the century. Now goddess only knows what will happen. This year we'll be monitoring pH, microorganisms, flow rate, nitrates; all the vital statistics. This won't be just a classroom exercise. The ecologists here will make real use of your figures. I'll be grading your work, but I'm easy. Remember that Life always gives pass/fail grades. Our ancestors didn't take care of the land, so now it's our job to do what we can with what they left us."

A doubtful looking girl raised her hand; I recognized her as one who arrived on the same day I did.

"Miz Jones," she asked. "What if we fail this class?"

"Honey," the short, intense redhead answered, "Where are you from?"

"Umm, Tacoma."

"Nice place. How was the water there?"

"It was OK. I like the water here better."

"I'm glad. Do you know where Tacoma gets its water?"

"No…. The Columbia River?"

"That's a good guess. Would you ever drink water right out of that river?"

"No. It was kinda stinky. Not as bad as this, though. We don't drink this, do we?"

"No, dear, not directly, but all our trees do. The birds do, too. So do the water-breeding insects. From them, pretty much everything living near the river ties into its waters."

She looked over the class. "Is anyone here diabetic?"

A lanky lad raised a hand.

"OK," the teacher continued, "What kind of regular discipline do you have to do?"

He pulled the neck of his shirt neck aside. "I've got to run the scanner over my pump once a week." He said. "That's here under my collarbone. It reads out what my blood chem's been doing. Sometimes it needs reprogramming. The med bladders need refilling sometimes, too."

"So, the diabetes has messed up your blood. If you don't watch the figures, you get sick. You could even die, right?"

He nodded.

"That's our job, folks. Rivers are Mother Nature's bloodstream. We're the med scanner in these parts. What happens if we fail?"

The girl from Tacoma grew pale, and all the class fell somber.

I asked Tina how a family had gotten all the way here from Washington State. She told me that the little girl, Lori, was the daughter of an intern from years before. Her family had returned about two months before.

We went to find the mother, Barb Lines. She was at the Recycling Center, supervising the piping of a mass of half-dissolved plastic bottles into the next vat in their processing. I asked whether she had a few minutes for an interview.

"If you don't mind waiting, once this slurry is transferred I can talk," she answered.

I was glad to wait. I watched as she directed a half-dozen workers in wrestling a heavy hose into position, clamping it and firing up a massive, whining pump. We went outside to find a quieter, shadier spot.

JO: We saw your daughter down by the river with Francie. Do you have any more children?

BL: No, just Lori.

JO: Why did you bring her back to Phoenix? Is her father along too?"

BL: Yes, he's here. His name is Loren: she's named after him. He's working on the plans for rebuilding the power grid in the LOOZ. We came back for the reality of this place.

JO: What do you mean? Isn't any place you go real?

BL: Like Karl says, people live in the world they believe they live in. For many, it doesn't have to be the real world. I'm not like that. I'm a chemical engineer. I have a low tolerance for deceptive drivel: Things are what they are.

I'll put it practically. "Out of petroleum" means "Out of petroleum." It doesn't mean "We need to prioritize acquisition of projected untapped reserves." "Poisoning the air" means "Poisoning the air." It doesn't mean "Unforeseen but economically impractical to correct side effects of necessary industrial processes." "We are paying UN reparations because we were a bunch of short-sighted, greedy bullies" doesn't mean "Our long-suffering nation is sharing its bounty with the less economically insightful." OK? Lori doesn't need the kind of brain-rotted doubletalk that passes for public discussion out there. Phoenix people are bright- I'm not worrying about starving or freezing or any of that. But more important, they mean what they say.

JO: I'm curious about how far you came. What was your original connection? What was the trip like?

BL: I'm sure that Tina told you that I was an intern here, while I worked on my undergrad degree at Moorhead State. Work, and love, took me back to Seattle.

What's happened to the Northwest is sacrilege. Half the time the rains don't come, and when they do they're full of acid from Asian smokestacks. The mountains look like dogs with mange; the trees are dying off so badly.

Things greened up for a little ways when we rolled into Montana- Ha! Think of that, "Montana" and "green" in the same sentence. That didn't last, though. All across Montana and the Dakotas people were on the move. Almost every day we had to stop for military convoys. We heard that the Blackfoot Nation had started a shooting war over their LOOZ status. Towns I used to visit, like Valley City, North Dakota, were just gone. I guess that floods got some, and fire the rest.

We were scared all the way. I tell you, coming through the North LOOZ Gate at Appleton was the greatest relief I've ever felt.

Tina then escorted me into the residential area. As always, flowers grew in profusion. It was like walking into a Tolkien fantasy; all the houses were underground, some even with round doors! Signs before them proclaimed BRADBURY, ADAMS, BUJOLD, TWAIN and other names. Although all of the signs were based on the same dark rectangles, each was unique, carved and painted with flowers, birds, or abstract symbols.

Tina led me to one with the name WALKER in large golden letters.

"Every house has the name of a writer, given by its residents," she said. "Those who write bring ideas to life, just as we are doing."

The round door of Alice Walker House was painted in a lighting pattern of yellow, orange and black. It swung shut behind us with a solid THUNK.

After a short tunnel, we came into an open area. The domed ceiling vaulted over our heads. Light came from windows around the dome's peak. Many plants hung in pots or twined their ways across the walls and ceiling. Chairs, a couch, and a TV Comp were arranged in one area. There were several curtained doors. On one wall was a small kitchen setup, where a woman with long red-blond hair was cooking. The air smelled of plants and the spices of her cooking. It was a warm, comfortable place.

"Hey, Krista!" Tina called. "What's happening?

"Ah, not so much," the woman said. "Just cooking up something to eat while I write."

Tina introduced her as Krista, a poet of some note. How she could market her poetry from the LOOZ wasn't settled yet. Even so, her visions would be valued within the LOOZ.

"Is it just the two of you here?" Jimmie asked.

Tina laughed. "Of course not!" she said. "Eight of us single women live here. This is our common space. The bathroom is through that doorway. We have our own rooms, although Kelly and Frieda share one. Come, I'll show you mine."

We pulled a black and yellow curtain aside and entered a space much like my quarters, although a bit larger.

The furniture was sparse, but not stark. The bed, desk, shelves and rug were ordinary enough, but in one corner hung a shelf with a very stylized female statue. I looked more closely, and saw that photos of African people surrounded it. A bowl-shaped incense burner and cones were in front of it.

"What's this?" I asked.

"That is my shrine. The Goddess is the Lady of Birth and Death, of Learning and War. From her I gather strength to be what I must. The photos are of great Africans, people I strive to be like."

"Oh, something like a traditional Catholic praying to Mary," I said.

"Something like that, yes."

136

We went back outside, waving at Krista. As we walked around the area, I noticed meditation benches, picnic tables and a playground interspersed among the mounds.

We saw Ben emerging from Volberg House.

"Ben," Tina called. "Have you got a few minutes?"

"Ah, the cub reporter wants his interview? OK. Come over here in the shade."

A small pavilion stood near the playground. Ben and I talked.

JO: The first question is always "Why are you here?"

BG: You saw what's left of that house on the ridge over toward Asyl? I grew up there. I got involved with the farm protests and the tractorcade as a kid in the Seventies. Later Marta and I farmed that land. We raised six kids there.

We stuck out the Eighties and Nineties, but George the Second's policies did us in. We sold out in 2004. I'd gotten to know Karl from trips to the Bait Shop. He knew the wider world, but respected our ways, too. He asked Marta and me to come on board here when we sold out.

JO: Why are you staying now? I'm sure that you'd rate a nice apartment in The Cities.

BG: Do you really not understand? I grew up here. I raised my kids here. Marta, two of my brothers, my folks, my grandparents and a whole slew of cousins are buried here. I'm in this land, and it's in me.

JO: You're clearly an educated man. Couldn't you nourish that better in The Cities?

BG: Yup- I'm educated; self educated. My folks couldn't afford college for me, so I read. Out on the tractor I listened to audio books. Later, the Internet helped a lot with finding materials. Then everything started to charge. Decent books and tapes got harder to find. Oh, yeah, Martha Stewart and Oprah and all those were easy to find, but solid stuff got scarce. That's part of how I got to know Karl. He had a good library, and let me borrow from it. Phoenix keeps expanding it, so I can find almost anything there, now. I doubt that I'd do better in The Cities, not for things that mattered.

One place I'd missed on my earlier quick tour was the livestock area. In a fenced-off patch of woods, horses, goats and chickens wandered freely. Along one side were several low buildings. Tina explained that some were foul-weather animal shelters, while others were roosting barns, a milking shed, and feed storage bins. At one end stood a stout concrete structure, much like the lab on the greenhouses. We entered it through a double door.

The room was large and clean, but with a lingering smell of barnyard and disinfectants. Small cages lined one wall. On the opposite wall were a commercial refrigerator, glass-fronted cabinets and a large steel table. This was clearly a veterinary hospital.

"Bom dia, Maria!" Tina called, walking toward a door in the rear wall.

The door opened, and a small, darkly tanned woman in a lab coat briskly emerged. She came right to me, her hand thrust out.

"I am Maria Carvalho," she said. "You'll want to interview me. Now is good, before one of those silly goats breaks a leg or something. Come into my office."

Before waiting for my answer, she turned and strode back through the door.

Tina looked amused, and gestured to follow her.

The office held a neat desk with flatscreen, some wooden chairs, and crammed bookcases. Maria offered us glasses of hot, aromatic tea that she called maté

We began:

MC: I am Maria Lucia de Carvalho. I come from Recife, Brazil. I am the veterinarian and biologist.

JO: OK. That's clear enough. How did you end up here?

MC: Like most people here, I came to do research. My specialty was goats and sheep. I had worked with the rural people in my state in Brazil. You know that my country was destroying our forests. Some of us were looking for other ways that the people could live. When our State University did a joint project with the Minnesota University, I came here. Karl asked me to stay. I became a citizen based on his statement that he needed my skills. What else?

JO: You didn't want to return to your home country?

MC: Certainly, my heart wanted to. My head told me that I could do more for the world here. In Brazil, I had to fight the bureaucrats, the Church and the traditions. In Phoenix, everything was focused on getting things done right. I hate ignorance and waste. So does Phoenix.

JO: What do you do other than animal medicine?

MC: The sunlight is changing. My animals will go blind unless we can strengthen their eyes. We have had some success in that. Many species here are becoming extinct. We must preserve their DNA so we can rebuild the ecology one day. I supervise that work as well.

We were interrupted when a young man ran in. He shouted that a goat had gotten out through a burst fence joint, followed by many chickens. What should he do?

Grumbling in Portuguese, Maria ran out behind him, throwing a "goodbye" over her shoulder.

Since we were near the greenhouses, I suggested that we interview Tami. We crossed some open space, and then entered through the same door as I had on the first day.

We found her in the chicken pen. The multi-colored birds surged about her feet, clucking madly, while she threw bits of green scrap to them.

"Oh, Hey!" she said. "I'll be with ya in a minute."

She dumped the last the clippings from her sack, then climbed over the short fence.

"So, it's my turn to spill my guts, then?" she said. Let's walk around while we talk."

We strolled up and down aisles. Tami paused her and there to examine leaves and stems. She would occasionally pluck a small plant; some went into her sack, others onto the rubbery grated floor.

JO: Tami, How did you come to Phoenix?

TS: I was at the University of Georgia. I'd just finished my Doctorate, and was thinking about teaching. I came to The Cities to check out a job at the U of M. I saw the notices about interns at Phoenix. I was curious, and came out for a look. After a while, I moved up here permanently.

JO: Why did you stay? With that degree, you could be anywhere. You could teach, or run a power plant greenhouse.

TS: I could've, sure enough. But I wanted something different. In a job-job, you're just a functionary. I like being motherly, knowing people, talking to my plants. You can't do that at a corporate greenhouse. They'll think you're a nut.

JO: So you don't like a scientific, production-oriented approach?

TS: (Laughing, then growing stern) Now, what makes you think nurturing isn't scientific, or production oriented? If I don't apply Science, these greenhouses don't produce. If these greenhouses don't produce, people's bodies starve. BUT, if we treat our partner life forms as mere things, resources to exploit, our spirits starve. That was the Outside's big problem when I came here- fat bodies and starved spirits.

By then it was time to go interview Jody. We drove my car back over the rolling ridges to Asyl.

The Corporates had finished refurbishing downtown; Main Street was deserted and quiet, except for the constant murmur of the corporate telescreens. The gaily-colored awnings of the Market stalls fluttered in a slight breeze; Tina mused that maybe the wind came from the hot air on the screens. Sounds of hammering and wood-chopping came from farther off.

Eventually we turned a corner and pulled up to the Art School building. Tina had explained its checkered history: from 1875 to 1950, a rural schoolhouse; from 1958 to 1989, moved to town and used as the high school band room; from 1989 to 1995, storage; in 1996, moved again, repainted and remodeled; from 1996 to 2008, a Folk Art School of international reputation. Despite its fame, the school had always been volunteer run, which led to some financially rocky times. When it finally failed, some of its last supporters and instructors refitted it as a commune. As an artists' colony it had continued to bring in students, but only on an ad hoc basis.

We found Jody out front, supervising the erection of a huge mobile-statue fashioned from bits of farm machinery.

"It's kinda cheesy," she admitted. "But Andre thinks it's a good representation of where we're at now.

"C'mon inside. I'll get us some bread and cheese. Sorry, the wine's still brewing, but we've got some apple cider from last year."

JO: I take it that you're a native Asylite?

JE: Yup. Born and raised. Like everybody else, I escaped to the outside when I was old enough. Mom and Dad stayed when we kids were gone. I taught at the U in Morris for a while, then moved back. When the U changed hands, I stayed, 'cause by then I'd gotten in with the local "Bohemians."

JO: Bohemians?

JE: You know, artists and such. Asyl, Minnesota had more artists per capita than anyplace but Paris, France or Milan, Italy. Some of the best Norwegian-style painters in the world lived here.

JO: Why are you staying even with the LOOZ closing in? Wouldn't The Cities be better?

JE: I'm just too cussed to leave. Why should I pay attention to a buncha stuck-up dorks who don't know Art from their arse? We've got everything we'll need here.

JO: What about all the Art opportunities in The Cities?

JE: Sure, they SOUND good, but how many people can afford to participate? How many average Joes and Janes can have a voice in running the show? It's all just a sham so you can say how cultured your City is. Phhhtt, all your city rats really want is pre-canned videos, and musicals based on old sitcoms. I'll take my Art raw and undiluted.

See that guy over there spreading mulch? He's a composer who specializes in neo-Baroque chamber music. He plays bluegrass fiddle, too. And he makes one hell of a pasta faggiole.

See her there with the big cat? She's a muralist. One of her best pieces was across there on the fire hall before the Corpos painted it over with The Administrator's portrait.

In some old movie, Robin Williams said, "Art is Life." This place is full of Art. Get it?

JO: I'm beginning to. Oh, I've seen a few cats like that one here and there. Something's different about them.

JE: Some of us call them bobbycats. Ask Jacko Stavanger about them when you see him. He's their "father."

JO: Father?

JE: Just ask.

Jody was another BSer, a more militant one than Ben. She could have talked all afternoon. Tina and I eventually managed to escape more conversation and caught US 59 back toward Montevideo. There was no other traffic for a dozen miles; the soon-to-be LOOZ was becoming a very quiet place. Some of the Living Waters folks watched us pass, but didn't wave.

Beyond Watson, we turned onto a gravel road. After a couple of turns we came to the Magic Pumpkin's woodlot. In the fields beside the road, we passed several dozen cattle, and a number of horses, including several huge, light-tan beasts. Tina explained that one of the Pumpkin's members had used them for farming for years. No big local wing-ding was complete without a hayrack ride behind the superb creatures.

There was still plenty of bustle in the woods as we approached, but it seemed less chaotic, centering on a couple of greenhouses. We parked near the Big House and asked a young woman whether she knew where Tommy was.

"Grandpa's down at the pond," She said. "I'll show you."

She showed us past a huge garden, then along a gentle downhill path through the woods. As we walked, she explained that her name was Sam, and her mother was Tommy's daughter. She'd grown up on the

Beanstalk Farm, the organic vegetable place, which was now outside the LOOZ boundaries. She and her husband had a farm along the lake, a few miles north of Phoenix. They were here helping with the Magic Pumpkin changeover.

Sam told me that although the farm had been in her family for five generations. When they had rented it out for a while in the middle Twentieth Century, the tenants had made a mess of it. Where the gardens were now had been filled with old machinery and trash, as had the woodlot. The creek had been fouled and eroded. Proudly she told us how her grandparents and their friends had reclaimed it, starting in the 1970s. I could imagine the crowd of college students hauling refuse and trimming dead branches.

Then we came within sight of the pride of the farm- the pond. Loving hands and strong backs had utterly transformed the manure-filled creek. With strenuous labor the new pioneers had built a thirty foot earthen dam, with sluice and gate, on the downhill side. Springs, once plugged with concrete rubble, were reopened. The result was a wide, clear pond, surrounded by grassy banks, with willow trees beside a sandy swimming beach.

That was where we found Tommy, sitting in a webbed lawn chair, scribbling on a flatscreen. He jumped up when he heard our approach.

"Hey, good ta see ya!" he said. "Hi Tina. It's Jimmie, right? Is it our time already? Boy! C'mon, I'll walk ya back up to the house. We'll get a little lunch."

We started the interview as we walked. Tommy waved his arms a lot as he talked, sometimes jumping aside to show us some interesting plant or insect.

JO: Sam tells me that you've done a lot to reclaim this land. When was that, and why?

TJ: Jimmie, first let me ask you what you think of when I say "soil."

JO: Dirt. Diapers. Laundry.

TJ: That makes sense, but I think of a living organism, a composite of sand and humus and worms and microbes. Now, how about "farm?"

JO: A Big, empty place with tractors and mean dogs.

TJ: That makes sense, too, for a city kid. For me it means "Home." A farm isn't just a place- it's an idea. It's a bunch of ideas. It's people growing strong by doing. It's togetherness in shared work. It's being a steward of the land, since we're only borrowing it until our children need it.

My family homesteaded this land. The Market made it just a piece of property. When I was at Macalister University, I met people who reminded

142

me that land is NEVER just a thing to buy and sell. All life comes from the land. That was in the Seventies, when talking about such stuff didn't get you in trouble- much.

When I came back with Lauren, I told my folks that we wanted to settle on this farm. We'd pay, of course. I told them that while I respected the work they'd done on their new place, here we'd try things a bit differently. We'd clean up the woodlot, refence the place, and run cattle.

It's funny, but for years people asked me when went to town, "Are ya still runnin' a commune out there?" It was funny because this always was a family farm. We did have some workdays when friends came out in the early years. We still have retreats and parties from time to time. Maybe that's what confused 'em. The only people living here are me, Lauren, and our kids. Well, that's who LIVED here for years. You see that it's finally really becoming a commune.

By now we had reached the Big House, a wonderful example of "American Additional" architecture. It had several rooms, balconies and decks built around an original small core. Its second-storey deck was reached by an outdoor iron spiral staircase. Tommy had us all traipse inside with him to retrieve snacks.

No one else was around.

"I guess they're all over across the woods getting the new folks settled in," Tommy said. "Hey, listen."

Beyond the woods came the sound of women singing.

"OK, the ladies are rehearsing." Tommy said. "You'll hear them on Sealing Day."

We emerged from the huge farm kitchen with bottles of home-brewed beer, a bowl of dried spiced apple rings, and a plate of beef jerky sticks. Tommy boasted that all had been grown, prepared or brewed on their farm. We went back out to sit on benches on the lower deck by the stairway. Cows mooed in the background, a flock of geese flew over, and two big cats stropped our legs, begging for jerky.

TJ: Now, where were we? Oh, yeah, we decided to run cattle. We'd learned how nasty monoculture was...

JO: Excuse me? Monoculture?

TJ: Ha! You've probably never seen anything else! Monoculture is where you raise just one crop in a big spread, like corn or soybeans. That kind of farming is bad for the soil, sucking out nutrients. Then you have to dump on chemicals, but they leech out other nutrients. That kills the worms and stuff that make soil alive. Birds and animals don't like to hang around stinky fields, either. It's just bad kharma. You end up tending a big chemical-soaked sandbox, not really running a farm.

We're doing a prairie-like system here. We plant solid grasses and things like alfalfa. The cattle graze in an area for a while, and then we shift them over. The relationship between cattle and plants is like the old prairie was, between bison and grasses. We have experimental plots for new cover crops, too. We've also planted hundreds of trees, and brought in bees. We've been certified organic since the '80s.

JO: What is that? Why?

TJ: It means that everything these cattle eat came out of the ground, not from a chemical plant. We use no chemical fertilizers or pesticides. We don't douse the steers with antibiotics or hormones to make them fat. People who buy our stuff get good, lean meat, and don't have to worry about slow poisoning. There are lots of studies showing that grass-fed beef is healthier for you; at least, there used to be.

Now "organic" means that we can keep right on operating when the gates go up. We can do just fine without outside input.

The interview was interrupted by a rumbling sound, which grew louder until it became a many voiced shrieking, like a choir of vengeful valkeries. We hit the deck as a blurry shadow passed over, cast by what looked like a swarm of enormous, supersonic bees. They passed boomingly overhead and over the northeast horizon. A few seconds later a great cloud of dust and smoke arose from where they had gone.

"Shit! That looks like it hit Holloway!" shouted Tommy.

As we found out later, they HAD hit Holloway. We had witnessed a small town just outside of the LOOZ being erased from the globe. The government has never released details, but it seemed as though someone programming the "Star Wars" defense grid made an error. The computers thought the town's grain elevator and fertilizer plant was a chemical weapons factory. Whatever the error, a town of 150 was obliterated by hundreds of twenty foot "crowbar" missiles.

Once we'd gotten up and dusted ourselves off, Tina and I decided to move along to Jacko's, to see what he'd seen.

"Geez," Tommy said. "Ya sure know how to make an exit."

Jacko was standing on his porch as we came up the drive, ready with drinks and nibbling food.

"A poor repast for weary travelers, but all this one can provide, even on a day when the sky is falling." he opined.

As we sat talking I looked at his cats; just as on our other visit, they didn't stray far from him. They clearly knew Tina, stropping her legs. They eventually let me scratch their ears.

Weighing as much as my full duffle bag, and with their heads on the level of my lap, they were awesome creatures, bundles of controlled lightning wrapped in fur. One was striped black, and the other, orange. They purred like chainsaws when Jacko offered them bits of jerky. When they picked the meat up, I was shocked to see that each had several extra toes on each foot, with two useable as thumbs; these huge hunters had HANDS.

JO: I've been told to ask about your cats.

JS: Ah, Louis and Aretha! No finer felines are to be found for far furlongs nor on foreign shores. They are the mighty warriors who rescued me! But that is a tale for later.

JO: OK, then tell me about yourself, first. I hear you've traveled.

JS: You could say that I have; and you could say that Neil Armstrong was a passing fair pilot. I was a freight man, rail and sea. As a mere stripling youth, I began working for passage all over our benighted and beneficent globe. I have seen the tropical sun come up in flashes of green, and arctic storms that left ice a foot thick on the fittings. I've contended with parasites and pirates, pursued crab and cod, maintained might and mien through untold hours of onerous effort.

Then I settled down to a more normal life: I just rode the rails. This very mandolin 'twas given to me by the great Hobo Billie, back when he was just Billie the Bum. Then I got a job as brakeman- not as much fun, but more secure and better paying. I kept watch where I went, and hit every jazz club on this side of the planet.

JO: Why did you retire from that?

JS: The fortunes of folly, my lad. The fortunes of folly. At one of those clubs I had a drop too much one night, but thought it all right because I was off the next day. We got a sudden midnight call to rebuild a mixed freight out of San Bernardino. I zigged when I should have zagged. I woke up with broken ribs and two crushed vertebrae.

In a most atypical fit of charity and compassion, aided no doubt by the gentle suggestions of my brother's law firm, the railroad saw it as their fault. I got a good settlement, enough so I could buy this place and hide from life. I stayed here for five years, only coming out for supplies.

Whatever else our Mother Goddess may be, She is an iron; as gluttons commit gluttony, so irons commit irony. When I first beheld these mighty ones their need was greater than mine. They struggled to suckle at their dead bobcat mother's teats. Their father, some local feral tom, was long gone, the cad. I took pity on them, which forced to leave my valley to seek aid.

I went to Phoenix, for they had been kind to me. Maria's potions restored the foundlings' health, and her instructions made my ministrations on their behalf fruitful. That was five years ago. Look at them now! I am told that their cloned kin grace many a fortunate farmstead.

JO: So why do you stay here? You say that you've returned to life, so why not move to The Cities instead of being trapped on the LOOZ?

JS: And be what? A worthless wino? A disabled, decrepit derelict? No, I shall preserve my poor dignity. Besides, my cats need me.

We arrived back at Phoenix in time for supper. Although I'd had a few conversations with Karl during my stay, we hadn't had a formal interview. That last evening we met back on the same platform where I'd first met him. In keeping with Phoenix hospitality, he had along a pitcher of tea and a basket of muffins. In deference to my city-bred posterior, we sat in beach chairs, with the food and drink on a table between us. As the sunset blazed, Karl began:

KM: Jimmie, tell me, is that a sunrise or a sunset?

JO: It's in the West, and it's late evening. It's a sunset.

KM: From here, that's a good answer. But, you know, people are looking at it in Japan, and calling it a sunrise. Are they wrong?

JO: That depends.

KM: Right again. I'm going to tell you some things this evening. You'll think that you understand them, but you won't really. Later you'll see that it depends on how you look at them. OK, you shoot- I'll dodge.

JO: You've said that I'm supposed to be an historian. What did you mean by that?

KM: An historian watches what's going on, then reports it as honestly as he can. A good historian can walk the blurred line between partisan slanting of his reports and trying to give insight into the "whys" of what happened.

Many people, from corporate flaks to vest-pocket Oprahs, are yakking about what the LOOZes mean. Somebody has to tell the truth about what's actually going on. I've read your feature work. You'll be a good Historian. So, besides what you've seen, what do you need to know?

JO: The obvious question is, Why Phoenix?

KM: Have you read many of my writings, Jimmie?

JO: Not many. Anything but the straight financial or technical stuff is hard to find.

KM: I'm not surprised. Do you know a book called "Fahrenheit 451?" If not, I'll give you a copy, along with a stack of mine and other stuff. The point of the book is that people are afraid of ideas. They'll shut out and destroy ones that aren't familiar or comforting; and my ideas are neither familiar nor comforting.

But that's all background. Why Phoenix? Because!

I'm a child of the Revolution, Jimmie. I was born while Sputnik I, the very first human-made satellite, was in orbit. I grew up with protests and peace symbols. There has been more change in my lifetime than there was in all of History before me, and that's no exaggeration.

Do you remember when you were a kid and it suddenly occurred to you that you had to make your own plans in life? You suddenly realized that neither Mom nor Dad nor God nor anybody but YOU had ultimate responsibility for your life?

JO: Yes, I remember that. I didn't like it. I'm still not sure about some of my choices.

KM: Exactly. That's the curse of my generation; the whole Human Species hit that point about when I did. All the rules were up in the air. It scared some people spitless, but inspired others to take up the challenge.

Phoenix was built to be a place for healing that wound. Humanity won't grow up and solve its problems without the fusion of Technology and Spirituality. Unless How To merges with How Come; with the number of bodies on the planet now, we won't even survive. That's the "Why."

JO: If that's "why," when did the idea of "what" come to you? And how did you decide to throw everything into it?

KM: You know that I was successful. I'd taken a failing hole-in-the-wall computer company and made it a multi-million dollar goldmine. But I was haunted by an image.

Back in college, I'd scraped together the money to buy my first computer kit, something called a ZX-80. It had an old TV for a monitor, and a crappy little membrane keyboard. It didn't have the power that a cheap watch does now, but I loved it.

Above my desk hung a poster, the cover of an old "Byte" magazine. The poster showed a nerdly guy working away at his homebuilt computer late at night. Behind him were the ghostly figures of Kirk, Spock, McCoy and other Star Trek characters, urging him on to create their future.

One night, many years and a fortune later, that image hit me in a nightmare vision. I wasn't creating their future- I was creating "Soylent Green" or "Blade Runner;" movies about nasty, nasty futures.

I remembered high school, when I'd admired the folks on hippie communes- at least they were trying. I knew that most had failed, but why? My gut told me that on some path like theirs lay my answers. Well thought out, that kind of thing might work as a living example of the fusion I sought.

My wife, who liked the house in the suburbs and her BMW, had a problem with it. I had to choose between Comfort and Life. I chose Life- she chose Comfort. The friction between us made a big fire.

When the smoke cleared I found myself poorer, ha "poorer," with two sons, and a lot of freedom. I nurtured the vision of a combined spiritual retreat and high-tech research center. When I heard that this place was up for sale I checked out the area. It had good transportation and communications links, it was reasonably close to two universities, and it had a tradition of attracting freethinkers and progressives. I had found my Phoenix.

I retired from business, but kept my stock. We came out here and started to build. It was tight at the beginning, but the right people showed up just when we needed them.

JO: So how did Phoenix end up in the Chippewa LOOZ? Why didn't you just sell out and go to The Cities.

KM: If Phoenix had been just a business, selling out would have been the right move; but Phoenix is a vision, an idea of how human beings are supposed to live.

Phoenix didn't end up in the LOOZ; Phoenix was the seed of this LOOZ. You know that all the other Zones in Minnesota are really work camps; I claim credit for the difference. You didn't know? You will.

I knew Administrator Erhart when he was just the local seed company rep. He wasn't a bad sort, at first, but he was good at what he did. He took those scared farmers and got them to buy his whole line. I think that he really believed he was doing them a favor, too."

JO: Wait, please. Scared farmers? Scared how?

KM: Scared of losing everything! Scared of what eventually happened anyway. They were stuck, with costs going up and prices going down. Big outfits like Cargill and ADM were building monopolies, squeezing out the independent, family operations. Scared when seed companies merged with chemical companies, so the reps basically told farmers exactly what to plant and what to spray it with, like it or not.

JO: But isn't that more efficient?

KW: Efficiency! The Great God of false Progress! Sure, it's efficient- if you're a naive bean counter! Jimmie, human beings are meant to take personal responsibility for things, to have both duties and authority. The

Family Farmer was the epitome of that ideal. City folks tended to think of farmers as dumb, but they weren't, they were smart and proud. There was a word for a dumb farmer: corpse.

Back to the point, Erhart was slicker than oiled snot. When the Feds came up with the idea of turning ALL Ag production over to the monopolies, he was right there. He had the experience and influence to administer rural Minnesota for the new cartel.

He had a rat's nose for profit, a cockroach's compassion, and the best back-slapping persona since Huey Long. I despised and pitied him, but when it came to talking deals with him, I dealt. I dealt with him as no one ever had. My friends and neighbors, my community, got to keep their freedom; Phoenix kept inventing- he got marketing control. I got to be guru to a bunch of independents; he got the prestige of being Administrator. He can paint us all as moronic misfits; I don't care, I'm free and he's not.

JO: How can you be free inside a fence?

KM: I'm free the only way a human can be free, Jimmie, inside and with my God. My life, my soul and my principles are in harmony.

You know, they'll never let you print that.

Chapter Seventeen (2020)

The End of the Beginning

Jimmie

I spent my last days in the Chippewa LOOZ in Asyl. Folks from all over gathered there for food, songs and stories, to cement their community in the face of the final rejection.

Everyone from Phoenix caravanned to Asyl, getting there about nine in the morning. Karl explained that there would be the usual awful speech and ceremony the next day, in which I had a small role to play. Today and tonight, though, belonged to The People.

Only crickets and stray cats paid any attention to the incessant telescreens on Main Street. Everyone else was across old US 59, beyond the abandoned railroad tracks and the grain elevators. Temporary structures covered the huge flat area where grain trucks had parked in former harvest days. It looked like a Renaissance Festival. At the camping end were modern tents, Indian tipis, yurts, RVs, even a couple of gaudily painted Romany wagons.

In the middle, several open-sided pavilions held food vendors. Their aromas of roasting meat and spiced vegetables enhanced the festive air. I had never seen so much food in one place. They were grouped around a roped off dance floor and low bandstand. The Phoenix crew was putting up tall lights around the dance floor. An impressive speakers' platform had also been erected at the far, southern end of the field, next to Old MN 40 and just below the Gate; my car was parked beside it, loaded and ready for my exit.

I helped set up the big Phoenix sleeping tents, and then went walking with Tina.

Many people wore Phoenix robes; others were arrayed in tunics, sarongs, dashikis, or batiked caftans. Musicians wandered about or sat in front of tents. I saw guitars, banjos, mandolins, fiddles, recorders, flutes, horns, drums, and marimbas, even a bagpipe and a koto.

People touched each other, a shocking change from The Cities, where we tried to pretend that others didn't exist. There were many hugs and kisses of greeting. People walked around arm in arm, even men with men and women with women. It wasn't naughty or obscene, but warm and welcoming.

I compared it with the street scene in my neighborhood. There, anything valuable would be made off with; here people left clothes, tools, musical instruments and cooking utensils out without fear of their disappearing. There, a young woman alone would be in danger; here, they promenaded laughingly through the throng. There, except for sneak thieves, children were rarely seen; here, children ran in and out, dodging boldly through the crowd. There, people's faces bore the stress of the constant fight to survive; here, they looked clean and confident of their future.

I discovered that the food was free; it was everyone's gift on that defining Day. I tasted goat gyros, vegetable kabobs, lefse with berry butter, baked apples- I lost track.

Even the Living Waters people had come, the men bearded and in plain work clothes, the women kerchiefed and concealed in long dresses. They were a bit tentative, but they had come. Eventually they were wolfing tacos, singing along to old songs and laughing with all the rest.

Impromptu concerts and dance parties erupted unpredictably through the day. A lone mandolin player would be joined by a conga drum and flute, and off they would go, playing old standards, Beatles, Woody Guthrie or Elton John tunes, or completely improvised stuff. People gathered around and started moving to the beat, or singing along. Then, after ten minutes or an hour, they would disperse, the musicians would drift away, and we'd search for another "happening."

Jody

It was a street dance, a wake, a christening, and a county fair. It was the end of the beginning.

Jody mused, *Who was it that said, "Knowing that you are about to be executed wonderfully focuses the mind?"*

She and about a thousand others were about to be effectively executed. To Corporate America they would soon be "unpersons."

Yet, things will work out, Jody thought. *We're strong. We have everything we need.*

Jody remembered another such scene, nearly thirty years before.

Many of Jody and Bill's friends had been involved in the Minnesota Renaissance Festival. They had convinced the couple to have the wedding as part of that late summer event. Jody's parents grumbled that their daughter should be wed at Asyl Lutheran Church. Eventually, though, they realized that her real community was now that of artists, not that of Norwegian farmers. Her new friends seemed nice enough, if a trifle peculiar, so they decided to enjoy the experience.

The Festival drew thousands of visitors to its recreated medieval market streets and squares. On the chosen day an open-air stage in the marketplace was covered in flowers. Garlands hung from poles at its corners. Musicians playing guitars and flutes wandered among the crowds, clad in the hose and tunics of bards.

A friar in his brown caftan ascended to the platform. Trumpets sounded, and a herald proclaimed, "Come all gentles to the marriage of Lord William and Lady Jody."

The rest of that day was a blur. How had she come from that to this, from playacting at castles and noble knights, to something that echoed it in reality?

Jimmie

The scene was disorganized and organic through the afternoon. About 5 o'clock, a young woman from the Magic Pumpkin set up a mic on the bandstand.

"OK, folks! Are we having fun, hah?" she called out. "Not to cut into your eating or whatevering…"

She paused for laughter, and then continued, "It's time to open up the stage. There's a signup sheet on the table over there. We have slots open until one in the morning, so grab the one you want. Any style goes, as long as you're good."

"To get things rolling, let's welcome the Pumpkin's own Grandma Turtle! And no, they aren't selling CDs today!"

The crowd cheered, stomped and otherwise carried on while half a dozen women in fringed buckskin outfits ascended the stage. Their instruments were wooden flutes and panpipes, hand drums and guitars. The lead singer and front woman carried a sort of lute made from a huge turtle shell.

Tina told me that the group was something of a legend on the folk music scene. The women followed Native American traditional spirituality, with a feminist spin.

"We have joy to be here today," the musician said, and then held up her instrument. "Great Spirit blessed me, years ago, by leading me to find sister turtle here. She'd been attacked by a dog while laying her eggs. I chased him away. While I watched, she gave up her strong turtle spirit. I covered the eggs for her, leaving a tobacco blessing beside them, and then brought her body home. Our band is named for her. May the feminine strength for life she showed bless all of you through our music.

"We'll start with a huayno, a sacred dance tune from Peru."

I'd never heard anything like it before. Rattles, a large drum, and huge panpipes provided a solid beat. Strings and high pipes wove a syncopated net of sound over it. The result was solemn and joyful, every bit as sacred as a Bach cantata, but making you want to move in its rhythm. Soon the dance floor was filled, and folks all over the campgrounds were dancing along.

When they finished, the crowd was very appreciative, hooting, stomping and clapping.

They followed this with a high, lamenting tune, mostly flutes, with a solo voice singing forlornly in some other language.

After maybe an hour, Grandma Turtle was followed by an R&B quintet, with a female lead vocalist. They put on a show straight out of the 1940s, the men in zoot suits and the singer in a slinky, sequined dress.

On through the night we heard bluegrass, choral music, classic rock, chanting, and Bob Dylan style folk.

Late that night I found myself dancing to a swing band with Tina. As I held her, swaying to a slow tune, I realized that I would miss her. Despite the terrors she'd endured, she was probably the freest, most confident woman I'd ever known. All of these people were like that- unburdened.

153

We woke up slowly the next day; the Sealing Ceremony wasn't until Noon, so there was plenty of time. Everyone was sleepy, but some early risers had started food cooking. I picked up a gyro from the Magic Pumpkin stall, and then walked about, dodging scrambling children, listening to music and taking in last impressions.

Finally, but too soon, Noon came. Like a scene from an old epic movie, horns blew and skyrockets flew from the gate complex. The AgriCorp anthem began to blare from huge speakers on the gate. We all made our way to the south end to watch the show.

A small vehicle, like an over-decorated golf cart, slowly made its way through the gate and down the hill, flanked by a squad of huge Augments marching in double time.

The cart pulled to a stop beside my car. Onto the stand strode Ehrhart. Half a dozen newsdrones buzzily hovered in the air around The Great Man. He was a greasy looking old man with a wide, loose smile. He took the podium and stood for a moment, looking out over the assembled crowds. Behind him stood the Augment bodyguards, in armor of bright corporate colors; each held a machine gun. Ehrhart spread his arms, as if to embrace the multitudes.

"My friends, people under my care, I come to you on a joyous day! We gather here to proclaim that America is greater than ever! Our actions prove that the System works! In our society of True Capitalism, all have Security! All have the unbridled right to seek plenty and comfort! Each settles at the level for which God Almighty has equipped him!"

He paused for the applause which never came.

"Today we show the mercy of our wisdom. Misfits are not persecuted, just isolated to find their own way. You choose not to strive, not to plan or grow, and we respect your right to that.

"You have turned your backs on the great Civilization toward which Humanity has been striving for ten thousand years, but we do not turn our backs on you! We have set aside this place for you in our mercy and benevolence! You are here fully free to explore your maudlin dreams, where you cannot slow the ongoing progress of Corporate America!"

He searched the crowd until he spotted me. He stepped to the side, spread wide his arms, and proclaimed, "Jimmie Olson, loyal corporate son, come forth from among them! Return to the bosom of Society!"

That was my cue. I shook hands with Alec and the others, hugged Tina, and walked over to my car. Erhart had come down from the platform to stand beside it. He gave me an exaggerated two-handed handshake. As I got in and drove to the gate, he followed in his cart.

154

My last view of my friends, over the shoulders of a squad of cyborg soldiers, was of hundreds silently holding their hands out to me in farewell and blessing.

Before boarding the waiting helicopter, Erhart strode up to my car.

"I will expect a full report from you, lad," he said, extending his hand with his famous smile.

"Yes sir, of course," I said a bit too forcedly. "I'll get right on it."

No, you won't. Erhart thought. *At least, you won't want to. I'll have my eye on you, boy.*

"I look forward to reading it." Erhart said. "Call my secretary to make an appointment. Soon!

Chapter Eighteen (2020)

Refugees from Paradise

Phoenix

The ceremony was over. Erhart had left. The Chippewa LOOZ was sealed. On the inner side of the gate, the party began to dissolve. Karl Mueller said to Alec, "I hope that Jimmie watches his step."

The mood was somber as the new LOOZers began taking down pavilions and packing away cooking gear. This was it, The Day. There were now no phone, no electricity, no insurance, and no shipments of outside goods. They were non-citizens, on their own, with only each other for support.

One night a week later, Karl sat on his favorite meditation platform, looking out over Lac qui Parle. It was late; most people had gone to bed, even those preparing for the upcoming Solstice wedding of Alec and Connie. Red lights slowly flashed every fifty feet on the opposite ridgeline, marking the security fence at the western LOOZ border.

Karl remembered how clean and living that horizon had once been. He thought about the changes he'd seen in his sixty-odd years. His youth in the nineteen-sixties and –seventies had been a time of hope. The eighties and nineties, though, saw the bizarre rise of neo-conservative politics, leading to the fascist coup of 2000 and the semi-declared World War Three, that absurdity called the War on Terrorism.

Karl enjoyed night meditation because of the quiet; he could easily reach out to sense the small creatures skittering about. On moonlit nights like this, he could even sense deer along the far fence line. But, no, that was something else, something human-feeling. He watched as that someone cut through the fence and slipped INTO the LOOZ. He quietly called out for the night watch. A young man came running.

"Have a look across there with your IR scope," Karl said. "Is that someone coming in?"

"Yes, sir," said Tim Johnson. "It looks small, like a girl."

"An exhausted, terrified girl." Karl said. "Have someone from the kitchen bring blankets and a thermos of hot chocolate."

As Tim ran to the Community Center, Karl watched their midnight visitor creep along the causeway. When she reached the footbridge over the narrow, smelly channel, he called out to her while projecting comfort and assurance.

"We see you. Don't be afraid. Come on over."

As the girl reached the Phoenix bank, Tina Dahingwa, Assistant Security Chief, and Helen Tomkins, Kitchen Chief, arrived with the supplies. They rushed to the slight, shivering form, wrapped her in a blanket, and hustled her off to the Community Center.

Karl turned to Tina.

"Young woman," he said. "I do believe we have a problem."

A few minutes later the group stood in the community kitchen. Their surprise visitor sat at a workbench and gulped soup from an earthenware mug. She looked to be about twelve and had long blond hair. She was dressed in a filthy, torn flannel shirt and jeans, and the remains of too-big cowboy boots. Sandy Lewis, Phoenix's resident doctor, hovered over her protectively. Ben had also joined them, since he knew everyone in these parts. She couldn't have come far, so maybe he could figure out who she was.

Karl gently touched Maria's shoulder.

"Has she said anything?" he asked.

"Not so much," said Sandy. "She says she's Kati Warner. She is afraid of the 'big robots,' and of 'Poppa.' She's in shock. You won't get much else until she's had a good sleep."

"Karl," Ben said. "I've heard of her bunch. Her mother went to school with my youngest. The Warner clan is from out by Madison. They're living-in-the-cracks kind of parasites, doing odd jobs, trading and salvage.

They've been caught in petty crimes, but nothing that can bust up their gang. They have the reputation of being nasty when crossed."

At that moment, a helicopter roared overhead. A few seconds later a squad of Augments burst through the Dining Hall doors.

"There is a trespasser here!" their leader shouted. "We require the trespasser!"

Karl calmly strode directly up to the huge soldier.

"You know me," he said. "You know that I am the negotiating authority here. The trespasser is a tired, cold little girl. The situation is not specified under contract. This requires a priority renegotiation. Are you authorized to negotiate?"

The Augment leader shook his head. He'd come to blast wrongdoers, not bandy words. His weapons itched to fire, but he couldn't make up his regimented mind once it was thrown off track.

"No. This one is not authorized. We will consult," He answered. His face took on a faraway look as he contacted his superiors.

"Do that," Karl said. "I will be prepared to travel tomorrow at dawn, no sooner. I require that two of my people accompany me."

"We will come for you at dawn," a voice said through the augment's mouth.

The next morning, Karl arose early to check on Kati. She was sleeping soundly in the infirmary, with Sandy close by. Karl could feel a chill fog of exhausted terror seeping from the girl. Sandy, looking haggard and disgusted, took Karl aside.

"I would speak to this girl's parents," she said. "I would speak with a baseball bat. This girl is malnourished. She has many old bruises. I think her left arm was broken about a year ago. She mutters in her sleep, sometimes screaming in terror."

Sandy looked Karl in the eye.

"Do Not Let Them Take Her."

A few minutes later Karl described Kati's condition to Ben and Tina, his companions for the day's journey, as they ate breakfast. They agreed that she should stay with them, but worried about the precedent that allowing a refugee into the LOOZ would set. How many would follow? What damage could they do? What rights and ethical responsibilities did the LOOZers have in defending their territory? They would rather accept those who came peacefully, but would Erhart agree to that? How would they approach these issues with Erhart?

And what preparations did Phoenix need to make for the likely confrontation to come?

At dawn, a corporate helicopter roared in from the east, and set down just outside the Phoenix gate. Before it had completely settled, an Augment sprang out. He took a fighting stance, scanned the area, and waved an "All Clear." A young man, immaculately groomed and utterly bland in his corporate suit, stepped out. He looked around, and then walked briskly up to the group.

"Karl Mueller, you are summoned," he said. "You are allowed two companions. We will board now."

"Just a moment, son." Karl said. "What's your name?"

"My name is not important."

"All right, Not Important, let's go."

As the helicopter approached the Twin Cities suburbs, it passed over the vast refugee camps, nicknamed "Kyotos." The three saw hundreds of acres of shacks, built from cardboard and scrap wood. Some lucky folks lived in rusted-out truck bodies. Eternal warfare, sea level rise, famine and storms had destroyed these peoples' countries. The Phoenix-ites were sobered to realize that for those folks this was far better than what they had fled; a slim chance is better than no chance. Karl had to shield himself from the miasma of stunned despair rising from the camps.

Finally, they reached the huge glass pyramid of the AgriCorp center, a few miles west of downtown Minneapolis. Its immaculately groomed grounds held a golf course, a pond complete with wing-clipped swans, and fruit orchards. It was surrounded by high, razor wire-topped fences, against which the refugee hovels washed like a sludgy tide. Augments patrolled the paths and along the fence. To Karl it felt crisp, cold and clean, like a steel tray full of scalpels.

The top of the steep-sided pyramid was a huge landing platform, pierced at its center by a mammoth ventilation shaft. Potted trees and vines grew all along the roof edges and the lip of the shaft. Not Important showed the Phoenixites to the secured entry door beside the open space. They looked down into the gulf; gusts of warm, humid air struck their faces, generated by the hundreds of offices below.

Cupolas with variously marked doors stood around the opening. Not Important used his card key to bring them through one into a long, cold stairway. The Augment from the helicopter followed them, while blatantly obvious cameras swiveled to watch. The walls and ceiling were painted bubblegum pink. The waffle patterned steps were painted deep green. The stairway reeked of acrid disinfectants. At the stairway's foot was another heavy, locked door.

They emerged into a cramped room. The color scheme and stench were the same. Besides the door they'd entered by, there were two others- one green, and one red. A guard behind a thick window told them to empty their pockets into a tray, and stand still for sensor scan.

"With this thing I can even tell what these lowlifes had for breakfast," he boasted.

Once the guard had cleared them, Not Important showed the three through the green door. He smiled a shark's smile as he pointed to the red door.

"Whoever goes through there doesn't come back out. Ever."

The change was dramatic. One wall of the hallway was glass, looking out into the ventilation shaft. The deep-pile carpet was maroon. The walls and ceiling were teal and taupe. A scent of lilacs was in the air. Gentle white noise, like a waterfall or the rustling of leaves, soothed the ear. It was in all obvious respects a pleasant, businesslike environment. Even so, Karl could feel that the people beyond the walls lived the poet's very "lives of quiet desperation."

They came to an elevator, marked with the AgriCorp seal. Not Important typed a code on its keypad.

"This will take us directly to Administrator Erhart's suite," he said. "Its exact location is secret."

Not after I've been there, Karl thought.

As they road in the small charcoal and silver box, Karl tried to get a reading on the Augment. The whole concept of these altered creatures appalled and fascinated him.

"Who were you before your conversion, guard?" he asked.

The hulking construct turned to answer.

"I don't remember," he said. "It doesn't matter. I serve."

After several jerks, stops and changes of direction the elevator stopped; Karl knew exactly where they were- out beneath the orchards. The doors opened on an opulent waiting room. The walls were of dark wood paneling. Light reflected from a textured gray ceiling. The floor was covered in thick burgundy carpeting. The doorknobs and other hardware were of brass. The receptionist, a beautiful blonde woman in a tasteful dark suit, sat at a glass and brass desk with viewscreens and touchpads inset in its surface. She touched an icon to announce their arrival.

"Administrator Erhart will be ready for you shortly," she said.

They sat in the overstuffed red leather chairs and waited.

In a few minutes the secretary told them to enter. The room beyond was again in contrast. It was large, with a red-painted concrete floor. Three walls were of light-green ceramic block. The fourth wall, facing the desk, was a massive video screen, dynamically divided into many smaller segments. Erhardt sat at the plain wooden desk, in an ordinary roller chair. He wore a command crown, which let him directly access the Company's computers with a thought. Behind him was a bookshelf; many of the books were on history or politics.

"So, Karl," he said. "Barely a week into the project and already you need concessions. Why am I not surprised?"

"No concessions," said Karl. "Just clarification. A new situation has arisen."

"Really?"

Erhart closed his eyes for a moment, and the video wall showed an Augment's eye view of the Phoenixites standing around Kati the night before.

"Hmm," he said. "A ragamuffin lands on your doorstep, a clear trespasser. You impede my guards in their duty of apprehending her. What's new?"

"What is new is that our agreement called for stopping invaders," Karl said. "You and we both need our borders secure. We need not to be overrun; you need the LOOZ not to become a hideaway for criminals."

"Again, what's new? This little scrap of flesh is an invader, a trespasser. Why should we treat her differently?"

Tina burst out, saying, "For the sake of Humanity, that's why!"

Erhart jumped to his feet. "Humanity!" he shouted. "Humanity is out there, beyond our fences. Thousands of tons of humanity! Shall I go out and pick apples for them? Girl, we don't help people for some vague notion of nicey-nice. Nobody does! We help because it brings power. That is how it's always been."

"Were Caroline and Anne just scraps of flesh, Ed?" asked Karl.

Erhart's lips whitened and his voice fell. He stuttered as he said, "That proves my point. I had no power, and so no insurance. The wife and daughter of a powerful man would have lived."

"You may be right," said Karl. "I don't deny the injustices of the old system. But you and I ARE men of power now, Ed. I have something to offer for the girl's safety."

"Phhttt! What could you offer that I can't just take?"

"My honor and my word. You know their value. I also have some information. I suspect that you've been having trouble with renegades out toward the South Dakota border, eh?"

"What if we are?"

"She's probably their kin. Do you have pictures?"

Erhart thought again. The wallscreen showed, in enhanced night vision, a group of men robbing a supply depot.

"Yup," Ben muttered. "That's the Warners"

"So," Karl said. "It's her family. I wager that they'll come looking for her. Your stake in the gamble is that we keep Kati. Ours is that we help you catch that bunch when they show up looking for her. Is it a bet?"

"Just this once. No more refugees. If you hamper my guards again they'll blow you away. I'm putting full sensors on the fence, with shoot-to-kill robots."

Life goes on. The presence of evil in the world is not an excuse to stop celebrating the good. Distraction is necessary, if sometimes risky. The wedding of Alec Mueller and Connie Winston had been set since long before LOOZ Sealing Day, and would not be put off.

It was a fine June evening. After sunset, in the long twilight, chains of paper lanterns glowed from the trees in the commons. Food was being prepared in the Dining Hall kitchen. The amphitheater had been readied for the ceremony; torches had been placed, but not lit, at the cardinal directions. Many colored lamps twinkled upon the Tetrahedron. Beside the stage, a quintet softly played light classical music.

It was a calm evening. The scent of flowering trees and shrubs was thick in the air. People had shed their daytime protective gear for the most riotously colorful outfits they could concoct. Beads, feathers and flowing silks abounded as they gathered in the amphitheater. Even Kati Warner, in the front row beside Tina, wore a bead-spangled dress and hat with her wide smile.

Karl ascended to the dais. He wore a royal blue hooded ceremonial robe with extensive embroidery and beadwork. He carried a small pine tree in a woven basket. Setting the tree down near the center of the stage, he stood behind it to address the assembly.

"We are here as a community," he said. "Let us declare our sacred space.

He raised his arms and gaze.

"We stand beneath our Father Sky, symbol and embodiment of The Ineffable, of Mind, Energy and Plan."

He looked downward.

"We stand upon our Mother Earth, at Whose bosom we are nourished, in Whom we live and breathe."

As he then pointed to each cardinal direction, an attendant lighted its torch and remained standing there as symbolic Guardian.

"We invoke the spirits of the East, our cousins, who embody Springtime, Morning and Beginnings, for all things are once new.

"We invoke the spirits of the South, our cousins, who embody Summer, Noontime and Maturity, for all things reach their apex.

"We invoke the spirits of the West, our cousins, who embody Autumn, Evening and Decline, for all things end.

"We invoke the spirits of the North, our cousins, who embody Winter, Deep Night and Renewal, for all endings are also beginnings, and all beginnings, ends."

Karl crossed his arms over his heart, and bowed his head.

"And we awaken the spirit within us, echo and spark of All That Is, that our path may lie in wise harmony."

He looked out at the crowd.

"Our circle is thus drawn. Let all within it know that they are in a sacred place and time.

"The custom would now be to call these lovers forth from their respective families, stressing that every marriage is the twining of two families. However, we are all family here; our recent bonds have been severed, yet we have the common heritage of being descended of 50,000-odd generations of humans. We are the descendants of those who survived all flood, famine, plague and war. We carry on being human beings. Through this ritual, and others, we pass on that heritage to another generation. Alec, Connie, please join me here."

Their clothing was in a Renaissance style. Connie wore a flame-red shimmering gown that complimented her pale complexion and red hair. Alec was clad in deep green and gold. There were no Best Man, nor Maid of Honor; all their community were witnesses and partners. The stood, holding hands facing Karl, the tree between them.

"My son, my daughter-to be, you are welcome here before the people. May this be only the first of many joyous gatherings.

Suddenly the Guardians of the Directions screamed; shotgun blasts cut them off. At that same moment, half a dozen scruffy armed men stepped out of the shadows. One of them, an older man with dirty yellow hair and several days' growth of beard, stepped onto the stage. He waved a sawed-off shotgun at the wedding party.

"You wimps are way too easy to sneak up on," he sneered. "Ok, old man. Where the hell's my grand daughter?"

Karl remained calm.

"If you're the Warners, you must mean Kati," He said. "She's right there in the front row."

163

"Come on up to grandpa, girl," the bandit said, gesturing to her.

"No! I won't!" Kati shouted.

He glared at a ragged young man in the shadows.

"Steve, you grab her," he snarled.

As the young invader moved to grab Kati, Tina leaped into a fighting stance in front of her. He tried to backhand the woman out of his way, but Tina had fought far worse foes than him. She grabbed his hand in mid swing, and then twisted his arm behind his back.

"Shit!" yelled the Warner patriarch, and then turned to Karl.

"Make her turn him loose!" he demanded.

Karl locked eyes with the raider.

"I don't think so," Karl said in an oddly echoing voice. "I'm afraid you've made a mistake."

As a half-disciplined group, the raiders were all watching Karl and their leader. They didn't notice that the assembled Phoenix-ites were staring at them strangely, spearing the invaders with iron gazes. They only knew that they were having trouble remembering where they were, and why they had come.

"Now," Karl said in a calmly commanding voice. "Wouldn't an agreeable peace be the best thing?"

"I s'pose," muttered the Warner leader, his eyelids drooping.

"Good. Now you and your boys put down your guns. We'll go over to the Dining Hall, have a little lunch, and talk about things."

Karl put his arm over the other man's shoulders in a comradely way. Just as they had left the stage a star-shell, a flare on a small parachute, erupted high above them. It cast the gathering in a monochrome of stark shadows and blue light.

A squad of Augments stormed over the hill behind Phoenix. Their leader shouted, "Nobody move! Surrender the trespassers!"

Everyone froze except Karl, who raised his hands and approached the leader. *Gods, no, not so soon!* he thought.

"You know me," he said.

The Augment pointed his weapon at Karl.

"There will be no negotiations!" the cyborg shouted.

"Yes, the prisoners are yours," said Karl, nodding. "Here they are. They will come quietly. BUT, you shall deliver them unharmed and well to your masters."

"That is not your concern."

Karl's eyes met those of the cyborg. He took a chance.

"I have the ear of the Administrator," he said. "My concerns are what I wish them to be. You will do as you are told."

The man-machine paused. "It shall be done." He admitted at last. "Prisoners, come!"

As the soldiers marched the marauders to the waiting helicopter, Karl spoke aloud.

"They were scum of the earth, but they valued family. This tragedy didn't have to be."

A few days later, when the physical damage from both attacking groups had been repaired, the people of Phoenix again gathered together.

They had burned the bodies of their fallen comrades on a great pyre, along with written prayers and farewells. Now they again assembled at the amphitheater. Again they called on the four directions, proclaiming a sacred space. But this time, rather than lighting torches, they planted a tree where each of the Guardians of the Directions had stood.

"We proclaim that their spilled blood shall nourish these trees," Karl said. "Their deaths were in vain only if we forget their lives, if we dishonor those lives by not upholding the principles by which they lived. The tough alloy of wisdom, knowledge and compassion formed their characters. An acid compounded of fear, desperation and callousness burned them. They have moved on, but are not truly dead."

In the following weeks, small robotic servitors worked all along the fencelines surrounding the Chippewa LOOZ, burying sensors and stringing new cables.

Chapter Nineteen (2020)

Back in "The Real World"

Jimmie

Eight-year-old Nochiko, lead singer of the Sáke Brats, gyrated through their latest Zock Bop video, "Give it to Me Now." She left little doubt about what she wanted to be given. I tried to tune out the wall screen behind us. The late night street scene two floors below was much more interesting- a parody of that last day in the LOOZ. Refugees, Homeless and revelers mixed in their throngs, filling the Old Lake Street Free Zone. Street hawkers shouted out the value of their wares beneath lurid signs. The police never came here after dark, so you could get anything you wanted- anything. Even at one AM the walking mall was filled; for many of these people it was home.

During the day the streets were empty of all but the most foolish or hopeless. Government press gangs grabbed homeless for work crews, Organleggers and brothel procurers grabbed whoever the government missed.

The money Karl had slipped me in the bundle of books wouldn't last long. If I didn't get my LOOZer stories finished to spec and on deadline, I could join those people on the street.

That's why I was here: writer's block. The Balcony Bistro was one of the perks of my total security apartment building. I sat sipping a Holy

Bartender with my friend George. I figured that talking things through might generate some inspiration. I had plenty of recordings, but wasn't sure where the handle was.

"You mean these people LIKED being on their own?" George asked.

"Yah," I answered. "They wanted to do for themselves, even if it meant jury-rigging things."

George gulped down the thick, red liquid.

"I don' geddit," he snorted. "I'll take security. The only independence I want is to independently choose my next drink. Your LOOZers sure are; they may as well be down there on the street."

"That's not how they saw it. It seemed less like we were sealing them in than that they were sealing us out."

For six months or so I managed to pay the bills, mostly. It was a newsletter here or some ad copy there, but just one-shot deals. I was running up some debt, but nothing I couldn't cover with one big assignment- or finishing the LOOZers story.

I was annoyed. I'd gone to Phoenix expecting to find a bunch of wild-eyed cultists, or elitist geeks. But I'd found the sanest, most open people I'd ever met. Worse, they'd sent with me a bundle of books that backed up their worldview. I'd only gotten permission to go so I could write an expose on a society of misfits; now, there was no way that I could write that story.

I'd tried to explain this to Erhart. He had sent many nagging messages, until I phoned him.

"Young man, you must consider the greater good," he said. "That area was my territory back in my seed rep days, so I know how attractive those people can look. It may seem romantic to play rugged individualist, but today we need order and dependability. Non-conformist attitudes just leave openings for enemies of the System. You don't want to endanger everything we're fighting for, do you?"

That's how it went. I was locked into my contract to write what AgriCorp wanted, with no escape hatch. I found other jobs to tide things over while I stalled, but I was blacklisted. My usual sources for jobs and leads dried up. They wouldn't even return my calls.

Feeling like a whore, I had actually tried to write a scathing indictment of the LOOZ misfits, but the words were like worm trails, meandering aimlessly. I literally couldn't do it.

The money was running out. Any day I'd be broke. Without a contract I'd be homeless. The tighter things got, the more I worried. I dreamed of Phoenix, of the people, of the greenery, of the open spaces. Then there was a nightmare in which Augment guards stormed the Phoenix dining hall. I was one of the guards.

I woke in a cold sweat, and went to the Balcony Bistro to think. I'd never known someone who'd been evicted. Sure, people I'd known had been evicted, but I'd never known any of them after they had been. I had no idea what to expect- which was more worrying than a certainty would have been.

I was reviewing my Phoenix notes in my wrist computer, when I noticed that the clock icon read 12:00. Midnight. Time of decision. I decided that I wanted another beer. I waved to the waitress.

"Have, Candy! Bring me another Corona will you?"

She came over to my table. A big guy emerged from the shadows and came with her. He stood with his arms crossed, staring.

"I can't do that. This place is for residents only," she said.

"Hey, you know me! I'm a resident!" I said.

"I knew you. You aren't a resident. You're a freeloader," she answered.

The big guy put a hand on my shoulder.

"Just move along, OK kid?" he said.

Shit. So it had started. I moved. It was about time I went to bed, anyway.

I went down to my apartment. The blue holosign beside the door, which should have said "OLSON," said "AVAILABLE." I put my chest tight up against the ID scanner. Nothing. I pounded on the door and shouted for Marilyn to open up. The border of the door lit red.

"You are unauthorized," Marilyn said. "Security has been alerted."

Two figures in riot gear, carrying shock sticks, came briskly around a corner toward me. They didn't say a word, but came up on both sides and struck me in the kidneys with their sticks. I collapsed in a red haze. I dimly noticed as they had dragged me to the elevator, then through a door in the front of the building. They dumped me there into the slush on Lake Street and went back inside.

I came to when someone waved an ammonia
capsule under my nose.

"Come on, softy," a feminine voice hissed, "unless you want to volunteer for a labor brigade."

"Who the hell are you?" I mumbled.

"Your only hope."

She tossed me a grubby old parka.

"Call me Stoat. That's all you're getting." she said. "Don't talk, follow."

I followed, shivering from cold and shock. Stoat looked to be around twenty- a hard, thin, wary twenty. She wore a dirty gray trench coat and wool cap. She was hard to see as she sprinted, froze and sprinted ahead.

We left Lake Street, passing from shadow to shadow. We went several blocks, stopping to avoid passing groups. We came to an enormous old 1920s pseudo-oriental house, the kind with a massive roof with wide overhanging eaves, and a porch supported on thick stone pillars.

We silently entered the kitchen door. Inside, the air was steamy, and thick with spices and the aroma of roasting meat. A serving window opened on a large, lantern-lit room, where many people were eating. I asked Stoat where they were able to get such abundance.

She said, "Don't ask."

Through the inside kitchen door, we passed down long, twisting hallways, and up a cramped flight of stairs. Finally, with our heads brushing the underside of the roof, Stoat slid open a low door, and waved me inside. The room was chilly, and filled with the smoke of floral incense. The only furnishings were a small desk and two chairs. Flickering light came from a fat candle in a wall sconce. Behind the desk sat a robed and hooded figure. Of its face I could see only the mouth, and the twin locks of blonde-grey hair that fell beside it.

"Thank you, Stoat," said the figure. "Please bring refreshment for our guest." Her voice was oddly familiar, and spoke of age and suffering. Stoat nodded and left, closing the door behind her.

"Mister Olson," she said. "Welcome. Have a seat."

She gestured to the straight-backed old office chair.

"Isn't this pretty melodramatic?" I asked.

She smiled, grimly, and leaned forward, her hands gripping the edge of the desk.

"Of course it is, my friend," she said. "For two reasons. Using symbolism and clichés provides the security of indirection. You also need to be impressed with the fact that you have left your world behind. Your trip to the LOOZ showed you some aspects of Reality beyond the world you thought you knew, but that was just a start. Be afraid, Mister Olson."

"Of you?" I asked.

She sat back. "No, not now," she said. "Never, I hope. Too many have feared me before. One becomes weary of being despised and feared. No, you and I are allies."

"You make it sound like a war," I said.

At this point Stoat returned with a tray that held a pitcher of water, two plastic glasses, some bits of roasted meat on sticks, and soft, hot, pretzels.

The hooded woman poured for us, then said, "A toast, Mister Olson. To Evolution!"

She raised her glass, took a long drink, then resumed.

"It is a war, Mister Olson, a very long war, and you are a draftee. You have my sincere condolences." She spread her hands before her in genuineness.

"Who drafted me?"

"I think that you know. Technically, you drafted yourself, but your abilities are highly thought of by a mutual friend."

I thought for a moment. The situation implied power and trickiness.

"Do you mean Karl Mueller?" I asked.

"Perhaps. You'll have to answer that for yourself."

"So, who are you? How do you know Karl? What are we fighting?"

She chuckled a bit, and then clasped her hands before her.

"Who am I? I am one who has been fighting since long before you were born. I know our mutual friend from those days. Our adversaries would rather see me dead, but I'm a tough old broad: call me Shoshanna."

"Mister Olson, what do you know of human history; besides what they teach in the schools, that is?"

"Some. I watch the History Channel sometimes."

"That's almost as bad. Mister Olson, behind the sinners and saints, the foolish and the wise, the cruel and the kind, human history has been a battle of horizons."

"You mean like the Cold War was the battle between Freedom and Slavery."

She snorted.

"That's correct, as far as it goes. Even that conflict wasn't exactly what you've been told. No, since the first humans became self aware, they have fought between fear and vision, in a thousand ways. They, we, could see far horizons, and dream lofty dreams, indulge in altruism and compassion. Some people saw, and did brave deeds. Yet, the comfort of retreating to chimp-like paranoia, conformity and conflict was always there. The wide plains, the oceans and the sky beckoned, but the comforting, dark forest of our primate past was ever with us."

"So, what does that have to do with me?"

"This is a forest time, Mister Olson" Shoshanna said. "We learned too much for our comfort in the last century. People became frightened, and retreated. The lure of narrow horizons, of control and blame is ascendant today, but the eternal war goes on. Humanity will look up and outward again one day. You have a role to play in preparing for that next round."

"Me? Come on! I'm just a feature writer!"

"Our mutual friend called you Historian, didn't he?"

I was suddenly struck with memories of Phoenix, of that first supper, of smiling, healthy, open faces. I remembered "Between the Candle and the Star." I felt my eyes widening, my breath catching.

"I see that you understand. We rescued you, Mister Olson, for a purpose."

She bowed her head, her voice sorrowful.

"We cannot rescue the hundreds of millions of our countrymen from the trap they willingly entered, but we can pull out a few here and there.

"Here is the deal. You are an observer and storyteller, Mister Olson. We want you to observe, and then tell your stories. That's all. You will go many places. You will write about what you see there. Eventually, you will return to Phoenix. You will continue to tell your stories as long as you are able. We will see to it that those stories get out."

"What if I don't want to be your errand boy?" I asked.

She shook her head.

"Your choice is not whether to serve," she said. "Whether they realize it or not, everyone works for the Erharts of the world, or for us. It has always been that way. You are lucky. You get to choose knowingly."

"What if I choose against you?"

"We are people of compassion," Shoshanna said. "But sometimes the most compassionate thing is a knock on the head. If you ever become a liability, you will truly disappear. Do you know where you are, Mister Olson?"

"In an attic, in a big old house in South Minneapolis."

"Granted. But more importantly, you are at a crossroads. When you go out that door, it will be to one of two paths. Will it be fear, or vision? Both ways are dangerous. Give your escort your decision. Fare well, Mister Olson."

Great, I thought. *I can let Erhart run me into the ground, or work with these people. I don't know where they'll send me, but it may do some good.*

The door slid open. A large hand beckoned. I walked out. The hallway was filled with two huge figures in robes like Shoshanna's. They waited for me to speak.

"Vision," I said.

One of the waiting men swiftly grabbed me. The other reached to press a hypospray to my neck.

"Vision!" I yelled. "I saiidd vi…"

I awoke slowly, muddily. My nose tingled to a hospital smell of disinfectant and ozone. My mouth had a sweet, rubbery taste. My breastbone hurt sharply, as though my chest had been cut open. I felt a surge of adrenaline. *Damn!* I thought. *They've sold me to organleggers! They've already taken my heart! NO, wait a minute, then I'd be dead. Am I dead?* I seemed alive enough. I tried to move my cramping arms; they were tied down. So were my legs. I tried to open my eyelids a slit, but they were gummed shut. I tried harder, and they popped all the way open. I was blinded by glare, so I quickly squeezed them shut again. After some trying I was able to open them just a bit.

What I saw could have been an organleggers chop shop, although it seemed run down for that lucrative business. I was in a cramped room, strapped to a high, narrow cot on one wall. The sheetrock walls had been painted white. A twin-basin steel sink and counter from some forgotten cafeteria stood opposite my cot. It looked clean, but age-stained. Above it was a shelf holding jars of pills, colored liquids, sticks and cotton balls. Along the front of the shelf, medical instruments –tiny knives, clips, long scissor-like objects- hung from hooks. They dripped as if freshly washed.

I craned my head to look at my chest. It had been shaved, and swabbed with orange antiseptic. A square of gauze was taped to its center. So, they had taken something.

I heard footsteps and a door opening out of sight behind my head. A man said, "Mister H, awake so soon? What's your hurry?"

Shit. I know that voice. I'm dead, alright.

An older man came to stand beside me. His gaunt visage, pencil mustache and gray hair were unmistakable. He smiled in a friendly way as he took my pulse, and then checked my pupils with a penlight.

"But you're, you're…" I stammered.

"Shhh." He said. "Yes I am, but don't say it. Names are too powerful to bandy about loosely. Call me 'Doc.' And you are now 'Mister H.'"

"But you're the terrorist doctor who killed all those patients!"

He clucked his tongue as he untied my straps.

"Come now," he said. "I hear that you're a writer, in trouble with the Administrator. You should know better than to believe what you read in the Corpo press."

"But I remember your case! They finally figured out that you were behind the death of those kids!"

He stopped his ministerings and looked me in the eye.

"I'll tell you, because they say that you need to know things," he said. "What killed those children were contaminated drugs. I found out, and was going to go public. I forgot that the Corporation is never wrong,

Mister H. Better that a lone doctor be executed as a terrorist than that fact be challenged."

He sighed. "A faked, remorseful suicide is far preferable to an actual execution- at least to the condemned."

"But how did you do it?" I said.

He pulled out a stethoscope and fitted it to his ears. "No more. You don't need to know that. You don't want to know that." He said firmly. "Now, how do you feel?"

I was massaging my arms and flexing my fingers to get the circulation back.

"Why am I here?" I asked. "What did you do to me?"

"You had a tracker on your sternum, Mister H. I removed it."

"HAD a tracker?" I said, while trying to sit up. "You can't go anywhere uptown without one. It was my apartment key and pass to secured buildings and comm links."

He smiled indulgently, as if talking to a slow child.

"Think about how your apartment reacted to you tonight." He said. "Every security scanner in the country will react the same way to your signal, now."

(NewsNet later said that I'd been tracked trying to sneak past the checkpoint on the St. Paul side of the Lake Street bridge that night. The guards had shot at me. I fell off the bridge. No body was found. I wondered who had been my stand-in, and where they were now.)

I realized that my wrist comp was gone. I asked Doc.

"You'll get it back later, as part of your kit," he said. "You'll be briefed and equipped as best we can."

"Equipped for what?"

"I haven't been told, of course. I surmise that it has to do with your becoming Mister H."

Stoat showed me my quarters; a tiny closet with barely enough room for a sleeping pallet and a bare light bulb. It was down the hall from the surgery, and across from a small library filled with old SF paperbacks, and books on social theory and history. No one wanted to talk about what was going on, so I mostly read for the week or so I was there. I ate in the big hall, with a stocking cap pulled low and my face dirtied for disguise. I didn't see Shoshanna again.

After about a week Stoat brought a small backpack and my wrist comp to me. The pack held a change of clothes, and basic survival gear such as matches, a compass, and a light foil blanket, along with a manual of wilderness techniques. She told me that my wrist comp had been rigged to auto-wipe all files if removed from my arm without entering a code. It would also wipe if I entered a "panic code."

"This is why you're going," she said. "Learn. Watch. Record. Then tell."

I practiced with the new operating system, recording sections of Doc's books using the built-in camera and microphone. I accidentally wiped the files a few times while practicing.

Late one December night, Stoat burst into my cubbyhole.

"OK, softy." she said. "Time to go. Put on your boots and grab you gear."

"But where are we going?"

She smiled a tight smile.

"YOU'RE going," she said. "I'm just sending you off. Come on!"

In a far corner of the huge basement was a pile of junk. Behind it was a door. Behind the door was a tunnel, carved through sandstone. My outstretched fingertips could just brush the opposite walls. Old steel rails ran along the center of its floor. In the light of Stoat's lantern it had a spooky, medieval feel.

"The Cities are full of old tunnels," Stoat said. "Mostly they're from the bootlegging and smuggling days."

"But why don't the authorities shut them down as security risks?"

She laughed, low in her throat.

"They need the underground economy. That's one of their dirty secrets. They howl about drugs and illegals, but they never really do more than make sure things don't get out of hand- and take their cuts.

"Watch it, we're changing tunnels now."

She opened a round iron hatch in the floor. We dropped into a smaller, round tunnel. We had to stoop to move forward. Its walls were of dressed stone, and were slimy to the touch. At the bottom of this tunnel ran, not tracks, but a trickle of smelly water. I thought that I heard rustlings just outside of the circle of light as I followed her.

"Hey! What's that?" I said. "I think there are animals in here!"

"Of course there are animals in here! It's an old storm sewer. Why do you think we gave you such good boots? Don't bother them, and they won't bother you."

"But where does this go?"

"We've got to get across the Mississippi. This tunnel comes out by what's left of the old Mendota Bridge. We can sneak across there."

"Why do we have to cross?"

Stoat threw a glance over her shoulder.

"Don't ask so many questions. You'll live longer," she said.

We slogged on for miles. My back and legs ached to numbness before a dim, orange light appeared far ahead.

"Why is it orange?" I asked. "Is something on fire?"

"Naw, we're coming out about half a mile from the big highway 55 bridge. The whole area is bright as day."

"So how do we sneak across?"

"You worry too much."

We emerged onto a rocky path high on the Mississippi River bank. I could see why Stoat knew we'd have cover. The ruins of the Mendota Bridge had been appropriated by homeless squatters. Though too weak to carry traffic, the crumbling old arches had sprouted rope catwalks and hanging dwellings below the old road bed, and shacks on top. I set off toward the bridge's near end. Stoat grabbed my arm.

"And how do you think you'll convince the guards not to just throw you off?" she asked.

"What guards?" I asked. "Who'd guard a place like this?"

"People guard what's theirs." She said. "There's a gang that runs things here. Just let me talk, and look harmless."

She looked me over.

"That shouldn't be hard."

We crunched up the wet path as it slanted toward the bridge's west end. It was like walking up a shallow creek.

Two well-wrapped figures emerged from the darkness, holding machetes.

"Hey, Trevor! Hey Major!" Stoat said, calmly, while walking right up to them. "I got another transient."

"What's he going for?" said one of the figures in a deep voice.

"The Man wants him." Stoat said. "You don't want to know why. You don't need the trouble."

"OK, he runs from The Man. Why should we risk it?"

"You don't get no shit on your hands." Stoat said. "You just get to smell it a little as it goes by."

She reached into a pocket, and pulled out a small paper sack. She tossed it to Trevor.

"This should deodorize things," she said.

Trevor looked in the sack, grunted, and waved us on.

He old bridge deck was covered with huts and shacks. Some were no more than shipping boxes with plastic sheets tacked on. One was a tent held up by a statue of a cartoon character; The Twin Cities had once been dotted with these memorials to a famous native son. Here and there were hung pitiful Christmas decorations: a glass ball, a bit of tinsel, a broken Santa Claus doll. A few people tended fires,

Gaps in the pavement were patched with plywood, stolen signboards, even old car doors. Stoat paused to lift one of these. A rope ladder descended into darkness.

"You afraid of heights, Softy?" she asked.

"I little." I said.

"OK, then you go first so you won't puke on me."

I laid on the edge, felt around with my feet, and went down the swinging rope contraption. Stoat came in after me, pulling the car door back over the hole. We descended through a few feet of shattered concrete. Twisted steel rods jutted from the mass, seeming to reach out to impale us.

Beneath the deck we emerged into what looked like a lunatic playground for giant spiders. A network of ropes, tied to the steel bars, hung beneath the bridge. Some ropes were just that, ordinary rope, but others were fashioned from strips of twisted cloth, electrical cable, even garden hose. Here and there swung hammocks filled with sleeping people. Stoat picked her way confidently toward the east end of the bridge, following paths of braided cable.

"Why are they under here?" I asked. "Isn't it dangerous?"

Stoat snickered.

"Dangerous? Think, Softy. It's out of the rain and the sun, and it's harder for robbers to sneak up on them here."

At the far end we descended to the river bank on another rope ladder, this one with rungs made from lengths of plastic piping. Another path ran along the bank for a few hundred feet. Then it was back to the tunnels. Behind a copse of dead lilacs loomed an opening large enough to drive to drive a car into. A few feet within, the tunnel was filled by a wooden barricade. A padlocked door stood at its center. Stoat produced a key on a string from around her neck.

"This tunnel is MINE," she said, grinning. "Not even Shoshanna knows about it."

She unfastened the lock, and we stepped through into another squared tunnel with rails. She relocked the door from the inside, and we followed the tunnel, gradually downward, for miles. Suddenly Stoat grabbed my arm, and doused the light.

"There's an opening ahead," she whispered. "Back in the late Twentieth, somebody cut a side tunnel into the old mushroom growing caves. Someone could be in there. Wait here."

Once she was a few feet away from me, I couldn't hear Stoat walking. In the utter darkness and silence I began to hear my heart thumping and my guts making tiny whistling gurgles. Shimmery illusions began playing at the edges of my sight. When her light again erupted before me, I was stunned for a moment.

"OK, clear," she said. We resumed our trek.

Soon we were beneath downtown St. Paul. I could hear the rumble of traffic and machinery, even in the middle of the night. I saw the orange light of floodlights leaking around another barrier in the distance, and felt a chilly breeze. The sound quality changed, becoming whinier, and a smell of dust was on the air. Stoat unlocked the door, and we emerged near a concrete pier on the Mississippi shore. The towers of downtown loomed a mile away. A massive rail yard was behind us.

The Mississippi barge shipping season used to be only from about April to November. Now that the winters were warmer, barge loads of grain were shipped all year around. The yard was busy as robotic loaders transferred grain from rail cars to barges. Yet it was strangely silent- there were no human voices among the humming electric bustle.

"Walk only where I tell you," Stoat said. "Some of these machines are too stupid to notice that they've squashed you to jelly."

She pointed out next to the pier, where something like a huge rail car on its side was moored.

"Listen up. There's a worker transport on this barge. See that bump down on the end? See that door? When I give the word, you run straight down that yellow line, jump on the barge, open the door and dive in."

I asked, "Then what? What if someone looks in there?"

"We've taken care of that," she said. "Just hunker down. In a couple of hours your barge will be lashed to a bunch of others and head downstream. It will have a little accident between Hastings and Prescott. When you feel it run aground, look for a red sailboat with a man in a bright blue coat. Don't ask questions, just jump aboard and do what he says."

"How will I know when it's run aground? Who will be meeting me?"

"You'll know, Softy," she said. "It'll feel like a train wreck, with lots of sirens and stuff. And even I don't know who's meeting you. It's safer that way, so get used to it."

"You're not coming?"

"No, it's your problem from here out. You'll have friends. Make it worth my having to talk to Trevor."

I moved to hug Stoat goodbye, but she backed away.

"Just move your ass. Don't get killed, Mister H. Don't blow it. GO. NOW."

I went.

The "worker transport" was a booth about as big as an elevator car. It smelled of old sweat, diesel fumes and dead fish. Benches ran down opposite sides. There was a tiny curtained alcove in one corner. Above the benches were open shelves with bottles of water and boxes of crackers. There was a radio, which I knew better than to turn on. The door had a hand-sized, grimy window.

I checked out the alcove. Yup. A bare toilet seat led down a pipe straight into the river. The rotten, chemical smell made me gag.

I couldn't have stayed awake, so I surrendered and lay down. My exhaustion at the underground walk, my tension about what came next, and the rocking of the barge sent me straight to sleep.

When I awoke, gray sunlight was oozing in through the window. The barge was smoothly sailing along, swaying a little. I looked out the window. High river banks covered in dead grass and trees crawled by. I snorted when I saw that some homeowners along the way had tied bundles of green fluff in the trees to simulate leaves. Many trees had fallen into the river; I wondered how often barges had real emergencies from ramming them.

It looked like we were out of The Cities, but still upstream of Hastings, I looked down. Shit! My barge was in the middle of the group, not on the edge! That could be tricky, later.

I decided to check out the supplies. I tucked a couple of bottles of water in my pack and opened one to drink now. I opened a box of crackers and wolfed some down, then took a handful to nibble.

I went back to the window to watch. Soon the Hastings High Bridge came into sight, beyond which we passed another barge marshalling yard. I knew that it wasn't far to Prescott, so I sat down on the rear-facing bench to wait.

After about half an hour I heard the engines' rumble rev higher. I sat up straight. There was a slight jolt to the side, then a heavier one straight forward. I was thrown back against the wall. The barge shuddered to a stop as sirens began to wail.

I grabbed my bag and looked out the window. A wedge of clearer water cut into the Mississippi's brown-green sludge along the far shore. Yup, this was Prescott, where the protected, wild St. Croix met the industrial Mississippi. We were aground. Angling toward me was a bright red sailboat, a big trimaran with sleeping cabin. Its mast was folded back and down. A man in a bright blue slicker stood at the tiller. He looked anxiously toward the barges.

I popped the hatch and sprang onto the catwalk that ringed my barge. The next barge was only a couple of feet away, but jerking up and down erratically. I got ready to jump, knowing that if I missed and fell between, I'd be soy burger.

I leaped- and fell flat on my face as the next barge rose to meet me. I scrambled across its corrugated steel surface, reaching the other side just as the sailboat bumped against it, then rebounded. The man in blue tried his best, but the distance between us swung from nothing to five or six feet, and the sailboat bobbed as much up and down.

The robo-barges were sending up a terrible alarm wail; I knew that Security would arrive at any minute. The man in blue knew it too, and was waving frantically for me to jump.

I flung my bag over my shoulder, took a few seconds to gauge the oscillations, sprinted for the side- and slipped. I managed to snag the safety rope that ran along the boat's deck with my right hand, barely. I swung, knee deep in the icy water, about to be crushed, drowned or both. The man in blue pointed the boat back into the channel, and ran to grab my arm. My flailing left hand grabbed his, and we managed to haul my carcass aboard.

He hustled me toward the stern, thrust a blanket into my hands, and shoved me toward the belowdecks hatch.

"Go. Get warm," he grunted. "Gotta steer."

He resumed his place at the tiller as I stumbled down the ladder. I was troubled- in those few seconds, he'd looked familiar.

As I descended the ladder, the boat's AI greeted me in a warm contralto.

"Welcome, guest. Make yourself at home."

The trim little galley was a welcome change. The floor, walls and cabinets were of real wood. The metal-framed chairs were upholstered in bright canvas. A coffeemaker burbled away next to a microwave oven. It was clearly a new boat, and nicer than many apartments I'd seen.

I grabbed a mug from its peg, and poured coffee. Then I noticed the family portrait on the countertop.

Jim Smith. Damn!

Two years before, I'd done a feature on the sailing crowd out of Stillwater. It had been a fluffy, don't-you-wish-you-lived-this-way piece. They were all management types and research scientists, folks the Corporation wanted to keep happy. I'd spent a few days hobnobbing, eating their food, sailing up and down the St. Croix and Mississippi.

One of them had been Jim Smith, a materials scientist at 3M, a fellow with a fistful of patents to his credit. Now, here I was on his new boat, the boat of a privileged company man. Had I jumped at the wrong time? Was our cover blown?

I sat, pondering, until he came below.

I greeted him. "Hi J…"

"No!" he snapped. "No names. Mister H. In the Movement, even YOU don't know who you know. Call me 'Bob.'"

He looked up. "Hey, Sophie," he said.

The boat answered. "Yes sir?"

"Maintain standard course to home base. Do not monitor cabin."

"Yes, sir."

"Is it really safe to have your AI here?" I asked.

"It's fine," he answered. "I have this friend in the computer industry. Sophie has selective amnesia. I select it. Now, I'm to take you home and pass you on north."

"Thanks."

"Don't mention it. I'm just doing what I can. They tell me that you're to observe and report. We need that. The Company won't let people like us know what's really going on. We're entertained so we'll keep working."

"People like you?" I asked.

Bob got a mug of coffee, and sat down opposite me.

He explained, "You know! You've seen! The comfortable ones. The moderately successful. Under no circumstances can we be allowed to realize that the rat race is rigged. Worse, that even if we win, it just makes us the meanest rats."

I thought a moment. *I guess that I just got kicked off the track- which makes me what?*

We sat, silent. After a long time Bob stood up, to look out the high windows.

"OK, we're in the Reserve," he said.

"What Reserve?"

He turned to look at me with anger and sadness.

"The 'It's all right, things are fine, work hard, play hard' Reserve."

"How's that?" I asked.

"Do you know what a Potemkin village was, Mr. H?"

"Umm, something to do with old Russia? I'm not sure."

"Close enough. Admiral Potemkin was in charge of building fake, prosperous villages along the roads where Empress Catherine went riding. Her advisors could tell her that everything was fine in Russia- while millions starved."

"So, how does that apply here?"

"The St. Croix was declared a 'Wild and Scenic River' decades ago. What that ended up meaning was that only the rich and powerful could live along it. The government still puts millions into replanting and painting the forests along its banks, so people in Stillwater, Hudson and Marine can still think that The System Works."

After another hour we came to the stand of artificial lilac bushes I remembered from my earlier visit. They hid a large garage door, which slid open at our approach. The floor of the boathouse was open to the water, so we motored directly in. Automatic grapples snugged the boat to the internal dock. While we climbed out, umbilicals plugged themselves into the boat's side to replenish its fuel and charge.

Up a long flight of stairs we came into the "back porch" of Bob's house. Though it was hidden from view of the river, huge windows looked out over the apparently untouched valley. Bob showed me how a wall panel could be slid aside to reveal a long hallway leading back under the house. I'd walked by it a dozen times before, unknowing.

"This house was built in about 2010," he explained. "This leads to the 'Terrorist hole,' a place to hide during emergencies. It's designed to care for a family of four for a month. It's also got a good library of books, movies and music. Our guests use it now."

"I'm not the first, then?" I asked.

Bob smiled conspiratorially.

"Not hardly," he said. "Since the fences went up we've had a steady stream of people. Now, go make yourself at home. I'll check up on you later. DON'T come out unless I give the all clear."

And that's ALL I'm going to say about anyone specific. The Corpos caught up with Bob a little after I left him. I don't want to take a chance on blowing anyone else's cover. I'll just say that people ranging from ancient hippies to Mexican migrant workers helped me along. I met people with a lot more guts than I have- and a lot more hope.

Chapter Twenty (2021)

WHO goes around comes around

Phoenix

Karl KNEW. It was time. He sat up in bed, sending his mind questing into the darkness. At two o'clock on this early spring morning, few of the Phoenix folk were awake. They had been working hard, preparing for their second summer in the LOOZ.

A familiar presence, Fear, Stealth, Hope, he sensed. Cold, Hunger.

The old man arose, pulled on a robe and sandals, and padded out of E. F. Schumacher House. The compound was silent, as only a usually busy place can be. A few night birds hooted. Some tendrils of fog drifted in from the lake.

Alec was at the Magic Pumpkin tonight, so Karl went to Alice Walker House to fetch Tina. As he expected, she was ready. They stopped by the Community Center for some blankets and a jug of hot tea. They piled these into a four-seater electric car, and quietly headed north along the lakeshore. They'd have taken horses, but their expected guest would be too tired to ride.

Eight miles north of Phoenix, they were within sight of the northern fence of the Chippewa Local Outlook Opportunity Zone. Red lights blinked along the top of the sixteen-foot chain-link barrier. Lawnmower-sized sentry robots scuttled back and forth along its base.

Karl and Tina stopped a few hundred feet from the fence, just downstream from the twisted pilings of the old Mud Lake Bridge. The robots swiveled scanning turrets toward them; they were more concerned with the outcasts trying to escape than with anyone coming in.

Karl and Tina sensed what the machines did not: something large was swimming under the fence, down deep, skimming the foul bottom muck.

"You keep an eye on the sentries," Karl said to Tina. "I'll go receive our guest."

Karl carried a blanket down to the muddy bank, where a seal-like creature was crawling ashore. He watched as it flopped over on its side, silently heaving from exertion. It touched its chest with the tip of a long flipper. Its dull black hide began to split and shrivel, revealing naked human skin beneath. In a few minutes the false pelt had curled and melted away. Karl helped the shivering young man struggle to his feet, wrapping him in a blanket.

"Welcome home, Jimmie," Karl said.

Jimmie Olson, intrepid freelance writer, laughed through chattering teeth.

"Sorry to wake you, sir," he said.

A few minutes later the three sat in the Dining Hall kitchen. Jimmie, still wrapped in his blanket, devoured flax bread and goat cheese. He wouldn't be mistaken for a fresh young writer. His face showed far more than a year of aging since the Phoenixites had bid him farewell.

Karl asked about the suit Jimmie'd been wearing.

"That was a semi-organic nanite composite," he explained. "It made me look to scanners like a big fish. It wouldn't have fooled a first-class barrier, but I knew Erhardt would be too cheap for one of those."

"Did you bring something dangerous in here?" Tina asked; bootleg nanotech was tricky stuff.

"No, it was a kind of one-shot symbiote. The design was lifted from the Israeli exile commando groups. Once released, it completely decomposes into simple proteins, starches and gasses. By morning, local life forms will have safely absorbed every trace. The grass might be a bit greener where I came ashore, but that's all."

"So, the outside got to be too much, eh?" said Karl.

"That and more," Jimmie said, grinning sickly. "But mostly, you folks were such good interviewees that I had to come back. I hear that you need a Historian."

"That we do," said Karl. "We knew that you'd be back, but how did it all happen? What's going on out there?"

"I'm the Historian," Jimmie said. "I remember."

He held up his wrist comp. A grim smile hardened his features.

"And I took notes."

A few weeks after Jimmie's return to Phoenix, subversive videos began to be hacked into corporate sites. Unsuspecting viewers got something they hadn't planned on...

Chapter Twenty-One (2021)

"A free Press is the backbone of Democracy."

Strength Through Joy, Version 2.0

News from Underground-

Hacked onto popular websites for your streaming multimedia pleasure!

Screw the Company!

Video:

Full-screen Resistance logo. Fade to panoramic shot of a rocky gorge. Climbers in bright gear scale sheer rock faces.

Narrator
This is Taylor's Falls Recreation Area. Some of you may have been here before. Back then you paid a couple of bucks and came on in.

Video:Dissolve to scenes of well-dressed tourists, wandering among vendor's booths in an enclosed arcade.

Narrator
But you won't be coming here again, not unless you've been a fortunate and loyal servant of the Company.

Video:
POV walking outdoors among tourists, approaching fortified park entrance. Handsome armed guards in corporate uniforms check travel permits, scan and frisk tourists.

Narrator
Even then, you'd best be ready for a spot of inconvenience.

Video:
Shots of booths selling typical tourist fare- carvings, blankets, souvenir plates, statuettes. Night shot of colorfully clad dancers doing "native" dances.

Narrator
Yes, this place has everything- rock climbing and cross-country skiing for the adventurous, oodles of shopping, and happy refugees sharing their culture.
Let's go see where those folks live outside of show hours.

Video:
Daylight again. Passing down muddy path in woods. A clearing opens up. It is filled with patchwork shacks. Morose-looking women wearing ragged coats are lined up before a water hydrant, jugs in hand. Trash is piled in corners.

Narrator

Don't worry, folks. They have changing rooms where they get cleaned, sanitized and scented before any of you will have to see them.

Video:
Proceeding past hovels, down another path. A high, electrified fence appears. Forty feet on either side is a clear-cut dead zone. The zone is dotted with graves.

Narrator
Did I mention that this place is hard to get into? It's even harder to get out of. But who would want to leave this Free Market paradise?
Let's see what some of our jolly holiday-makers think.

Video:
Approaching attractive young woman in short skirt, shell top, and billed cap- all in Red and White Company colors. A dark-skinned young man in vaguely Caribbean clothes stands by her.

Narrator
Excuse me, Miss. I'm with the Net. Where are you from?

Woman
I'm from Coon Rapids.

Narrator
I take it that you're here on a package deal?

Woman
Sure. You bet! Two years of perfect attendance at the factory, and I get a weekend here with all the trimmings.

Narrator
And this fellow is part of the trimmings?

Woman
(giggles) Oh, I'd get lost without Jaime. He tells me the best places to go, and keeps me away from boring stuff, tucks me in at night, gets my meals, the works.

Narrator
Do you know where he's from?

Woman

Aw, just one of those sunken island places, I guess. (Faces man) Right, Jaime? It's so romantic- Lost World and all that.

Jaime

As you say, Missy. Now, you must see the jugglers. (takes her arm, walks off)

Narrator

I guess that Jaime's easily embarrassed.
(pause to look around)
You, sir, do you have a moment?

Video:

Approaching a portly, graying man in all green and gold.

Man

I guess. What about?

Narrator

I'm with the Net, gathering people's impressions.

Man

(puffs up chest and smoothes hair) Ah, OK, when will this be on?

Narrator

I'm afraid that I have no control over that, sir. You seem to be having a fine time. Where are you from?

Man

You bet I am. I'm up here from Lakeville.

Narrator

Then you would have passed some refugee camps on the way.

Man

(scowls) Lazy sons of bitches. Come running to the US of A, looking for handouts. (Eyes passing "native" woman in skimpy costume) If they'd just get off their butts and work, like these kids here, they'd be out of those dumps in an eye blink.

Narrator
Thank you, sir, for those wise words.

Video:
Three-way split screen- Happy tourists at lower left, crying child in front of hut at lower right, glaring sun at top.

Narrator
Taylor's Falls recreation area. From the folks who brought you Global Warming, perpetual war, pesticide-laden food, and punitive social conformity. I'm your roving reporter, and that's the way it is in 2021.

"Five hundred years of the same old shit."

News from Underground-
Hacked onto popular websites for your streaming multimedia pleasure!
Screw the Company!

Video:
Full-screen Resistance logo. Fade to panoramic shot of a huge lake. Dying trees line the banks. The far side is invisible over the horizon. People are walking along the near shore. Teenagers toss a Frisbee. In the middle distance figures on a small boat are laying a fishing net.

Narrator
This is Red Lake, a center of Ojibwe culture in northern Minnesota. It's been this way for centuries- people gathering food, enjoying the air,

and going about their business. Oh, and something else has been going on for centuries.

Video:
The harsh roar of an approaching aircraft. People flee from the beaches. Figures on the boat don life jackets and helmets. A young woman runs onto the beach, carrying a shoulder-launched rocket.
An attack helicopter skims over the trees from the east. It fires missiles, striking and exploding the fishing boat, then turns toward the woman with chain guns blazing. She raises her missile and fires, just before her head vaporizes. The rocket strikes, and the helicopter explodes.
Dissolve to: Stock scene of 19th Century cavalry battle.

Narrator
They've been at war. Didn't you know?

Video:
Tall, broad-shouldered man

Narrator
This is Tribal Chair Thomas Whitefeather. He is elected head of several thousand Ojibwe citizens. Thank you for talking with us.

Whitefeather
I'm glad to. I'm a US citizen, or I was. I was proud to serve in both the Iraq wars. When the Federals said that the deficit meant they'd have to drop services on the Rez, we said that we'd take over and run things, semi-independent, you know? We'd trade with them and everything would be fine.
Then they went back on that promise. They said we weren't producing enough whitefish or lumber. Who could, with the acid rain killing the fish and weather changes screwing everything up? Their answer was that a forced-labor camp would cure us of our complaining. We've fought back as best we can. So far, we're still free people.
So we're right back to my great grandfather's time- but now we're smarter. We can hold our borders, mostly.

Video
Images of forest and wildlife. Focus on group of houses and teepees.

Narrator

This is Ponema, home to several spiritual leaders, making it the heart of the Ojibwe Resistance.

Video
Old man in buckskins. His hair is white, and his face dark and rugged as tree bark. He sits beneath a tree, smoking a long pipe from which feathers dangle. He sets the pipe down and faces the camera.

Elder
Now's where I get to say all that "Noble Red Man" crap, huh?
I was a young man during the "Dances with Wolves" fad in the '90s. I know it's all been said before. The Earth is our Mother, Circle of Life, all that. But you guys just don't get it. It's not a game, a fad, or a cartoon. For us it's life. You don't get that, so you get death. It's simple.
Don't tell me that my attitude is "incompatible with progress." Plenty of people showed you how to go Green without living like peasants. Plenty of books were written about Earth Spirituality. What you've got for progress is slow death. It was your own choice.
We don't want to die with you. Leave us alone.

Video:
Scenes of families together, playing and feasting; holy people doing ceremonies; soldiers in camouflage patrolling in the forest.

Narrator
The Minnesota Ojibwe Nation- people who just want to be left alone. However, Corporate needs take priority in the Land of the Free and the Home of the Brave. I'm your roving reporter, and that's the way it is in 2021.

Bad neighbors make good fences

News from Underground-
Hacked onto popular websites for your streaming multimedia pleasure!
Screw the Company!

Video:

Full-screen Resistance logo. Fade to panoramic shot of a fortified dam. Pan to show security fences and a concrete moat, with armed soldiers patrolling on both sides, stretching to both horizons across the prairie,

Narrator

The US/Canada border. For two centuries the longest undefended border in the world- Until the War on Terror. The US first began building this barrier, supposedly to keep out terrorists. But watch more carefully...

Video:

Night infrared shot. Small bands approach the fence from the US side, trying to get through. They are shot by guards from both sides.

Narrator

After 9/11 and the first Patriot Act, Canada began to more tightly restrict US immigration. After the flood of political refugees began in 2005 the US countered with barbed-wire, trenching and guards.

Video:

Night shot- guards come running from the US side to retrieve bodies.

Narrator

We watched the border for several nights running. We saw many incidents like this one. We never saw, nor heard of, anyone trying to cross from Canada into the US.

Video:

Close up of guard tower.

Narrator
Canada, our good friend and neighbor to the north. Are they trying to tell us something? I'm your roving reporter, and that's the way it is in 2021.

It can't burn if it ain't there no more.

News from Underground-
Hacked onto popular websites for your streaming multimedia pleasure!
Screw the Company!

Video:
Full-screen Resistance logo. Fade to shot of a mile-wide swath of clear-cut forest. Not a tree or bush is left standing. Muddy ruts score the ground. Surrounding trees are brown and dying, many fallen over. The carcass of a deer rots in the foreground.

Pan to small mobile home in the midst of desolation. A pickup is in front, a large flatbed truck with a grabbing crane stands to the side. Fade to interior shot of stocky, blond man in plaid shirt, jeans, and heavy boots.

Al
Hey. I'm Alphonse Bergman. Call me Al. I'm a logger, my daddy was a logger, and his daddy was a logger, but it ends with me. Welcome to my home.

Video:

Pull back to reveal interior of trailer. Old family photos hang above the TV. Dirty dishes and laundry rest on furniture. A shotgun leans on the TV.

Al picks up shotgun, uses it to gesture around room, keeps holding all through interview.

Al
Oh, don't mind my shootin' iron. It's just for worthless varmints.

Video
Focus on photos in turn as Al talks.
First, a burly, dark man in coveralls stands before the large truck in winter.

Al
This was my Daddy. He taught me how to take mature trees without messing up the young ones. He told me why, too. A healthy forest keeps producing, and is good for wildlife.
"Son," he told me, "The good Lord put us here to use the Earth, not to ruin it."

Video:
Photo: A blond woman mugs for the camera near the trailer. The trailer stands in thick forest.

Al
This was my wife, Britney. (Al's voice becomes slightly choked.) She took off after we lost Kaylin.

Video:
Photo: A small girl, perhaps ten years old, is feeding a raccoon. The trailer is visible in the background, again in thick forest.

Al
Yup, this was my sweet child, that last summer. We took this when we knew the clearcutters were coming. She had a way with animals. They were never afraid of her; they even followed her around sometimes. This whole forest was her home- until they cut it down. When they cut it down, they cut out her heart. She was dead of sorrow in a month.
(Breaks down crying)
You'd better go now.

Video:

Pan for full 360 shot, starting with trailer. Part way through, a shot sounds from the trailer. Camera POV bounces, running toward trailer. Cameraman's hand reaches into view, opening door. There is a glimpse of scarlet spattered walls.

Cameraman
God, no! Call 9-11! Shit!

Narrator
The great North Woods, spirit nourishing wilderness and inexhaustible source of lumber and pulp. I'm your roving reporter, and that's the way it is in 2021.

It didn't have to be this way.

News from Underground-
Hacked onto popular websites for your streaming multimedia pleasure!
Screw the Company!

Video:
Full-screen Resistance logo. Fade to shot of a deep green pasture. Huge cattle graze across its width.

Narrator

This is the Chippewa Local Outlook Opportunity Zone, the LOOZ. You've heard of it. You call its residents LOOZers. For losers, they live pretty happy, healthy lives.

Video:
More pastoral scenes; scenes of picnics and outdoor concerts; scenes of apple trees thick with fruit, being picked and eaten by a half-dozen young people.
(one half second of static and dark swirling colors)

Narrator
This is what we get when we play God.

Video:
Scene of city towers bathed in smog; refugee camps; faces with cancerous growths; foul rivers; crowded streets.

Narrator
This is what we get when we open our eyes and take our position seriously.

Video:
Lush grain field, houses in the background

Narrator
The Chippewa LOOZ- miserable, festering nest of malcontents and misfits. Yeah, right. I'm your roving reporter, and that's the way it is in 2022.

THE END

Appendix:

Excerpts from the writings of Karl Mueller

From "How Did We Get Here?"
Ballantine
1999
p 5

During the last half of the Twentieth Century people worried that 'God Is Dead.' They felt terrifyingly alone in a Universe of cold equations and Physics. The majority fearfully turned their backs on the changing world. They couldn't accept that their comfortable Grandpa in the Sky wasn't there any more, that even the sky wasn't what they had thought it was. They talked more about 'things Man is not meant to know' than about their own new responsibilities.

They sold themselves short, like walking out of a movie just when the hero's in the worst trouble. They missed the resolution completely. God wasn't dead. Their image of Him was like a small child's image of a parent; when that child grows up, the parent must grow in their eyes, too. They refused to let their image of God grow, so they couldn't grow as people. Like children throwing tantrums, many fell into Fundamentalisms or raw Materialism, which are basically the same thing. Fear of the knowledge that challenged them made them chop off any part of reality that they couldn't shove into the old idea boxes. They fought for comfortable ignorance.

Ibid, pp 35, ff

I'm part of that whole gang of people like Bill Gates, Steve Jobs and The Woz. We saw that in this system no good thing, no social justice, no moral improvement, ever, ever, ever happened until it was economically profitable for someone. Take abolishing slavery, creating Medicare, enacting Child Labor Laws- whatever you like, MONEY was behind it. And things don't suddenly become profitable: they do when Technology makes the path. So, we got into Technology. We surfed the wave of change. We hemorrhaged ideas and enthusiasm, adding our life's blood to the river of newness.

However, many of us got sidetracked. Some of us succeeded too well with our schemes; we made tons of money, and forgot why. We were outsiders who bought into The System- and the price was our souls. We ended up strengthening just what we had wanted to change. I suppose that was understandable; as Rabbi Jesus said, "The love of money is the root of all kinds of evil."

As pitiful as we were, sadder still were the people who really, really wanted to make things better, but never learned how the world actually works. Their kites of idealism flew on winds of misunderstanding and downright ignorance.

They wanted to "Save the Whales," or the trees, or the wild mustangs, or whatever noble thing, God love 'em. They put up posters and stuck on bumper stickers. They had fundraisers and 'awareness raising events.' They confronted whaling ships in sexy little speedboats. They chained themselves to fences. They were heroically well intentioned, but pretty much all they accomplished was to annoy the people they really needed to reach.

The vital thing they didn't notice was that, for instance, the countries that had actually stopped whaling were the ones that had found substitutes for whale products. These same so-called Greens even blockaded and protested at the research labs which were creating the technologies that would have made whaling unnecessary. Neither did they see that the pressure for logging came from the legitimate needs of Society. I'd stake my fortune that the invention of e-publishing and -mail has saved more trees than all the redwood-spikings and chaining-to-trees protests put together.

They didn't get much help from us successful ones; we had our heads up our butts, inventing a crazy, sterile future just for kicks. They rightly saw us as sellouts, moneygrubbers, techie bastards. We saw them as willfully ignorant "fluffy bunnies." Impasse. Both our philosophies were bankrupt without the other.

From "Now What?"
Self-published
2003
pp ix, ff

This is the first era of Humanity to actually KNOW what's going on in the world. We know what makes the sun shine. We know how life works. We have better maps of Mars now than we did of Earth when I was a boy. We SEE that we're a part of all that is.

There is only one valid response. We accept the responsibility of being fully human. We accept that perilous knowledge which is ours. We accept the hard work that our human-ness demands of us. We accept that God is with us, because God IS us. We accept that we are Mother Earth's eyes and hands. We accept John Kennedy's words, that "God's work on Earth must truly be our own." We accept that nothing is truly real until it is known and cherished. We accept that our Responsibility and Destiny is to learn, to love our world, to use every tool we have or can invent to make it better.

From "My Path"
U of M Press
2004
pp 7, ff

When I hit my crisis on conscience in the '90s, something Buckminster Fuller wrote went to the core of things. As a young man he had realized that God had put him on Earth with his engineering and design gifts to make the world a better place. He knew that if he was true to that calling, everything else would fall into place. He resolved never to strive for money or recognition; he trusted that they'd happen in the natural course of being who he was.

It sounded pretty hokey- except that it worked. He followed that philosophy for many decades, until his dying breath, and it never failed him. He just thought about human needs and invented ways to meet them; becoming wealthy, famous and respected sort of happened by themselves along the way.

I resolved to follow the same Path from then on. I didn't shirk work or responsibility, but trusted that things would work out. They did.

Ibid, p32

When I was designing Phoenix, I studied the literature of other "utopian" experiments. Most Twentieth-Century examples tended to be based on a kind of shallow spirituality that made people feel good and morally superior. They celebrated "egalitarianism" and "consensus" run amok, thus making sure that the entire organization functioned at the level of its least competent member. As noble as their intentions were, they had no staying power. They were pretty little castles in the sky, with no solidity or real power in society. That's why they failed, and are survived only by the parts of their ideas that could be profitably absorbed into pop culture.

I vowed not to make their mistake. Phoenix's core would be a cadre of scientist-mystics, built on a solid foundation, with long-range planning.

From "Reaping the Whirlwind"
Asyl Publishing Group
2008

Introduction

People love conspiracy theories. There is almost no limit to the outlandish and simplistic terrors they'll believe in. From Planet X to reptilian space aliens to the Illuminati, the more bizarre the better. The trouble is that real threats aren't "sexy." Early alarms about resource depletion, climate shift, corporate power, and the time bomb of colonialization had been sounded since the late 1800s. The Common Man found them hard to grasp, and the powerful saw no profit in worrying about them.

So, here we are in the Twenty-First Century. That whole flock of birds has come home to roost. Many commonplaces of our youth are alien to our children and grandchildren. They have a hard time picturing huge flocks of birds in migration. Swimming in lakes and rivers is a stupid idea to them. They can't believe that we never heard of sunscreen until the 1980s. That farmers would be independent small operators is a fantastic concept. That we had aspired to a world without want or war is ludicrous in their world filled with both.

Some of us saw this time coming, and acted. We may have done too little, too late, but we tried. I pity those who never even tried.

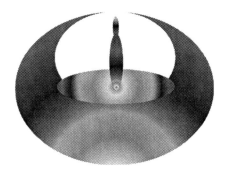

About the Author

One foot's planted in vanishing rural Minnesota. The other taps time in the science fiction worlds of Heinlein, Clarke and Asimov. Chuck Waibel straddles two very different influences to create his first novel, Phoenix, Minnesota.

The northern prairie village of Milan (population 326 at last Count), can claim Waibel as one of its livelier citizens since the year 2000. Watching a town struggle to maintain its identity and survival while appreciating the world influences pressuring its destruction got him to thinking about "and then what?" A personal interest in non-conventional spiritual paths spiced up a book full of familiar characters that seek a sustainable answer to this puzzler about human survival.

Chuck Waibel gives appreciative nods to influences Buckminster Fuller and E.F. Schumacher.

Printed in the United States
133208LV00003B/172/A